"Unc

We used to live with him."

Thea's spirits deflated as quickly as they'd risen. The twins rarely mentioned their uncle. He hadn't called since she'd begun taking care of them. He hadn't written to ask about the girls, hadn't sent them birthday cards. If she had to guess, Thea would say Uncle Logan didn't care what happened to his nieces.

"Please." Hannah touched Thea's hand with one finger before stepping back. The gesture said so much more than the reticent little girl ever would. The twins tolerated Thea's hugs, but didn't seek out physical contact.

Dear Reader,

We all start our lives in different places and situations. Some of us have the advantage of coming from a secure, loving home. Some of us have a less picture-perfect upbringing. Most of us turn out all right, either through love or our own determination.

Neither Logan McCall nor Thea Gayle was raised in the ideal family. Their families and the amount of love they gave have shaped who these two are. Logan is convinced his harsh upbringing makes him unworthy of having a family, while Thea is not sure she knows what a real family is. He's heartless. She's a kindhearted, lonely do-gooder. It will take a lot of determination to turn their unlikely attraction into a lasting love.

I enjoy hearing from readers—about this book or some of my others—either at my Web site (www.melindacurtis.net) or via regular mail (P.O. Box 150, Denair, CA 95316).

Melinda Curtis

The Family Man
Melinda Curtis

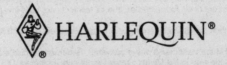

HARLEQUIN®

TORONTO • NEW YORK • LONDON
AMSTERDAM • PARIS • SYDNEY • HAMBURG
STOCKHOLM • ATHENS • TOKYO • MILAN • MADRID
PRAGUE • WARSAW • BUDAPEST • AUCKLAND

ISBN 0-373-71241-3

THE FAMILY MAN

To Judy Ashley, Sarah Palmero, Anna Stewart and Geri Wells
for listening to me ramble and giving me advice
about the Tin Man in the early stages.

To my family, for showing me what enduring love
is all about.

Books by Melinda Curtis

HARLEQUIN SUPERROMANCE
1109—MICHAEL'S FATHER
1187—GETTING MARRIED AGAIN

Don't miss any of our special offers. Write to us at the
following address for information on our newest releases.

Harlequin Reader Service
U.S.: 3010 Walden Ave., P.O. Box 1325, Buffalo, NY 14269
Canadian: P.O. Box 609, Fort Erie, Ont. L2A 5X3

CHAPTER ONE

EVICTED. THEA couldn't believe it.

"Can we go home now?" Hannah asked as she plucked a dandelion from the sparse grass at her feet. A gentle breeze lifted wisps of blond hair that escaped from her braid.

Hannah, one of Thea's ten-year-old charges, was perched on the corner of a black suitcase so large she could have fit in it, had it not been stuffed with everything the girl owned. They hadn't moved beyond the cracked sidewalk, edged with crabgrass, upon which the apartment complex landlord had left them fifteen minutes ago.

"We don't have a home," Tess announced in a wobbly voice. She stuck her little chin out, daring Thea or Hannah, her twin, to contradict her.

Swallowing a pang of despair, Thea stepped over her laptop computer and drew Tess to her. Not that the cramped, dark apartment had ever felt like home to Thea. This Seattle apartment was just one in a string of places she'd stayed since leaving home nine years ago. No, Thea hadn't lived in a place she'd call home in a long time.

Next to Thea, Tess kept her body stiff, staunchly refusing to show any sign that she was comforted in any way. Tess had to be the brightest, most standoffish child Thea had ever come across. And despite Thea's best efforts these past two months, she'd been unable to break through the barriers Tess and Hannah had erected around their hearts after their mother died.

"Home is where the heart is. You know, where you hang your hat and park your flip-flops." Thea tried to keep the words light, knowing she failed. Their mom was dead and their dad had gone missing. And since Thea could relate to mothers leaving and dads not caring too much, how upbeat could she be? Still, she had to try. "There's a better home for you out there. One with a…a backyard…and trees."

Since she was a kid, Thea Gayle had tried to go through life looking for the silver lining and encouraging those around her to do the same. She wouldn't let a few minor setbacks—like being evicted or not knowing where her employer was—get her down. At least, she hoped she wouldn't.

Thea forced her gaze away from the mocking piles of chaos that surrounded the twins she'd been hired to care for. Three bulging suitcases, a laptop computer, several boxes of textbooks and notebooks, two pink scuffed backpacks and one box with the meager remnants of their pantry were scattered in disarray around the porch of what had formerly been their sparsely furnished apartment.

"A house." Hannah made a wish, blew the white dandelion fronds into the air and shut her eyes tight, adding in a whisper, "A house with a staircase leading up to a magic room."

"With lots of friends nearby," Tess added, to Thea's surprise.

"That's the spirit." Thea managed a weak smile before the trio descended back into a lost silence.

"You won't leave us, will you?" Hannah turned her big blue eyes to Thea, her bottom lip quivering.

"No," Thea hastened to reassure Hannah. She might only be their nanny, but she cared about them.

If only they'd let themselves care in return.

"This is all *his* fault," huffed Tess, turning her back to Thea and crossing her skinny arms over her thin chest.

Assuming Tess referred to her father, Thea didn't refute her words. The girl was right. If Wes Delaney had paid the rent, his cell-phone bill—or even paid Thea—in the past few months, they'd be on the other side of that apartment door right now. If Thea could turn back the clock, she'd never again complain about the peeling paint on the door or the walls so thin you could hear the couple next door fighting. She'd be sitting contentedly at the kitchen table, studying for her Ph.D. exams while the twins did their homework on either side of her.

Two months ago, Wes's advertisement for a nanny/housekeeper had seemed a blessing. Working on her Ph.D. in textiles had taken Thea longer than she'd planned. She'd finished her coursework and was studying for her written and oral exams. Her savings had dipped dangerously low, so she'd taken the position with the Delaneys, which would have been fine if she'd been better at prioritizing the needs of the twins against progress on her studies. Now her exams were rapidly approaching and she was woefully unprepared.

And a lacking place to sleep.

Uncertainty, sour and unpleasant, clutched Thea's heart. No place to live. Less money than ever. Running out of hope that she'd ever fulfill the promise she'd made to make something of herself. And with Wes gone to heaven knew where—he couldn't be dead, could he?—what was she going to do with the twins?

As if aware of Thea's rising panic, Tess walked down the front path to the curb where Thea's yellow Volkswagen Beetle was parked. After a moment, Hannah followed her sister, stopping a careful distance from her twin. Neither spoke. Neither touched. But Thea had the distinct impression that they knew what the other was thinking.

What had the twins been like before their mother died? Thea closed her eyes as she tried to envision Tess's small face with a joyous grin or scrunched up in tickle-induced laughter. She tried to imagine a more outgoing, confident Hannah. Or the two sisters holding hands as they walked home from school, giggling and sharing confidences as siblings were supposed to do.

Much as she tried, Thea couldn't quite picture them that way. Having buried their mother six months ago and being raised—if you could call it that—by a malingering father, who didn't seem very interested in his daughters the four or five days he was home every month, it was no wonder the girls were so withdrawn.

Turning them in to the police or some impersonal social agency was out of the question. They'd just be passed from one foster home to another. Tess would continue to refuse to eat more than kept her alive and Hannah would continue to eat to salve her pain. They may have been identical twins, but their grief had taken its toll on their bodies in different ways.

Unfortunately, Thea knew she couldn't take care of them forever. As it was, she'd have trouble figuring out a way to keep them fed for more than a few days with less than one hundred dollars to her name.

"I want to go home." Hannah turned back to Thea, fingering the hem of her yellow sundress. "To Idaho."

"He won't take us." Tess shook her head without facing them. She shoved her hands into the back pockets of her jean shorts.

"Is that where your father is? In Idaho?" Thea asked, her spirits rising. Maybe this was just a huge misunderstanding. Wes could wire them some money and the landlord would let them back into the apartment. She'd spend more time studying and a little less time trying to coax the girls out of their shells.

Tess snorted.

Ignoring her sister, Hannah stepped around a box of Thea's books, something uncharacteristically bright shining in her eyes. "Uncle Logan lives in Idaho. In Silver Bend. We used to live with him."

Thea's spirits deflated as quickly as they'd risen. The twins rarely mentioned their uncle. He hadn't called since she'd been with them. He hadn't written to ask about the girls, hadn't sent them birthday cards. If she had to guess, Thea would say Uncle Logan didn't care what happened to his nieces.

"Please." Hannah touched Thea's hand with one finger before stepping back. The gesture said so much more than the reticent little girl ever would. The twins tolerated Thea's hugs, but didn't seek out physical contact.

Why on earth would this uncle in Idaho help them now?

An ant crawled up the side of the box containing the bread, peanut butter and cereal. If Thea didn't decide to do something soon, the ants would claim the last of their food.

Perhaps the twins' uncle was the only person they could turn to.

Lifting her gaze to the blue spring sky above, Thea refused to think about the folders filled with notes at her feet, or her looming exams, or the balance on her credit card that was already too high to pay off.

And she would *not* think about the penalties for taking the girls without their father's permission. She'd filed a missing persons report on Wes three weeks ago. As far as she was concerned, if Wes Delaney was alive, he'd abandoned his daughters.

"Let's load the car." Thea brushed the ant away, picked up the box of food and headed to her car.

She was taking the twins to Idaho.

"THEY'RE DECLARING this fire a runaway," Golden announced, sliding on a patch of ice as he came down a slope on Hyndman Peak, east of Sun Valley, Idaho.

Logan McCall tensed, reliving his own tumble last year that had snapped his femur. Without thinking, he rubbed his thigh, which still gave him more than an occasional twinge of protest at the physical demands of his work. Then he realized he was drawing attention to his injury and stopped. He couldn't afford to show any weakness. If you couldn't keep up, you couldn't be a Hot Shot.

With a quick sideways glance to see if anyone had noticed, Logan lifted his arm to wipe the sweat off his forehead with the long sleeve of his shirt. It might be less than forty degrees on this sunny spring day in the mountains, but the fire above him had warmed everything here to above ninety sweat-dripping degrees. The Hot Shot fire crew kept perspiration-soaked bandannas and shirtsleeves busy in between flinging dirt and snow on the flames at their feet. Their clothing may have been fire resistant, yet all that coverage didn't keep them cool.

Logan's body felt the fire's heat from head to toe, but the flames could never warm his heart. He couldn't get over that one regrettable choice he'd made five months ago.

"Did the fire jump the line somewhere else, Golden?" Logan asked his best friend as he flung snow at the flames with a shovel. He wished he could control the pain in his chest with the same straightforward manner he controlled a fire.

Golden nodded, clipping his radio onto the front strap of his pack. "Winds pushed it across the road to the east. It's heading down the mountain to the ski resort."

Some of the other Hot Shots stopped tossing dirt and snow at the flames above them to listen. The Silver Bend Hot Shot crew was working with two other fire crews on a prescribed burn above the Sun Valley ski resort. The Department of Forestry had decided they needed to set a controlled burn in a timber area that had been weakened by two years of drought and ravaged by bark beetles. Without water, the pines had been unable to produce enough sap to protect themselves against the hungry insect, which bored into the bark and ate the dry trees from the inside out. The large percentage of dead pines on this side of the mountain was a huge risk for wildfires later in the year. Some bureaucrat seemed to think that the snow and rock farther up the ridge would stop the fire from crossing over to the other side of the mountain.

But they hadn't figured on winds changing direction and pushing the fire down the mountain, had they?

Gazing up the slope, Logan shaded his eyes against the

glaring spring afternoon sun. He saw nothing but orange pine swaying in the wind—orange from the flames consuming dry branches or orange needles indicating the tree had succumbed to the beetle. Succumbed. Given up. Lost.

"Are we being reassigned to the east?" Spider asked. He was a wiry firefighter about Logan's age. Seeing him in Hot Shot garb—a yellow button-down shirt and forest-green khakis—was always something of a shock. Off duty, Spider preferred the black color usually associated with the creepy crawly that was his namesake.

All the Hot Shots had nicknames—Jackson was Golden because he was lucky; Nick was Steve, short for Stephanapolis; Doc because he went to medical school during the winter; and The Queen, so dubbed because she was a redhead named Victoria. Logan's nickname was Tin Man, a name he'd earned by being the most confirmed bachelor among his crew. They gave each other monikers to lighten the mood when battling the deadly flames.

Not to say that they weren't businesslike on the fire line.

"Lots of ski bunnies down that slope at the ski lodge, Tin Man." Chainsaw nudged Logan with his elbow, his namesake resting on his broad shoulders. He, Steve and a bulldozer had cleared a twenty-foot wide path through the trees that cut across their side of Hyndman Park. "We'll look like heroes."

Well, they might not always be businesslike, but they got the job done.

"Send my group out first, Golden, before Tin Man starts breakin' hearts and makin' all of mankind look bad." Spider's words were baiting, almost itching for a fight.

Logan looked away, heat burning in his gut near as

hot as the fire above them. Since losing his twin sister six months ago, Logan's temper rarely receded. He'd taken to avoiding his friends because he couldn't escape the cloud that seemed to shadow him everywhere.

Golden shook his head. He was the superintendent of the Silver Bend Hot Shots based in Silver Bend, Idaho, and had the patience of a saint. Logan and Spider were his two assistant superintendents, each in command of a team of nine men and women.

Last year, Golden had volunteered to train firefighters in Russia, and while he was on leave, Logan had taken over the superintendent position. At the time, Spider had seemed to accept Logan's advancement over him. Then, just after Golden returned from Russia, the team had fought a huge fire in Garden Valley, Idaho, and things had changed.

Logan had been baby-sitting some of NIFC's Incident Command team when they'd been trapped by a fire on a steep slope. NIFC, short for National Interagency Fire Center, coordinated fire crews and resources in the United States when a fire outgrew the capabilities of a local fire district. The incident commander, Sirus Socrath, who went by the Hot Shot name of Socrates, had bounced down the slope toward the advancing flames like a rag doll, breaking his arm. Logan had slid after him in the hopes of saving him, only to take a tumble and break his own leg. They'd waited out most of the fire in a cave until Golden showed up and saved Logan's ass, cracking his own ribs and noggin in the process.

While Logan and Golden were on the mend, Spider took over the team. Shortly thereafter, he'd started giving Logan nothing but his own dark brand of bullshit. Logan was finding it increasingly hard to ignore his friend's digs, increasingly hard not to plant a fist in Spider's grinning face.

"Our team is watching the line *here*." Golden banished any hope of recreational action at the ski lodge, eliciting a series of muffled grumbles among the team. "They're sending the Snakes," he added, meaning the Snake River Hot Shot crew from Pocatello, Idaho.

The groans weren't held back at this news. Three-quarters of the Hot Shots were single and under age thirty-five.

"Let's do what the boss says," Logan called out to his team even as the wind whistled past him from a new direction. "Spread out and make sure this beast doesn't jump *our* line."

"Come on, let's go help the Snakes, Golden," Spider was saying, disregarding Golden's command—that they get back to their jobs. Then he turned to Logan with that infuriating grin of his. "To look at you, Tin Man, I wouldn't think you'd be so heartless and give up so easily. It's been a long winter for some of our crew."

"Shove it, Spider," Logan said through gritted teeth, trying to rein in his explosive temper even as it burned its way through his veins, trying to force his feet in the opposite direction, away from the challenge Spider continued to flaunt in his face.

Neither effort worked. His body shook with nearly uncontrollable energy.

"I'm just saying you're colder than ever," Spider continued, a mild smile on his face, as if he were making a joke Logan was too stupid to understand.

Before Logan realized what he was doing, he had Spider by the straps of his backpack and his face pressed almost into Spider's. "I said, shove it!"

Hands yanked Logan back, away from Spider and his

taunts. Then Golden dragged him farther down the road, away from the others. But the anger came with him.

"Damn it, Tin Man." Jackson looked him square in the eye before lowering his voice. "Logan, what the hell happened to you? Your temper was never as bad as this."

The anger was choking, making it impossible for Logan to form a reply. How he wished he could rid himself of it.

The person he'd been closest to in the world, his twin sister, Deb, had known how to ease his anger with a word. But she was gone. And Logan hadn't been able to honor her request and be a guardian for her two girls. While Logan was lost in grief, Deb's slimy husband had taken them and disappeared. It was probably for the best, considering Logan's temper, lifestyle and upbringing.

Still, Logan had never imagined that doing the right thing would tear him apart.

"I'M SORRY, ma'am. There's no answer."

Thea thanked the operator and hung up the pay phone at the gas station on the outskirts of Boise. Things didn't look good. Hannah was insisting that her uncle lived in Silver Bend, Idaho. There was a listing for Logan Mc-Call; however, the guy never answered his phone. Thea had been trying to call him every four hours since they started on their trip. Now they were less than two hours away from Silver Bend and the twins' uncle was nowhere to be found. Just like their father.

Which meant they'd come all this way for nothing.

"Thea! Thea, come quick!" It was Hannah, standing over by the gas station's rusty garbage bin. She looked okay. Her white T-shirt was a little dirty, but...

Tess. Where was Tess? Thea's heart stopped until she caught a glimpse of Tess's head bobbing up in the Volkswagen. Nevertheless, Thea ran over to Hannah.

"What is it? What's wrong?"

Hannah pointed at something between the garbage bin and the brick wall. "There."

"Are you okay?" Thea struggled to catch her breath, more from the scare that something had happened to Tess or Hannah than the run.

Hannah bobbed her head. "There's something back there. I think it's a puppy. I think it's stuck." She'd stepped back and pointed behind the bin.

"Let me look." Thea put her head near the wall and looked into the narrow gap. All she could see was a pile of greasy rags stuck between the brick wall and the bin's corner wheel.

"Hannah, there's nothing—"

Something whimpered beneath the rags, interrupting whatever protests Thea had been about to voice. Still, it could be a rat or something equally nasty back there.

"It's a puppy, Thea," Hannah repeated stubbornly. "I think it's stuck."

Ooohh-ooohh-ooohh. It was a weak dog's cry for help.

There was no mistaking it now. Thea didn't think rats whined like that when they heard people.

"All right, we'll get it out." But how? There was no way Thea or Hannah could wiggle their way into the narrow opening between the trash bin and the wall. Thea gripped the cool, rusted metal and tugged.

Nothing budged. Hannah set her feet against the wall and pushed the trash container.

The bin groaned forward, maybe an inch. The dog's pleas for help became louder.

"What are you doing?" Tess had come over from the car, and stood with her arms crossed in familiar, obvious disapproval.

"We're saving a puppy." Hannah grunted with the effort of pushing and talking at the same time.

"We'll be done that much faster if you help, Tess." Thea stepped back and looked at the imprint of the metal bin on her hands. It figured that the trash bin was full and as heavy as an elephant.

Tess rolled her eyes and seemed about to refuse when the dog whimpered again. Then she, too, was pushing on the bin.

In the end, the gas-station cashier, a reed-thin teenage boy, came out to help them push, pull and tug the bin away from the wall enough so that Tess could slip back and pick up the bundle of rags.

"Be careful. It might not realize you're rescuing it," Thea cautioned. All she needed was for the dog to bite one of the twins to cap their string of bad luck.

Tess backed out of the gap and handed the bundle to Thea. It either had to be a puppy or a small dog, as it seemed no larger than a cat.

"Someone's wrapped it like a mummy," Thea noted as she knelt and carefully peeled away the rags from the dog in her lap. The more she unwrapped, the stronger the unpleasant smell of urine.

The dog was crooning to them now, a constant, weak complaint. He didn't snarl or move to escape when the final layer was lifted. He just blinked up at them in the bright March sunlight.

"That's harsh." The gas-station cashier turned up his nose in disdain before returning to his duties.

Thea agreed, angling her head to the side in an effort

to avoid the stench. Whoever had done this to the little dog had been unspeakably cruel.

Hannah reached down to pet him.

"Don't," Thea warned. "We don't know if he's going to bite." Or if he had rabies. Plus, he was covered in a layer of pungent yellow pee, not all of it dry.

"What are we going to do?" Hannah asked.

Thea gazed down at the defeated little dog in her lap. "We'll have the cashier call animal control or whoever takes abandoned animals around here. They'll clean him up and find him a home."

"No! It's an orphan. Like us." Hannah's face crumpled as she began to cry.

And that's how Thea found herself driving into Silver Bend with no place to go, a car full of her possessions, two abandoned girls and a clean, small white terrier with brown spots.

"Stop! Stop!" Hannah cried as they drove through town. "If Uncle Logan's not at home, he's at the Painted Pony."

The little dog in her lap perked his ears. He was cute, once they'd washed him, and seemed to have the sweetest disposition, which made Thea wonder why anyone would have treated him so horribly.

Thea parked in the lot next to the Painted Pony restaurant. A life-size plastic painted horse waited for them on the wooden porch. But Hannah didn't head to the front door. The little girl ran around to the back, dragging the terrier behind her with the braided leash Thea had made with scraps of material. The little dog kept his nose to the ground and frequently lifted his leg to try to mark his territory before being yanked farther along by Hannah.

"Hannah, where are you going?" Thea asked, hefting her straw purse onto her shoulder.

"Rufus has a dog run in the back," Tess explained.

Thea tore her gaze away from Hannah, who was disappearing through a back gate, to look at Tess. "You know who runs this place?"

"Heidi's grandma." Tess leaned back against the dusty car and crossed her arms over her chest, jutting out her chin.

"Who's Heidi?"

"A friend from school. When we lived here." She shrugged.

"And she's got a dog?"

"Yeah."

Hannah returned, panting for breath. "Hurry, let's see if they're inside."

"No one's here, Han. None of their cars are here," Tess said, and followed her sister.

"Whose cars?" Suddenly, Thea wondered if the twins had put something over on her. They seemed to be speaking in code. What were they talking about?

"The Hot Shots," Hannah said over her shoulder, as if that explained everything.

"The hot who?"

Tess shot Thea a scornful look. "Hot Shots. They eat at the Painted Pony before they leave and when they get back." Noting Thea's blank stare, she added, "Uncle Logan is a Hot Shot. He fights forest fires."

"Hurry." Hannah jogged ahead in an ungainly way that Thea found endearing.

"So someone inside should know where your uncle is?"

"Yeah." Tess's steps slowed.

Thea didn't understand why Tess didn't seem

happy at the thought that they were close to finding her uncle.

As soon as Thea stepped inside the Painted Pony, she felt oddly at ease. Most of the place was taken up with black-and-white linoleum tiles, faded Formica tables and booths with worn green bench seats. There was a sturdy-looking bar, a jukebox on the far wall near a pool table and a small, scuffed dance floor.

Even the elderly woman with short gray hair, a weathered face and kind eyes who was hugging Hannah seemed graciously welcoming. Tess hesitated when the woman called her over, but finally submitted and received her embrace with much the same suffering expression as she did when Thea hugged her.

"I'm Mary Socrath. I own the Pony." The woman extended her hand as she came toward Thea, her expression curious. "We haven't seen these two angels in quite some time."

Before Thea could shake her hand, Hannah asked in her soft, polite voice, "Where's Uncle Logan?"

"I thought I saw you two dart in," observed a tall, slender woman coming in the door behind Thea with a gait as stilted as a pigeon's.

"Birdie, come in and meet..." Mary looked expectantly at Thea.

"Thea. Have you seen—"

"Where's Uncle Logan?" Hannah interrupted Thea.

Ignoring both Thea and Hannah, the thin woman stepped closer. "What brings you to Silver Bend, Thea?"

"Introduce yourself, Birdie," Mary gently chastised, then did it for her. "Birdie runs the general store across the street."

Thea's head started to ache. Two days ago finding

Logan McCall had seemed like the logical thing to do. And now?

"Thea's our nanny. We're looking for Uncle Logan." Hannah's voice trembled.

"Oh, not Wes's wife, eh?" An old man pushed his way past Birdie, flashing Thea a grin beneath his bulbous nose. He extended a plump, gnarled hand. "Smiley Peterson, town barber."

After shaking his hand, Thea retreated to Hannah and draped her arm protectively across her shoulders, wishing everyone would just slow down. With a huffing noise, Tess slumped into an empty booth, perhaps realizing that the townspeople seemed more interested in Thea than in helping them find Logan.

"We're looking for Logan McCall," Thea clarified, trying to hold on to her resolve to remain strong for the girls when she only wanted to sink into the booth next to Tess and cry. "He still lives in town, doesn't he?"

"Yes, he does." Birdie smiled, and Thea thought they were getting somewhere until she added, "Are you here long, dear?"

"I want my uncle Logan," Hannah wailed, unable to contain herself any longer.

Everyone in the room seemed to freeze. The third-degree questioning blissfully stopped. Thea led Hannah to the booth Tess had claimed and had her sit down. Hannah cried hysterically, testing Thea's resolve to hold herself together.

"Please, give her a little room," Thea pleaded, pressing a napkin into Hannah's hand. The locals' onslaught, combined with Hannah's tears, put Thea off balance.

"I'll get her something to drink," Mary said.

"You aren't saving these chocolate-chip cookies for

anyone, are you, Mary?" Birdie asked, even as she plucked several cookies from under a covered dish.

Smiley patted Hannah on the top of her head. "The boys are up in Sun Valley fighting a fire. Heard on the radio that it jumped out of bounds, but that the Hot Shots contained it."

Hannah blew her nose, then accepted a cookie. Tess pushed the cookie Birdie offered to the middle of the table, where Thea was sure it would remain untouched.

"When is he coming home?" Thea prodded.

"I'd say another day or so," Birdie chirped.

"Oh, my." Thea felt her heart sink to the tips of her toes. *Another day or so.* That could be a week. *A week!*

"You can probably get a room over at the motel," Smiley suggested.

No. They couldn't. Thea didn't have to take out her wallet to know they couldn't spend one more night in a hotel. One night had been enough to drain her funds significantly.

"Dad's gone and we don't have any money," Tess announced, causing Thea's cheeks to heat with embarrassment and another ripple of activity among Mary, Birdie and Smiley.

"I'll make lunch for everyone," Mary offered before disappearing.

"Where's that father of yours?" Birdie's expression hardened with disapproval.

"Ought to be shot, that man," Smiley grumbled.

Later, after Hannah polished off a cheeseburger with fries and Tess picked at a similar plate, Mary pulled Thea aside. "I've called Lexie, my daughter-in-law. She's got a key to Logan's place. She'll be here after school lets out to take you over. Don't worry about a thing. Logan will put things right."

"THIS IS BEAUTIFUL." Thea followed Lexie Garrett's SUV up Uncle Logan's steep gravel driveway, staring at the dark green pine trees, huge rocks and the occasional patch of snow as if she'd never seen a forest before.

Tess didn't say a word. Slumped in the back seat, she had a knot the size of a football in her tummy. At least when Mrs. Garrett and her daughter, Heidi, had shown up at the Pony they were in a hurry to get baby Henry to the doctor, so they hadn't gotten out of their SUV and tried to talk to them. Tess had been worrying about what she was going to say to Heidi since they'd left Seattle.

Tess couldn't pretend she was still Heidi's friend, just as she couldn't pretend with Hannah that everything was okay. Every once in a while, Tess would wake up and feel almost normal. And then she'd remember that her mom was dead and there was no one that loved her, least of all Uncle Logan.

Her eyes filled with tears, which she quickly blinked away.

Tess wanted her mom back. No one knew her favorite cereal was Cocoa Puffs or that she liked red more than pink. Her mom had always made Tess smile. Now she didn't have anything to smile about.

Tess wanted to go back to the way things were before, when she was just another kid. She used to like lots of things, like watching TV, kicking a ball and making friends. She didn't do any of those things anymore.

Which made Tess think again about Heidi. They used to laugh together a lot in school and at each other's houses. Now Tess couldn't laugh, hadn't laughed in months. So, what would she say when she saw Heidi?

They continued up Uncle Logan's driveway. Whizzer put his front paws on the passenger window and scratched. Hannah put the window down an inch and helped hold him up so he could get air. The little dog breathed in deeply several times, pressing his wet nose to the window and wagging his tail as he dreamed of peeing on all those trees. At least, that's what Tess imagined he was thinking. The darn dog peed on everything. He'd even tried to go on her right after they washed him in the sink in the gas station bathroom.

"This is where your uncle lives?" Thea asked as she shut off the engine. She had her head down so that she could see the huge two-story house in front of them through the windshield. "It's got trees, and a mountain for a backyard…and friends."

Tess used to think Uncle Logan's house was a castle or a mansion. She'd loved pretending that she was a princess or a movie star who lived there with lots of servants. She didn't have those silly dreams anymore. Bad things didn't happen to princesses.

"This is where my mom died." Tess bit her lip, wanting to stay in Thea's small back seat forever. She didn't want to be here.

Mrs. Garrett and Heidi climbed out of the SUV. Thea, Hannah and Whizzer jumped out of the Volkswagen. Tess couldn't move.

"I'll introduce you to Glen," Mrs. Garrett said to Thea. "She's a sweet thing."

Tess had almost forgotten Aunt Glen was staying with Uncle Logan. She was old. Really old. Tess had heard Uncle Logan complain to her mom last summer that Aunt Glen didn't have all her bulbs screwed in. It took Tess a couple of days to figure out that Uncle Logan thought Aunt Glen had gone crazy, which was fine with

Tess because that meant Tess didn't have to pretend nothing was wrong when she was around Aunt Glen.

"I check in on Glen a couple of times a day when the guys are on assignment. I'll feel better that someone's here with her all the time," Mrs. Garrett was saying. "I'm sorry we can't stay. Henry's got a doctor's appointment down the mountain in less than an hour, but you'll be fine. We'll come by tomorrow morning to check up on you."

"Hi." Heidi stepped into the Volkswagen's open car door. Tess hadn't seen her walk up.

She managed a strangled "Hi" back, which was followed by a painful silence.

Heidi wasn't looking at Tess and Tess didn't dare look Heidi in the eye. She wished she could just disappear under the quilts on the seat next to her, but that would be more embarrassing than not knowing what to say. Hannah had gone inside with the adults, so she was no help. Whizzer was busy running around and peeing on every bush he could see. And so Tess was left trapped in the back seat, unable to move or say a word.

Then Mrs. Garrett raced down the steps, saving Tess from further embarrassment. "Heidi, come on. You can catch up with the twins later."

"See you," Heidi called as she left.

Tess slumped over onto the quilts, buried her face in them and tried to stop the tears.

CHAPTER TWO

THE VIEW WAS SPECTACULAR, with snow-covered peaks standing out in sharp contrast against the smoke-softened sunset. One of the things Logan loved about being a Hot Shot was being close to nature. Only he could no longer enjoy it. Logan sat on an icy tree root with his back against the trunk, looking out over the Sun Valley base camp as it settled down for the night.

He had a birthday coming up soon. A birthday he'd be celebrating alone. He'd never been alone. Deb had even been born first. Growing up, she'd been the strong one when things got ugly with their father at home, which was often.

No kid should have to live through what Logan and Deb had. The harsh words. The fear. The bruises.

Shouts of laughter rippled through base camp. A group of firefighters from several different crews had gathered amidst the low tents that dotted the meadow's snowy landscape. The wind was really blowing now, and this far from the fire line, it stole the breath right out of Logan's lungs. His watch showed the temperature as twenty-nine degrees. Standing up and moving around would be smart. Too bad Logan wasn't smart. As hot as he'd been the past few days on the fire line, he was an ice cube now. Which suited him just fine.

He stared back down at camp. For tactical purposes, NIFC had brought in portable toilets, a large canvas tent for Incident Command, and Jose's Taco Truck, which had the best tacos in the Northwest, or so their signs proclaimed. Base camp provided firefighters with some of the amenities they didn't have nearby. Camps didn't get much more minimalist than this one, though.

Golden leaned his shoulder against a pine tree a few feet away from Logan, following the direction of his gaze. "Only the finest cuisine for our firefighters."

"Breakfast burritos aren't so bad." At least the food was hot.

Golden rubbed his stomach as if it was empty. "It takes a lot of tacos to fill a man's belly at the end of the day."

Logan couldn't argue with that. He shrugged deeper into his down jacket and thought longingly of a hot shower. Smoke and sweat had combined to form a sticky layer on Logan's skin. NIFC hadn't deemed the Sun Valley burn of a long enough duration to pay a vendor for portable shower stalls.

"How are you doing, Logan?"

Uh-oh. Logan shifted on the root. Even though they were best friends, Jackson and Logan tended to call each other by their Hot Shot names unless it was a social occasion or they felt the need to speak on a personal level, as Golden did now. And as he'd done over the past few days when Logan had lost his temper.

"I'm fine, *Jackson*." Which was so far from the truth that the words nearly echoed in the hollow area once occupied by Logan's heart.

"Don't bullshit a bullshitter."

Logan sucked on his cheek to keep from saying anything.

"I need you out there one hundred percent. What I don't need is you and Aiden going head-to-head every time I give an order. It's not good for safety or team morale."

Jackson knelt down until he could look Logan in the eye. "This is going to be a tough year on the crews as it is. Two other states set early controlled burns that blew over the line. We were fortunate that we contained ours with less than a ten-acre loss. California and Colorado weren't so lucky."

Logan perked up. He could talk about work. Work was his savior. "They lose anything other than tree husks? Was anyone injured? Did any structures get burned?"

"No. We were lucky this time. But public opinion is against us, budgets are tight and I don't want any mistakes on my team." His jaw had that firm set to it that warned, "Mess with me and you'll be in for a world of hurt."

Relieved that the crews were okay, Logan gave a jerky nod to indicate he understood, that he would try harder to toe the line. Then he waited for Jackson to go away.

He didn't.

"I know that losing Deb hit you hard, but you have to snap out of this."

"Is that an order?" Something bitter climbed up Logan's throat. He told himself it was just bad tacos, not the fact that his best friend since high school was disappointed in him. "Or am I missing something?"

Jackson shook his head. "You know what I miss? I miss my right-hand man. I miss my friend. There are a lot of us that miss you, buddy. You might want to think about that while you're checking out that sunset."

Logan would like nothing more than to do just that.

Only thing was, he didn't know how to find that person Jackson referred to—the man he used to be.

STANDING IN LOGAN'S driveway later, Thea breathed deeply. The green scent of fir and pine filled the air. The dark green and brown colors set against the dusting of snow on the ground were calming. This part of Idaho was breathtakingly beautiful, so different from the skyscrapers of Seattle.

She could forget her goals up here, set aside the dream of earning a degree that would put her at the top of her field as her mother had done. Here she could listen to her little inner voice, the one that occasionally piped up at the oddest times with a twenty-seven-year-old's desire for a family, a white picket fence and PTA meetings.

She let herself stare at Logan's house just a little longer before she went back inside. It was a perfect house, straight off a Christmas card. The big log home was blanketed in snow, with smoke curling out of the two-story brick chimney. Part of Thea longed for the storybook life that had to go along with living in such a house. But she'd promised her mother when she was ten—right before her mother left—that she'd make something of herself.

Thea retreated to the kitchen and sank into a spindle-backed chair that felt unsteady enough to be an antique, her notes in piles next to her laptop, her study plan tacked to the wall. She needed to be reviewing her advanced technology notes. She should have reviewed them two days ago. She swung her foot, causing a ripple from the bells she'd attached to her shoes. According to her grandmother, vibrant noise was supposed to keep her spirits up, because the light notes reminded her to believe in sunshine and happily-ever-afters, of dreams being achieved. The sound didn't help. She couldn't focus on her studies.

The kitchen table was adorned with a deep brown crocheted doily. The hardwood floor was dark wood, as were the cabinets, and the countertop was brown tile with brown grout. Brown. Dark. Corners. Even the coffeemaker was made of black plastic.

The effect of the room was downright depressing, not at all the homey atmosphere the exterior of the house promised. Thea needed to dive into her notes, but she couldn't concentrate in this gloomy environment. She pushed back her chair.

"Brown," she muttered as she moved into the shadowy living room. Brown hardwood floors, brown velour couches—brown, brown, brown, brown, brown. Not a bit of other color in the place. The same neatness and lack of knickknacks in the kitchen pervaded this room—nothing to indicate anything about the man who lived here, his family, his roots. No photos of smiling relatives and friends or mementos of any kind. With the blinds closed in every room, it was more sterile than the furnished apartment she and the twins had been evicted from. And, despite the neatness of the place, everything was coated with a layer of dust.

The house had seemed so promising from the outside. Thea wandered dejectedly down the dimly lit hallway toward the bathroom.

"Deb, is that you?" an elderly, shaky voice called out as Thea passed another dark room.

"It's me, Thea." Thea poked her head in the bedroom.

Glen, Logan's maiden aunt, a gray-haired beauty, was sitting in bed knitting something with dark brown yarn.

The coffee mug Thea had filled earlier and a half-eaten piece of apple pie rested on the nightstand.

"Do I know you, dear?" Glen asked in a tremulous voice that sounded close to an elderly Katharine Hepburn.

"I'm taking care of the twins until Logan comes back."

Lexie had warned Thea that Glen's short-term memory was unreliable. She might have said nonexistent. Glen didn't seem to remember Thea at all.

"Now, my boy Logan, he's a man you can rely on. Cares about folks, he does." Glen's blue eyes were dull, faded, and a bit lost. She sighed. "Have I ever told you that I raised Logan and Deb after my sister died?" Glen gestured to her bureau of dark wood. Several pictures blanketed in thick dust were displayed there. It was the first place in the house that Thea had seen pictures.

"No, you haven't." Thea stepped nearer for a closer look, carefully brushing away the dust on an old, square-framed picture of two similar-looking young women leaning close, with seventies beehive hairdos and psychedelic orange and lime-green dresses.

"That's me and my sister, Meg." Glen shuffled out of bed and stood next to Thea. She smelled of soiled clothing and sweet coffee. This close, Thea could see her complexion had the tawny hue of unwashed skin. "And this is Deb and Logan."

Thea closed her eyes for a moment to collect herself as anger at the old woman's neglect threatened to overwhelm her. Lexie, with her own family and responsibilities, couldn't be blamed, but the absent Logan McCall could. Already, Thea was thinking about what needed to be done—linens washed, everything dusted, swept and vacuumed, and Glen needed a bath, along with a complete brushing of her hair and teeth.

Thea drew in a steadying breath before peering at the photo Glen indicated. Logan wore a tuxedo and Deb a princess-style wedding dress. Two impeccably groomed blond heads leaned close together, both sporting picture-perfect smiles. Their expressions were so alike…

"They're twins," Thea said, noting the resemblance.

"Yep," Glen confirmed. "Runs in our family thicker than the plague. Meg was my twin." Her hand stroked the picture of the two women, seeming to tremble more with each breath she took.

Thea took Glen's arm in case she collapsed. "Are you all right?"

The old woman nodded with a sniff. "Doc says my asthma medication gives me the shakes. Can't complain. Well, I could complain, but what good would it do me?" She returned to the bed.

Glen's face seemed deathly pale in the shadowy bedroom. Thea thought Glen could use more than some occasional light. Giving in to impulse, Thea spun the plastic handle on the blinds to let sunshine stream through the window.

Glen frowned. "Logan doesn't like them open."

"Why not?" Thea couldn't understand why Logan would want to keep this sweet old lady in the dark.

"Sometimes it's easier not to look." Glen waved a hand at the bureau again. "Those blond beauties in the back are Deb's little girls—Tess and Hannah."

When it seemed Glen was waiting for a reaction to the girls, Thea obligingly leaned in for a closer look. The twins were younger, sporting bright bathing suits and smiles. Everything about the girls in the picture sparkled with energy and happiness. Thea longed to see them that way again.

Glen settled back against the pillows. "They light up this house."

It was comforting to know that the girls had been happy here. Thea hoped they would be again. "I'll leave you to your crocheting and go check on the girls."

"I may as well go with you, just in case their room's not as clean as it should be. I wouldn't want the girls to get into trouble." Glen scooted back off the bed. She turned the handle on the blinds to bring the room back to shadows. "Logan prefers the house dark," she explained again as she shuffled ahead of Thea down the hall.

"It's neat as a pin," Glen announced with apparent relief as she paused in the doorway.

Peeking around the door frame into the dimly lit bedroom, Thea had to agree. Like the girls' room in Seattle, there were no stray shoes, no scattered scrunchies for that long blond hair, no half-dressed Barbies with hair that was frizzed from being carried about in backpacks, cars and pillowcases. The room was as impersonal as the rest of the house, from the quilted pink bedspreads to the white dressers each holding a lamp and a small clock radio.

Thea noticed untouched toys stacked neatly in the closet. Now Hannah sat on the floor playing quietly with Whizzer, while Tess lay on her bed staring at the ceiling.

Thea had hoped the girls would thrive in their uncle's fairy-tale house. But now her heart filled with doubt.

How could she leave them here?

"WHO TAUGHT YOU HOW to make Barbie clothes?" Hannah asked, leaning over Thea's shoulder while she sat in one of the dull living-room chairs creating a new wardrobe for the two Barbie dolls she'd found in the twins' closet. "Did your mom teach you?"

Thea paused midstitch, staring into the fire. Her mom hadn't been supportive of Thea learning any homemaking arts.

"My grandmother taught me. I've loved sewing since I was a kid." Thea remembered her mother looking at her handiwork and saying how those neat stitches meant she'd be a wonderful surgeon one day. All Thea had wanted was for her mom to say her baby doll quilt was beautiful. Thea shied away from the memory. Her mother had never understood Thea, not that she'd had more than ten years to figure her daughter out. The painful memory had Thea reaching for a change of attitude.

"I once met a man who created Barbie ball gowns for a living," Thea said, glancing at Hannah to gauge her interest in the story. The twins never watched television, which made for long nights. Thea had learned to rely on her knack for telling odd stories to engage the twins and help pass the time.

"A *man?*" Tess blurted. She sat in the corner of the dark couch, her limbs pulled up tight, her small forehead creased in disbelief.

Glen looked up from her crochet project. Thea had yet to figure out what the older woman was making. It was long and brown, every stitch making it longer and browner.

"A man," Thea confirmed, wondering briefly when they'd see the elusive Uncle Logan and if he'd be good for the girls.

"Why would a man want to sew?" Hannah reached across Thea's lap to finger the small red dress, until she saw Thea watching her. With a quick glance at Tess, Hannah drew her hand away, tucking it behind her back.

"People should pick jobs that make them happy," Thea said, pretending to be intent on finishing Barbie's hem, while trying to ignore the rising panic that she should be studying if she ever wanted to pass her exams. She couldn't even propose a dissertation topic until she received a passing grade on both her written and oral exams. She shook her foot, eliciting a soft jingle. "What do you want to be when you grow up, Hannah?"

Hannah shrugged, looking at Tess, then stared at the fire. Thea was convinced that the two shared an unspoken bond. Neither would get over her grief without the other. And Tess wasn't done grieving.

"I always wanted to be one of those secret agents, with the slinky dress, spiked heels and a real kick-ass gun," Glen spoke up, rearranging her yarn chain in her lap. "Only Eldred came along and I didn't think I could leave Silver Bend."

Assuming Eldred had been Glen's beau, Thea smiled. "It's nice to dream big. How about you, Tess? Any plans for the future?"

Instead of answering, Tess got up and left the room.

AS HE DROVE HOME toward Silver Bend, Logan McCall ignored the streaks of golden light peeking over the horizon. A new day may be dawning, but it would be the same gray, colorless day that he'd faced yesterday and the day before that.

He drove in silence up the long, steep grade before he reached Silver Bend, passing the ramshackle, abandoned house where his parents had died. Where his father had killed his mother.

In that house, he'd learned how low a man could sink when ruled by a hot temper regularly fueled by alcohol. In that house, he'd learned that the only person he could depend on was his twin sister, Deb. Together, they'd survived the verbal abuse and physical beatings. When they'd left, Logan vowed he'd never have a family of his own.

Deb, lucky enough not to have the gene that carried their father's destructive temper, had lived an almost normal life, married and produced two girls Logan adored, only to die much too soon. Burdened with his father's shameful legacy—a fiery temper—Logan couldn't trust himself to honor Deb's request and be the girls' guardian.

What if he lost his temper or did something stupid? Like go on a drunken binge. Or get so blitzed he wouldn't know who he was hitting or why.

Logan wiped a hand over his face.

No. He didn't know how to be a father. It was best that Tess and Hannah were being raised by someone else. Even if Wes wasn't the best father around—he sure as hell hadn't been the best husband—he had to be better at it than Logan.

So he continued to his house and the life that was emptier than he'd ever dreamed possible.

"ARE WE THE FIRST VISITORS from Silver Bend this morning?" Lexie stood on the front porch with plump little Henry propped on one hip. Her smile was dazzling, but as genuine as her little boy's. Lexie's brown hair was pulled back into a mother's utilitarian ponytail. "We just dropped Heidi off at school, so I thought we'd come by to check on you. Did you make it through the night okay?"

"We were fine." Thea let them in, taking the blue quilted diaper bag from Lexie. "Am I going to get more visitors today? The casseroles yesterday were…interesting." They wouldn't need to cook for a week—if she could get the girls to eat them.

"Small town. Half the population over fifty." Lexie rolled her eyes. "Oh-ho, are you going to get visitors. Each one will dust off the old family recipe." She shuddered, then sank onto the couch and settled Henry on her lap.

"It doesn't sound so bad." Cities were so impersonal. Even at her university, you could pass by hundreds of students without anyone ever looking you in the eye, much less be concerned about you.

"She doesn't suspect, does she, Hot Shot?" Lexie played with one of Henry's chubby fists. "They'll know where she was born by dinnertime."

Thea was reminded of the relentless questioning from the trio in the Painted Pony.

"So, if you have any secrets you want to keep, practice your poker face and changing the subject." Lexie continued, "Not that we aren't fond of them all, it's just that…well, we love it when there's a big political scandal to keep them busy."

"Thanks, I think." Thea sat on the opposite end of the brown couch, catching sight of Tess lingering in the hallway as she did so. "How old is Henry?"

"Nearly eight months." Lexie blew a raspberry in his fist, and he giggled. "We nearly lost him when he was born. But you're a fighter like your dad, aren't you, Hot Shot?"

"And your husband is a…uh…Hot Shot, too?" Thea was becoming incredibly curious about Logan and his Hot Shot job.

Lexie nodded. "Firefighting runs in Jackson's veins. He'd be miserable if he couldn't fight fires."

Henry sneezed. Lexie efficiently wiped his nose with a tissue, dodging the chubby hand that batted hers away.

"I'm a Hot Shot, too," Lexie blurted. After a moment of uncharacteristic hesitation, she pulled a jar out of her diaper bag and handed it to Thea.

"Hot Shot Marinade." Thea read the colorful label. "How cool. Are you a saleswoman?"

"I *am* Hot Shot Sauces. I'm head cook, bottler and salesman." Lexie drew Henry closer, eliciting a squawk out of the boy. She laughed self-consciously. "He's right, I'm taking myself too seriously. It's just that I've never done anything except be a wife and mother."

It took Thea a moment to sort all Lexie's achievements—wife, mother, businesswoman. "Don't put yourself down. I'm even a bit envious. You have it all." Even though they seemed about the same age, Thea had years of study and work ahead of her before kids were a possibility. In her eyes, Lexie had set the bar as high as Thea's mother had. Still… "Isn't it hard? Glen said something last night about Hot Shots being gone a lot. And running a business when you have two kids…"

"Sure, it's hard. Forget seeing any Hot Shot in the summer for more than twenty-four hours at a time. It's pretty steady nine-to-five work in town from November to March." She laughed. "I mean, they're in town if they're part of the permanent staff, like Jackson and Logan. But I've tried living without him, and it just wasn't what I wanted." Lexie grinned. "What can I say? I love the lug."

Thea found herself grinning back, even though her heart gave a small, envious pang. What would it be like to have a love that strong? "You must be brilliant as well as lucky in love."

"Your time will come. If you stick around, you can have your pick of the other Hot Shots." Lexie bounced Henry gently. "Not that it's easy to catch one. Most of them don't know the meaning of the phrase *settle down*. Or, they're stuck in a rut."

"A rut?"

"That's a nice way of saying some of them have yet to grow up. Some got dumped and have sworn off women. Others don't realize they weren't put on this earth to sleep with as many women as they can." She sighed. "Then there's Logan. He's always been a ladies' man, but he can't seem to get past his grief or his anger over losing Deb. He had a temper before, but now he's got the shortest fuse known to man."

Cognizant of Tess eavesdropping in the hallway, Thea lowered her voice. "He'll be fine with the girls, won't he?"

Lexie looked Thea directly in the eyes. "He'd do anything for those girls."

There was an odd sound in the hallway, followed by retreating footsteps.

"I'm so glad you're here, Thea. I know Logan's going to need help with Hannah and Tess."

"Whoa. Wait." Thea shook her head. "I'm not staying. I'm getting my Ph.D. I brought the girls here because Wes is AWOL and they had nowhere else to turn."

"They'll still have nowhere to turn. Fire season is starting. You can't just leave them." Lexie's expression dimmed.

Thea thought about the untouched pile of textbooks and notes in the kitchen, about the physical condition and mental state of Glen, about the bare interior of the house, and two little girls with broken hearts. In her mind's eye, she saw her mother leaving for good, but not before she wrenched a promise from Thea to reach for the stars and refuse to settle.

"Well," Lexie said finally. "Things have a way of working out, don't they?"

THE RED CAUGHT HIS EYE first as Logan rounded the bend toward his driveway.

Red giving way to a slender pair of legs.

Then the other colors hit him. Yellow, blue, orange. The spectrum of the rainbow glinted against the light dusting of snow on the ground and the yellow Volkswagen in his driveway.

By the time Logan got out of the truck, it had registered that a woman did indeed belong to the car. A woman with killer legs and a dog.

Said dog was little and white with brown spots and short fur. At the moment, he was lifting his leg over the shrubs edging Logan's porch.

"Good morning. Are you Logan McCall?" The woman's voice was melodious, as colorful as the red denim skirt she wore topped with a bright orange T-shirt. Totally inappropriate attire for early spring in the mountains.

Not that he didn't appreciate the view. He just didn't appreciate the invasion of his privacy.

Logan pushed his sunglasses higher up on his nose and emitted a gruff reply. "Yeah, I'm McCall." Thoughts of coming home to silence, a hot shower and twelve hours of sleep faded. Why was this woman here?

"It's a beautiful day, isn't it? Not a cloud in the sky." She laughed a little self-consciously and shifted her feet.

Logan stared at the woman's bright red sneakers. She'd laced her shoes with little silver bells so that her feet tinkled every time she moved.

He made the mistake of looking her in the face for the first time. She had warm brown eyes that crinkled when she smiled. Somehow, he'd known she'd have the kind of expression that made you want to smile back. No one could drive a Volkswagen like that and not be cheerful.

Something was wrong. He could feel it. Women like this didn't show up on his doorstep unless… "Where's Aunt Glen?"

"She's inside with the girls." The woman had a way of standing still that made it seem as if she were moving. Maybe she did move. A thin layer of snow crunched softly beneath those red shoes. There was something about her that was…intriguing.

As if he'd heard a car coming, Logan looked down the driveway, taking his time before asking, "What girls?" Part of him wanted to believe she had a carload of women in his house, but he suspected that wasn't the case.

The dog trotted over to sniff Logan's mud-caked Black Diamond fire boots.

"Whizzer, no," she warned the dog.

Logan bent down and petted the friendly dog. Ignoring the woman's bare, slender ankles that led up to shapely, fine legs, he craned his neck around until he could see the Volkswagen's license plate. Washington. Last time he'd seen Wes, his truck had sported Washington plates. His hand stilled as the dog danced away.

"That explains a lot of things," he observed as the anger pooled in his belly, welcome in its ability to obliterate all other feeling. His nieces were inside, which meant that Wes was close by. "Where's Wes?"

"I don't know." The joy seemed to have gone out of her tone. Even the bells on her feet were silent. "I haven't heard from him in over a month."

Logan snorted in disbelief. From where he knelt on the ground, he could look up and see her over the top of his sunglasses. She didn't seem so bright and sunny now. In fact, her eyes darted around as if she was starting to panic. Maybe she was going to cry.

The last thing he wanted to witness was a female display of emotion—from Wes's girlfriend, no less. When Deb died, he'd locked his own emotions away so their intensity wouldn't break him.

But instead of bursting into tears, the woman cried out and sprang forward. "Whizzer, no!"

At the sound of spray hitting something behind him, Logan leaped up and away, with only a brief twinge in his leg. His reflexes were sharp after having dodged many an angry bee fighting fires in the mountains. Bees didn't like fire and they wanted desperately to take their anger out on someone. Snakes, at least, seemed to have the sense to dart out of the way when they heard twenty firefighters moving toward them.

"Whizzer, no," she reprimanded the prancing dog before turning those deep brown eyes his way. "I'm so sorry. He didn't get you, did he?"

Logan just stared at the woman, unwilling to embarrass himself by looking for wet spots on his backside. If the little rodent had pissed on him, he couldn't feel it yet through his grubby pants and boots.

Rather than back off from his stare, the woman closed the gap between them with a soft ripple of bells, grasped him firmly by the shoulders, turned him around and checked him out.

At least, Logan assumed she was checking out his ass. That's what most women did. And most of the time, he didn't mind. Not a bit.

But that was before Deb became sick and died. Before Logan became the legal guardian of his nieces. Before Deb's lowlife, trucking husband had disappeared with the twins because Logan wouldn't stop him. Before Logan had sunk into despair because he'd let the most important people in his life down.

The woman turned him one way and another, her touch commanding yet distinctly tender. "He didn't get you." Her hands fell away as she stepped back.

Logan blew out the breath he'd been holding. He hadn't been on the receiving end of an attractive woman's touch since…last summer. He suppressed a groan. He didn't even want to think about it.

Logan was selective. Ample assets, that's what he liked. Lots of blond hair—didn't even matter if it was natural blond—and full, red, pouty lips that whispered with the promise of a night or two of fun. But this woman…

She was thin, small breasted, with chestnut hair that tumbled past her shoulder blades and dimples that only made those crinkly smiling eyes that much more appealing. He could see the freckles dusting her nose because she wasn't wearing any makeup, not even lipstick. She was the kind of woman who stayed home and baked apple pies to spoil her man upon his return.

She wasn't his type at all.

"Where's Wes?" he repeated irritably, thinking that she wasn't Wes's type, either.

"I told you, I don't know." She hugged herself against the chill. It was nippy out, yet she only wore that thin

T-shirt—bright orange with a yellow sun—and an in-
digo-blue jean jacket over that almost knee-length red
denim skirt. Dressed like that, she had to be from California or Arizona originally. Add the Volkswagen Beetle and she had to be a second-generation hippie.

"Wes stopped paying the bills and we got evicted,"
she added. She looked at him tentatively, as if waiting
for him to bite her head off.

Logan swore. He'd known it was wrong to let the
twins go, but he'd been unconvinced that he was the better alternative. "Are they okay?"

"See for yourself." She spun away with her bells jingling, striking his nerves as she walked toward the house.

"Whizzer, come on." She opened the front door as if
she, not Logan, lived there.

Whizzer jumped up onto the porch with superdog-
like agility.

"Are you coming?" She hesitated in the doorway.
Sunlight glinted off the silver threads in her red skirt and
the bells on her feet. One shoe continued to jingle.

Whizzer stood on the porch panting, as if peeing
were an Olympic sport in which he was competing and
which required a lot of effort.

Logan almost smiled at the lighthearted picture they
made until he remembered she was Wes's girl, which
meant her friendly, upbeat manner was probably just
an act.

"They've been waiting to see you," she added when
he didn't budge.

Logan scratched his grimy neck, more than willing
to bet they had. The girls probably blamed him for every
crappy thing that had happened to them since their mom
died. And they had every right to. If anything bad had

happened to them while they were in Wes's care, it was Logan's fault.

Guilt and frustration pulsed in his veins. Suddenly, Logan couldn't face Tess and Hannah.

THEA WAS INCREDIBLY RELIEVED to have food for the girls, a roof over their heads, and to have found the twins' uncle. Or she had been relieved until Logan stood staring at her as if she'd just landed from planet Mars and might be dangerous.

"My name's Thea Gayle. I've been watching the girls," she managed to say, assuming he was waiting for her to introduce herself. She thrust her free hand in his direction, then pumped his hand vigorously, until she realized how nicely his large hand felt wrapped around hers—callused, warm, comfortable. His friendly grip was at odds with the melancholy expression in his eyes that said stay away, keep your distance, don't want any.

Against the play of light and green shadows of fir trees, Logan McCall looked magnificent as he hesitated on the porch. Like a young Robert Redford, with soot-streaked angular features and eyes as blue as the cloud-less sky above him.

They stared at each other across an awkward bit of silence while Thea struggled for something to say, which was unusual for her. She was seldom at a loss for words. Stories to ease the mood usually came easily to her lips. It had to be those eyes of his, so blue, so sad.

They stepped into the house. The clock ticked on the living-room mantel. Thea could hear Aunt Glen talking to Tess and Hannah in the kitchen. Whizzer circled the hardwood floor behind her before plopping down with a big grunt.

Thea shrugged apologetically, grateful for any break in the tension. "We had quite a time finding you. It seemed like the whole town took us in."

The gorgeously grim-looking firefighter stared down at her with distant eyes. It was clear that he'd come directly from a fire. He wore a yellow button-down shirt in need of a washing, dark green khakis and grimy work boots. Her fingers itched to touch the Nomex fabric his clothes were made of. It was fire resistant, an advance that she'd explored in a section of her textile studies.

As they continued to stare at each other, Logan's golden eyebrows hovered low over those attractive peepers, as if he couldn't quite believe what he was seeing. She bet women far and wide fell at his feet begging to be lost in the deep blue of his gaze, which was compelling despite his obvious reluctance to smile.

He was the kind of guy who didn't need anything or anybody. Here was a man who could pick and choose which women he spent time with. And she'd bet Whizzer's kibble that he was choosy, all right. He was the type who didn't give her a second glance, with her plain features, plain coloring and plain body. Heck, he didn't think enough of her to speak to her.

Or it was as Lexie had implied. Logan was too burdened with grief to care about much of anything.

Thea sighed, telling herself it was a good thing that Logan didn't think much of her, even better that he didn't need her. She'd fulfilled her obligation to the twins. She had to get back to Seattle and her study schedule.

She slid her cold hands in the pockets of her jean jacket and retreated farther into the house. Thea was so intent on keeping her distance from the man that she missed his question.

"Did Wes treat them right?" he repeated, words heavy with scorn as he pushed his sunglasses back up his nose. "Did you?"

Thea sucked in a breath, torn between an unusual feeling of loyalty toward her employer—even though he'd turned out to be a deadbeat—the need to tell the truth—that Wes was so neglectful it was hard to call him a dad—and indignation that he'd think she'd mistreat the twins.

"If it's money you want, you've come to the wrong place." Logan spread his hands, palms up, his gaze burning with hurt and accusation. "I'm just a poor Hot Shot."

There was that temper Lexie had warned her about. Be smart and say as little as possible, she counseled herself. Don't make a joke of it. Logan McCall didn't want anything to do with optimism. If anything would work with him, it would be sarcasm, something Thea avoided.

Only, all that intensity directed at her from those blue eyes was disconcerting. And her mouth engaged itself before she had time to heed her own advice.

"A hot-who? Is that like some sort of male stripper?" At his startled expression, Thea continued, rolling her eyes dramatically. "Because I've only met one male stripper. His name was Cowboy Temptation, but I don't think he was a real cowboy. I mean, he wore a holster with pop guns."

Logan's jaw worked. "I'm a Hot Shot." He emphasized each word carefully, then added, "A wildland firefighter."

Too shell-shocked at herself to answer intelligibly, Thea could only echo, "Wildland?"

"My team fights forest fires. I'm not a city firefighter."

She smiled as if she'd missed his irritation, as if she

didn't know there wasn't a city anywhere close to here. Thea wasn't going to kid herself. Logan, with that icy, wounded reserve of his, wasn't going to help her get back to Seattle. In fact, she didn't think she or the twins would be welcome in his house at all.

"Oh, I get it," she said, playing the dumb brunette because he might be the kind of hero who wanted to come to the aid of a helpless woman. "You put out fires in parks, like Yellowstone."

"Close enough." The firefighter chewed on the inside of his cheek.

Thea's conscience tsk-tsked her. He'd been showing all the signs of a man shadowed with grief. Now she'd upset him even more with her "don't worry about little old me, my IQ hovers safely below yours" routine. He didn't know if she was ditzy, kidding or seriously intellectually challenged. That tended to yank the carpet out from under a guy.

"You really shouldn't do that," she found herself saying as she studied him.

"What?"

Because she was a touchy-feely person, Thea came forward, and stroked his jaw with her forefinger. His skin was stubbled and rough to the touch. Of its own accord, as if entranced by the texture of his cheek, her finger continued to trail over his skin.

The Hot Shot froze.

Mortified, Thea snatched her hand back, oh so aware that her finger had started to stray toward his lips. She never reacted to men this way, as if she were a brazen woman of the world. For crying out loud, she was Thea Gayle, dateless Ph.D. candidate. Everybody knew that. Happy, harmless, lonely Thea Gayle. Well, that last lonely bit was her descriptor, but in the dating world, she was definitely not a player.

She shoved her hands back into her pockets to keep them occupied, out of trouble and away from the fire-fighter. Her face felt warm. "You shouldn't chew on your cheek. It must be painful for one thing, but it can't be healthy."

He must think she was an idiot. She was a talker by nature and babbled to ease awkward situations. Usually, her babbling didn't bother her, but this time Thea longed to escape. Only, she couldn't leave the girls until she was sure Logan would care for them better than Wes had, and not turn them out.

He wouldn't turn them out, would he?

She peeked at the man through her lashes. He opened his mouth, about to say something, then snapped it shut and shook his head. His jaw worked, as if he was try-ing not to bite the inside of his cheek again.

"What do your friends call you?" she managed to say, trying once more to put him at ease.

"Logan McCall." There was the barest trace of a tease in his voice, as though he was reluctant to admit her question amused him.

That teasing note meant a lot to Thea. It meant he wasn't heartless. The girls would be fine. "You don't have a nickname or something? Lo? Mac?"

After a telltale pause, he denied it. "Nope."

Thea grinned, grinning wider when his mouth turned ever so slightly up at the corners in an almost smile.

From the kitchen, she heard Glen's tremulous voice.

"Oh, I almost forgot them." Thea grabbed Logan's arm and tugged. "They can't wait to see you."

Well, that wasn't quite true. Still, Thea wanted to believe in happily-ever-afters, even if she knew firsthand they rarely existed. She could hope for Logan and the girls. The sooner she got this reunion over with and smoothed things out for them, the sooner she'd be able to get back to her own life.

The thought was unexpectedly distressing.

"I THOUGHT I HEARD VOICES." Aunt Glen pushed open the swinging kitchen door with one sticklike arm, smiling when she saw Logan. Much as Logan had tried to keep meat on Aunt Glen's bones this winter, she was skinny as a rail. "Back so soon, Logan?"

Moving past Thea, Logan swept his fragile aunt into a careful hug. "Can I get you anything? Coffee? Something to eat?"

"Not a thing, dear."

Logan released her, more than a little annoyed by the arrival of his nieces and Wes's ditzy girlfriend. She'd thought a Hot Shot was a stripper? The sooner Logan found out what was going on and sent her on her way, the better.

Glen's voice stopped Logan in the doorway. "Well, perhaps you could make a fresh pot of coffee. Deb drank the last of it before she went on her walk."

Logan gripped the kitchen door frame. Aunt Glen spoke of his sister in the present tense. Glen was slipping further and further into her own reality, just when Logan needed her to hang on to his.

"I'll make some." Thea slipped into the kitchen.

Aunt Glen seemed to sway as Thea passed her. Afraid she might fall, Logan put his arm around her back and, with one hand on each of her elbows, guided the frail old woman to the couch.

"You treat me like I'm old," she said, setting her mouth in a tight line.

"No, I treat you like the lady you are."

Glen's expression eased. "When I was younger, no one treated me like a lady. I was a broad and proud of it."

"You've always been both to me." She'd always been there, trying to shield Deb and Logan from the horror that was their childhood. She'd taken them in when their parents died, and tried to give them a normal life.

"What a sweet little dog," Glen said, reaching down to pet Whizzer. "Is he yours?"

The kitchen door creaked behind him and Logan turned.

"Uncle Logan?" Hannah took a tentative step forward.

Logan's eyes watered as he saw his sister in her daughters' faces. Tess had her chin jutted out in Deb's stubborn manner and Hannah's lip trembled just like Deb's did before she cried. But they'd changed, too. Hannah had filled out a bit and Tess looked almost anorexic.

Part of Logan wanted to hug them, part of him burned with guilt over letting his sister down and not fighting to keep them in his home, and part of him wanted to shatter with the physical reminder that his sister was gone.

"I need to take a shower." Logan escaped to the back of the house rather than face his nieces and admit—again—that he wasn't the man he needed to be.

CHAPTER THREE

AFTER HIS SHOWER, Logan pushed through the kitchen door in search of caffeine. Thea stood at the counter wiping down a coffee cup, humming a tune and moving her body almost imperceptibly to some beat only she could hear. The coffeepot was gurgling with life, but it was Thea's energy that held Logan spellbound.

Colors. Bells. A woman's voice.

How long had it been since he'd felt happy enough to go out dancing? Never mind that he'd spent much of the last eight months recuperating from his broken leg. When was the last time joy of any sort had surged through his blood and energized his body?

Logan yanked at the neck of his T-shirt, which suddenly seemed to be choking him. His sister had died in this house. Her two daughters had witnessed Deb growing weaker by the day. There was nothing to celebrate here. How dare this woman—this *stranger* who had replaced Deb in Wes's life—come into his kitchen and bop around as if she hadn't a care in the world.

The kitchen door creaked softly as it settled into place.

Thea started and turned, stopping when she saw Logan staring at her. She gave him a half shrug and a half smile as though he should understand that she couldn't help herself.

But she did stop moving.

"Are you through?" he asked between gritted teeth.

She blinked those milk-chocolate eyes of hers. If he was expecting a fight, he wasn't going to get it.

Logan struggled with his temper. Lately, anything could light his fuse. He'd been yearning for a good fight, and had even considered hitting a bar down the mountain in the hopes of finding trouble. Lately? Who was he kidding? He'd battled his temper since the day he was born.

With more than ten years as a Hot Shot, Logan had been in his share of brawls—mostly after long days on a fire when he was too keyed up and exhausted to sleep. The Sun Valley fire, with Spider riding his ass every day, had been tough. Coming home to his nieces had been tougher.

"Coffee's ready. Milk or sugar?"

Logan didn't have to look at Thea to see the smile on her face. Cheerfulness filled her voice.

"Half a cup with both," he managed to say, biting back his irritation.

"One sweet cow, coming up." She'd already found the milk and sugar. In no time, she'd fixed his coffee. "Would you like a slice of apple pie? Mary brought it by yesterday."

"No, thanks," Logan mumbled as he took the cup. He tried sitting, but he was too strung out to relax. His body demanded movement or total release. Besides, the kitchen table was cluttered with books and papers. He paced the kitchen. "Where is everybody?"

"Outside with Whizzer." She pushed back the curtains over the kitchen windows to let in more light, filling the room with tinkling bells and rays of dust-ridden sunshine.

The command *"Don't,"* died in his throat as the suddenly too-bright room dazzled him. He blinked and squinted. "I thought Wes hated dogs."

"We rescued him along the way. He's a sweetheart if you don't make him nervous. And he has a tendency to mark things, which is how we came up with his name. I'm hoping that with a little love and stability, he'll settle down."

Without much sleep and without his sunglasses, the light was almost too much to bear. "I suppose strangers make him nervous," he said, recalling how the terrier had tried to mark him.

"And new places, loud noises and too much excitement." She added in a dramatic whisper, "I'd keep your voice down if I were you."

Was she teasing him?

She couldn't be. But she did seem to be flirting.

The idea that Thea was treating him as if he was an old friend or her big brother, when she didn't even know him, didn't seem possible. Or flattering. He was the Tin Man, damn it.

"Aunt Glen seemed to like Whizzer." *She probably likes you.* The thought rose unbidden and unwelcome. For whatever reason, Thea was with Wes and, therefore, not to be trusted. "What did you ever see in Wes?" Logan demanded, hoping her answer would put the kibosh on whatever it was about her that intrigued him.

"A place to live and a steady paycheck." She sounded almost relieved to be talking about it.

The thought of Thea sleeping with Wes turned his stomach. Wes must have really put one over on her.

Thea smiled, but it was an apologetic smile. "Maybe I wasn't clear before. I'm the girls' nanny. I took the job because I'm working on my Ph.D. in textiles." She gestured to the mess of books on the table. "Wes is my employer. Although Wes hasn't paid me since I started, hasn't been home in more than four weeks and his cell phone is disconnected." She blurted it all in a rush and then blushed, as if embarrassed to admit the extent of their problems.

Which were really Logan's problems.

The good news was she wasn't shacking up with Wes. It was just her legs and Logan's lack of sex that had his mind in the gutter. But...Logan sank into a kitchen chair as the meaning of her words sank in.

Heaven help him. With Wes out of the picture, Logan had no choice but to take the girls.

"Why didn't you call me sooner?" he asked when he managed to speak.

She smiled apologetically. "Believe me, I would have loved to have called you sooner. The twins didn't tell me much about you until we got evicted. I kept us going as long as I could." She hesitated. "Listen, I'm working on my Ph.D. and the exams are looming. I've got to take the tests starting in May, but it looks like you're in a bind." She laughed self-consciously. "If you wanted me to stay on, I wouldn't turn you down."

Invite all that noise and color to stay? "No, thanks."

Logan shot up out of his chair. Swift steps took him to the window next to Thea. He wrenched the curtains closed.

"I don't allow sunlight in here." It reminded him of his sister's sunny disposition—strikingly similar to Thea's. "Or anywhere in the house."

"I thought they were only closed when you were gone." The dimples disappeared.

"No." This close, he could smell Thea's sweet perfume. He'd bet the fragrance had an optimistic name like Joy or Happy. He crossed to the other side of the kitchen.

"How do you know how to dress for the day if you can't see outside?"

The question came out of the blue and had Logan's usually quick tongue stalling on words for a couple of seconds. "I just wear jeans," he finally answered, tugging the neck of his shirt.

"But—"

"Look, lady…Thea…deciding what to wear isn't that big of a deal for me every morning." His words were crisply delivered with just enough bite in them to have most people backing off. "We'll do fine without you."

Thea blinked, but didn't retreat. "I would think that putting your clothes on right-side in or wrong-side out would be a big deal."

Logan sucked on the inside of his cheek in an attempt to ignore the desire to yell. This woman was obviously a few volts shy of a full charge.

"Your T-shirt is on inside out," she clarified. "And backward."

That explained why his T-shirt seemed to be choking him. The heat of humiliation flushed uncomfortably under Logan's skin, followed by a quick bolt of anger. He resisted the urge to tug the neck of his shirt again.

"Sometimes a little bit of light helps avoid embarrassment later." Her smile was gentle, not triumphant, which was maddening considering he was itching for a good fight.

"I am not embarrassed." To prove it, he stripped the shirt off in front of her, snapped it right-side out and pulled it back on. Then he stared at her and sucked on the inside of his cheek, waiting for her to lose her temper.

"Well—" she smiled easily as if they weren't two strangers who'd just almost argued about something as inane as sunlight and inside-out shirts. "—about me staying…"

LOGAN MCCALL WAS out-of-her-league gorgeous.

Thea had been trying to make him laugh, or at least loosen him up so that he'd realize how much Tess and Hannah needed her here because he didn't seem to want them. And then he'd gone and done that angry striptease and her mouth had gone dry.

He'd just ripped off his T-shirt to reveal a sculpted chest straight out of a magazine. Forget the Robert Redford comparison. The famous actor had never achieved such hard planes of muscle that tapered downward with a sprinkling of golden hair. And Thea had never come close to dating someone with such solid-looking arms, either.

With a physique like that, Logan must be the firefighter that carried damsels in distress out of windows or down ten flights of stairs without breaking a sweat. He had hero written all over that body. Why he acted more like a hermit living in a cave on a deserted island was beyond her.

Unfortunately, being a brooding hunk didn't score points for Logan in the caregiver department, nor did the dark, sterile, incredibly uncluttered house. Thea sensed he cared for the twins. If he could just get past his grief, everything would be okay. But it had been more than half a year, and he appeared to be in a worse emotional state than Tess and Hannah. Leave them here with Logan, who could barely care for Glen? Thea's conscience wouldn't allow it.

"At this point, I'll work for room and board, and gas money to get back to Seattle in May," Thea offered.

She watched Logan pace the limits of the kitchen, wondering if she was pushing him over the edge or if he'd been dangling there these past few months. She hoped it wasn't the latter.

Logan scowled at her. "You can't stay."

"Why not?"

"Because…because…" He looked stricken. "I don't even know you."

"But the girls do. I know they need family right now." Thea's throat clenched with the admission. "But they need some stability, too."

"You can't…I can't…" He was all doom and gloom. He blew out a breath. "Look, I don't think it would be good for Tess and Hannah if you stayed." He wouldn't look at her. "You've got those tests to study for and a life to get back to."

"I understand. You're all they have. Your sister would want you to take them," Thea said because she did understand—she wasn't wanted here. Still, she racked her brains for an argument he'd accept. She wouldn't just walk away from the girls.

Logan's keeping Tess and Hannah was almost as bad as Wes having them. And Logan wasn't warm and fuzzy with the twins. Their reunion hadn't been a happy one. Thea had listened on the other side of the kitchen door after the girls went into the living room. He'd been great with Glen, but he hadn't lasted two minutes with his nieces.

Thea squared her shoulders and gave her foot a little shake, setting off her bells, trying to think happy thoughts. Logan wasn't hopeless. He could learn how to be a dad. He'd get over his grief in time. And the temper? Well, he was a firefighter, wasn't he? His temper couldn't be that bad or they wouldn't keep him on that Hot Shot crew.

"I'm sure you'll be able to find a baby-sitter fairly quickly. Someone's going to jump at a twenty-four-hour-a-day, seven-days-a-week job." She curbed her smile.

"I've got Glen," he said stubbornly.

Despite herself, Thea blurted, "Glen needs a baby-sitter of her own."

It took Logan a moment to nod. "She's been a little out of it lately, but she's been grieving. She raised Deb and me."

"You can't be serious." Thea had a vision of the fairy-tale house burning down. Logan needed a little less attitude and a lot more reality.

"She's good with the girls," he argued, as if that trumped whatever argument she might have. He set his jaw and did that thing with his cheek.

"I don't doubt she loves Tess and Hannah. But I doubt a woman who can't take care of herself—even the basics of bathing and going to the bathroom—will be able to take care of them."

Logan drew back. "She does that."

Laying a hand on Logan's arm, Thea shook her head. "I've been making a shopping list. I put adult diapers on the list."

He backed away, rubbing his biceps where she'd touched him as if burned. "Glen has been taking care of herself for years. She's perfectly capable—"

"How do you know?" Irritated that he couldn't see what was happening to Glen, Thea propped her fists on her hips.

"I ask..." His expression wavered. "When I hugged her—"

Thea met Logan's gaze. The truth was going to hurt. "I helped her take a bath last night. Her clothes were stained and crusty, as if she'd been in them for days."

Logan opened his mouth, closed it and then looked at her as if she'd boxed him into an unpleasant corner.

The fact that he planned to leave Glen in charge of Tess and Hannah only strengthened her resolve to stay. If she had to be blunt and rattle his beliefs, she would. The twins had been in her care for two months. She was responsible for them.

After a moment, he said, "I just don't think this will work."

The urge to shout some sense into him became almost palpable. Thea fought it. "Trust me, Glen can't do this alone. Whoever helps you will be shopping, driving, cooking, cleaning and doing laundry, plus keeping the girls up with their schoolwork *and* watching out for Glen. It's a full-time job."

He sucked on his cheek, his eyes a well of unresolved sadness. For whatever reason, he didn't want her.

The knowledge stung. It was as if she'd been unwanted and lacking her whole life, and this was the last straw.

"You're going to make me beg, aren't you?" Thea said half jokingly as she blinked back tears of regret for Glen, the twins and herself.

For a fleeting moment, he smiled.

Oh, my. Something warm and intimate fluttered in Thea's belly.

He gave her a rueful look, innocent and heartrending at the same time.

"How about a compromise? I'll ask the twins if they

want me to stay. If they don't, I'll help you find a sitter and be out of your hair with no more than a small loan for gas money."

"And if they do want you to stay?"

"I'm your new sitter until things settle down." Thea tried to keep her voice from trembling. Staying wouldn't help her studies or fulfill her promise to her mother. Yet, Thea knew in her heart that she'd fight to stay because it was the right thing to do.

"I've got another idea." He crossed his arms over his chest. "I'm sure Glen's going to come through. Since you seem so attached to the girls, I'll let you stay a few days just to ease your mind."

Thea didn't understand why Logan was so reluctant to agree to her plan. Maybe her assessment of him as the hero who charged to the rescue had been in error. If so, she had just a few days to prove Tess and Hannah's recalcitrant hero wrong.

"WHY IS SHE STILL HERE?" Tess wondered about Thea aloud. Tess didn't understand why Thea hadn't gone home. Sprawled across her bed, Tess stared at the ceiling while Hannah played with Whizzer on the floor between their two beds, talking to him as if he were a baby. "I know she wants to leave."

"Maybe she doesn't have anywhere to go," Hannah answered.

Tess rolled over and faced the wall. "Who asked you?"

Uncle Logan didn't seem to like Thea much. He frowned at Thea the way he frowned at Tess and Hannah. Well, mostly Tess.

Mrs. Garrett had told Thea that Uncle Logan would do anything for Tess and Hannah. Tess knew that wasn't true. Uncle Logan was always grouchy and silent around them now. Nothing like the fun man who used to spoil them. Tess didn't like him and didn't know why anyone else would, either.

So why was Thea here?

"I hope Uncle Logan lets her leave Whizzer." Hannah continued to talk baby talk to the dog.

Someone knocked on their bedroom door. Whizzer pranced over to it and scratched at the wood with his short little legs.

"I bet that's her," Tess whispered, rolling over. Something not so good happened in her stomach.

The door opened slowly on its creaky hinges and Thea poked her head in, those bells she always wore jingling. "I think we need to take Whizzer outside. He can't hold it very long."

"I'll do it." Hannah popped up.

"Just a second, Hannah. I have something to ask the two of you."

Tess's tummy clenched again. There was only one reason that adults wanted to talk to kids—bad news.

"Your uncle Logan invited me to stay for a few days. Before I say yes, I wanted to make sure it was okay with you girls. If you don't want me to stay, you just say the word."

Hannah picked up Whizzer. "Are you going to be Uncle Logan's girlfriend?"

Thea opened her eyes really wide and shook her head quickly. "No."

"Why would you want to stay here?" Tess asked. If Tess had her choice, she'd go stay with the Garretts…as long as it was okay with Heidi. Her mouth went dry. Well, maybe not the Garretts since she and Heidi weren't talking. But she'd go anywhere there was a real family with a mom and a dad.

Tucking her hair behind her ear, Thea smiled. Thea's smile made Tess's stomach ease, but didn't make the pain go away.

"I made a promise to take care of you. A promise is a very important thing. But I think you need to say yes." Thea looked around. "I'll be doing a lot of studying, but maybe we could sew something for your room."

The way Thea talked had Tess wondering. Did Uncle Logan want her to stay?

"My mom used to sew," Hannah said, wiping her nose. "She made us dresses once."

Tess remembered. Her mother had sewn matching blue dresses with pink ribbons that the twins had worn on the first day of school in the third grade. That was when it was really cool to be Hannah's twin. Now Tess wouldn't wear the same color shirt Hannah was wearing, much less the same dress.

Thea's smile faded and her voice got real soft. "I bet your mom did a lot of special things with you."

Suddenly, Tess could barely fill her lungs with air. Her face started to feel numb and tingly. "Why are you being nice to us?"

Thea started to say something, but Tess drew in a shaky breath and cut her off. "You don't have to be nice to us anymore. Ask Uncle Logan. We're not nice." That's why no one wanted them.

"Hmm. Your aunt Glen thinks you're nice." Thea didn't correct her or try to be too cheerful the way the teachers did at school when Tess talked back at them. She just looked…serious.

It would have been better if Thea had given her a fake

smile or argued with her. Hannah was sniffing, crouched on the floor at her feet. Tess struggled not to cry.

"Tess, I've taken care of you for two months and I've never seen you do anything mean. I don't think you realize what a special girl you are, how special you both are. You worked together to save Whizzer, didn't you?"

When the door closed behind Thea and Whizzer, Tess wiped her nose, listening to Hannah cry. She couldn't make herself reach down and touch her sister for fear she'd start crying herself and never stop. She ached with loneliness.

Why did Mom have to die?

THEA SAT on the front-porch step watching Whizzer make a frenzied circuit around the sun-dappled yard, but she was seeing something else. Her mind replayed memories of her own past—lying on her bed in a dark room and wondering how she'd make it through the next day without her mother. What would she have done if her father hadn't wanted to take care of her? At ten, she'd been running the household, striving for perfection in the hopes that her father wouldn't find fault with and abandon her, too. At ten, Tess and Hannah had gone in the opposite direction, withdrawing into shells so tight they might never open.

"Whizzer must be marking his territory against the raccoons," Logan commented as he lowered himself onto the step next to her.

Lost in thought, Thea hadn't heard Logan come outside. She hugged her knees tight as she attempted to push the painful childhood memories to the far corners of her mind, along with the strange flutter she got in her stomach from looking at Logan. Being attracted to him was almost more disconcerting than her memories. He'd already made it very clear he didn't want her around.

"Should I be afraid of letting Whizzer out at night? He won't get eaten or anything?" She'd only had the dog for a few days, but he now had a permanent place in her heart.

"Might." He shrugged. "Cats need to be kept in at night, too. Not because of the raccoons, but because of coyotes and wolves."

"Wolves." Thea shivered.

"We're out in the middle of the woods. This is their turf, not ours." Anyone else would have smiled when they reminded Thea that she was in the midst of a forest. Not Logan. With the sun on the other side of the house, his face was cast in late-afternoon shadows.

She should have been put off by the closed, withdrawn expression he wore to cloak his grief. Instead, Thea's heart went out to him once more. His distant demeanor was very hard on his nieces. It wouldn't help them deal with the death of the most important person in their lives, or the apparent abandonment of their father. Thea had gone through counseling to deal with her own sense of loss and knew that Logan needed to talk about what had happened in order to move on. And if he didn't move forward in the grieving process, he couldn't help the girls.

In his isolated mountain home, Logan was clearly not working through his grief, hiding in the silence and darkness he so obviously craved. For some reason, Thea couldn't shake the thought that Logan needed people to heal. The three of them—Logan, Tess and Hannah—stood a chance if he'd just open up.

"It seems a little lonely up here. No sirens. No music from your neighbor's apartment. No garbage trucks lumbering by," Thea said to fill the silence.

He looked at her shoes, before admitting, "Some call it peaceful."

If it was peace he wanted, he wasn't getting it from Thea. For two months, the twins had put up with her questions and stories. Maybe her efforts to draw them out weren't successful, but Thea wasn't going to stop trying.

"I once met a woman who couldn't stand silence. She carried a Walkman everywhere she went, with just one earphone plugged in." There. That ought to get a reaction out of him. Thea couldn't resist staring at Logan.

Logan looked shell-shocked, and then he dead-panned, "What did she listen to? Religion? Talk radio?"

"Rap music." Thea allowed herself a small smile at the memory of her grandmother. "She was a black belt and said it kept her on her toes."

He rolled his eyes. "So, you're saying silence is overrated?"

"For some people."

"You, for instance. You're never silent or still. Why is that?"

This was definitely going in a direction she wanted to avoid. She was who she was, and she didn't want to explain herself to him. By rights, he shouldn't want to pursue the subject, either. His house was silent as a tomb. "Were you close to Deb?"

Logan chewed on his cheek, making her wonder if he was going to answer. "Yeah," he finally admitted.

"Was losing Deb…was it sudden?" The twins rarely spoke of her.

"We knew." Two words spoken incredibly slowly, an indicator of his tremendous grief.

As he stood, Thea watched Logan erect barriers

around himself as clearly as if they'd been made of brick. He was shutting her out.

"And Wes? Were he and Deb—"

"They were separated. He was never here. He never called." Logan's words were more guarded than usual. "When he showed up in November and wanted to take the girls, I knew it was wrong, but I couldn't seem to stop him."

Frowning, Thea rubbed her hands over her eyes. How horrible that must have been for Tess and Hannah, being passed along and cared for by two men who didn't express their emotions easily. Thea's father, a police detective, had been much the same.

"Are you staying or not?" There was no invitation in his tone.

"The girls warned me I wouldn't like it here," Thea hedged, filled with second thoughts. She didn't really want to tiptoe through this family's grief if it meant dredging up all of her own baggage. And yet, how could she not?

"Why did they warn you?" Logan hung his head and answered his own question. "Never mind. It was Tess, wasn't it?"

Thea rushed to explain. "Tess was more curious as to why I'd want to stay than telling me I couldn't."

"I don't know why you'd want to stay, either. I don't know what I was thinking even offering to let you stay a few days. I would have run in the opposite direction if I were in your shoes."

"Then why did you ask me?"

HE HESITATED. Why indeed?

Logan's muscles bunched. Any more pressure and he

just knew he'd crack. Deb. The twins. His leg. His entire body vibrated with the need for a release. Thea placed a hand on his arm. Her fingers were cool against his skin. Despite himself, the tension in Logan's muscles eased.

"Do you want to tell me more about Deb?"

Looking into Thea's solemn gaze, Logan wanted desperately to say no. Anything he said was just going to make him look weak. He had his rules, which was how he kept it all together.

Don't talk about Deb. Don't think about Deb.

With effort, he made his head move in something that might have resembled a stiff shake.

"I know it sounds like a cliché, but sometimes it helps to talk about it. Especially to a stranger."

Logan's lungs wouldn't fill with air. Sister Mary Sunshine was here to fix him?

He swore.

At her.

Thea's cheeks filled with color. "I shouldn't have pried. I'm sorry."

"You're sorry." His muscles tensed again.

"I was just trying to help. It's like you're wearing this sign that says go away, and yet underneath it you've written don't go—"

"Like hell I did."

"And I'm such a sucker for strays." Her bells echoed on the porch, mocking his indignation.

What right did Thea have to be upset? Logan's body began to shake. "I'm not asking for help and there's no sign on me, clear?"

"Perfectly."

"I could have sent you on your way first thing." He

should have brawled with Spider in Sun Valley. At least then he'd have taken the edge off.

"I appreciate it."

She was almost infuriatingly polite. Logan flexed his fingers.

"Did you also try to fix Wes?"

Thea blinked, barely pausing. "No."

She was cooler under fire than Logan would have thought for someone emitting all that color and noise. "So, based on a few hours with me, you've decided I need some therapy?"

"I think you need to talk about your feelings." She straightened, looking aside. Her cheeks turned pink. "Yes."

"And Wes didn't."

"No." Her gaze rose to the stairs at his booted feet.

"Did you know that Wes can't keep his wallet or his dick in his pants? He's always broke and sleeping around. And you didn't see any signs on him?"

She paled, looking at a point near his knee. "No."

His throat threatened to close, but he forced the words out anyway. "Did you know that Wes Delaney is a heartless, selfish, son of a bitch who doesn't care for his girls and didn't care for my sister?"

"No."

"Did you know that he left the day Deb was diagnosed with cancer, took all the money out of their bank account and disappeared? Leaving them no choice but to move in with me?"

"Or that when he showed up months later and took the girls that I didn't raise a hand to stop him?" Logan leaned forward and raised his voice. "Knowing what I do about him, I still let them go. I'm just as low as him. Signs? I'll tell you what you can do with your signs."

"Is that true? About the girls?" Thea didn't back down, but she wasn't in his face, either—surprising, because most women didn't let the door hit them on the way out after he unleashed just a hint of his temper.

And Mary Poppins was getting more than a hint of temper. He didn't break away from her stare when he nodded.

She placed her hand on his arm again. "I can help if you'll let me."

"Maybe I don't want your help," Logan said quietly, "although heaven knows Wes needs someone to help him."

"I'm staying for the girls until you find someone *appropriate*." She arched her eyebrow. "Unless you'd like to rescind your offer."

As much as he wished it, Logan couldn't form the words telling Thea to leave.

"Is this Birdie's succotash?" Suspiciously, Aunt Glen moved the yellow goopy concoction around her plate, which was more than Tess and Hannah were doing.

Logan frowned at his own plate. It did look nasty.

"Can I have a grilled-cheese sandwich?" Hannah asked Thea in a soft voice.

"No." Logan shook his head. "You know the rules." That had been his father's rule, Deb's rule and Logan's when the twins had first moved in. "Eat what's on your plate. You'll need energy for school tomorrow." That sounded lame even to Logan. He was signing them up for school in the morning and breakfast would give them the energy they needed. Not this poor excuse of a dinner. He should have agreed to take Thea into town to pick up groceries at Birdie's store earlier, but that was just asking for trouble. Birdie, Mary and the rest would pry his life open for inspection.

Tess moved her plate forward an inch, indicating she was done. Without looking at her directly, Logan recognized the stubborn set of her chin. Hannah turned sideways in her chair, facing Thea. None of the adults had touched the yellow goop on their plates. The only sound at the table came from Hannah's heavy sighs and the occasional clink of a fork on a plate.

Logan sat at the head of the table facing a huge paper calendar tacked up to the brown paneling. He didn't want to ask about it. He'd rather have his empty, quiet house back. But he found himself asking anyway. "What is that?"

"It's my study planner," Thea explained, pushing her plate aside. "See, it lists a different class to cover each day, along with the key sections that are rumored to be on the tests."

"So, you're taking the tests the first week in May?" The first Friday in May had been boxed in red. Logan noticed another day was boxed as well. "What's the blue box for on the second Friday?"

"The first Friday is my written test and the second the orals. I only get to take the oral exam if I pass the written portion." With her freckled nose scrunched and her eyebrows pulled together, Logan could tell Thea was worried. "Both tests cover every topic I've taken in the past three years."

"What did you say you were studying?" For the life of him, Logan couldn't remember.

"Fabrics. And she's going to pass," Hannah said solemnly. "She studies more than anyone I know."

"At least, more than anyone in the fourth grade," Thea amended, gently touching Hannah's nose.

Without smiling, Hannah snuck a quick glance Tess's way, then looked at her hands. Tess sat back in her chair with her arms crossed, her disapproval of everything and everyone at the table apparent.

The twins hadn't always been this way. Logan could remember them giggling at his jokes and running like screaming banshees when he played Tickle Monster. He couldn't remember any jokes appropriate for ten-year-old girls. And the Tickle Monster was hiding in some cave along with his heart. Still…

He looked around the room at the unhappy faces. Even Thea looked sad as she stared at her planner.

"I'm going to revolutionize the textile industry," Thea stated, eyes glued to the wall. "Someday."

Logan cleared his throat, staring at the yellow goop that Birdie had made. "Does anyone feel like having pizza? I'm thinking some pepperoni sounds good about now."

"Don't have to ask me twice," Glen said. "Just make sure to tell Birdie her succotash was yummy when you see her."

Thea was already clearing the plates. Hannah helped.

"I'll eat pizza," Tess said. "But you won't fool me this time."

"Fool you?" Logan frowned.

"Fool me into trusting you," Tess explained, jutting out her chin. "You don't want us any more than Dad does."

"HANNAH DELANEY! Let go of Aaron's neck this instant!" Miss Kalidah's high-pitched command cut through the excited voices of children in the school yard, as the orange-haired vice principal made her way through the crowd ringing Tess, Hannah and Aaron.

"You better let him go, Han," Tess advised her twin sister.

Panting from the effort it took to keep the boy still, Hannah released Aaron from the viselike chokehold she'd put on him after he'd said some evil things about Tess and Hannah.

Aaron stumbled and fell to the damp, muddy ground. The mean, hurtful smile was no longer on his face and Tess couldn't help but feel a bit relieved.

"Are you all right?" Hannah asked Aaron, tears in her eyes.

Aaron tilted his head so he could look up at Hannah, while one hand rubbed his red throat. "You nearly killed me!"

The circling children parted for Miss Kalidah. They were just as eager to see punishment doled out by the vice principal as they had been to see Hannah's version of justice. Miss Kalidah frowned as she stared coldly first at Hannah, then at Tess.

"I should have known." The vice principal's voice grated like boots on gravel. Miss Kalidah had come to Silver Bend Elementary School last fall, right about the time things fell apart for the twins and they'd moved to Seattle.

"What happened?" Miss Kalidah demanded. She was a tall, wide woman with shocking orange hair and yellow eyes. The kids called her the Tiger Lady behind her back.

Aaron and Tess pointed at each other. "*He* started it! *She* started it!"

"One at a time." Miss Kalidah scrunched her pale face, shook her frizzy orange hair and bent over until Tess could see the dark hair at her part. "And I want the truth."

Tess crossed her skinny arms over her chest and flattened her lips together, willing Hannah with a serious look to keep quiet, too.

Ever the baby, Hannah bit her lip and blinked back the tears, but amazingly said nothing.

"Tess told Hannah to *get me*." Aaron scrambled to his feet. "I didn't do nothing."

Miss Kalidah stared at Tess and Hannah with an accusing yellow glare. She paced around the twins, eyeing them while she made her punishment plans.

"That's a lie, Aaron." Heidi Garrett stepped into the circle. Heidi turned to Miss Kalidah. "Aaron said bad things about Tess and Hannah. Really bad things. A couple of us told him to stop, but he wouldn't."

Tess's heart swelled at Heidi's effort. It felt good to know someone cared. Uncle Logan certainly didn't seem to anymore.

Miss Kalidah turned her icy stare in Aaron's direction. "What do you have to say to that?"

"I didn't say anything no one in town isn't already saying. And what do I get for it?" He pointed to Hannah. "Hannah the Hulk's arm wrapped around my throat."

Hannah took a step back and sniffed at the insult. No one would know from looking at her that she'd just practically squeezed the pulp out of Aaron Fischer. She'd grown two inches, gained a few pounds and become a crybaby since their mother had died. Tess, on the other hand, was never hungry, hadn't grown a bit and never let herself cry.

"That's enough, Mr. Fischer. I'll see you in the office. You have two minutes to get there." Miss Kalidah called the office on her walkie-talkie and told them to expect Aaron. She turned to Tess and Hannah. "As for you two, this is a very disappointing first day. Both of you may also report to the office. I'm sure your uncle will have a lot to say about this."

Hannah couldn't stop a tear from falling this time. Last year, Tess would have thrown her arm around her sister and comforted her. But that was a heartache ago.

The entire upper grades at Silver Bend Elementary stared at them with interest as they trudged toward the office. Tess imagined she could hear what they were whispering to each other.

Tess and Hannah's mom got sick and died from a brain tumor. Their dad left home with a cocktail waitress. Their uncle cares for them now, but he'll leave as soon as the fires start, because he's a Hot Shot and they're never home. Then the Delaney sisters won't have anyone but their crazy old aunt Glen to take care of them.

Aaron had said they'd be put into foster care and no one would ever adopt them.

Tess walked several feet in front of Hannah, fighting the anger at her mother for dying, at her father and Uncle Logan for not being around or caring, fighting the feeling of loneliness, and losing herself to everything.

CHAPTER FOUR

"IT'S A VERY OLD family recipe, my dear," Aunt Glen said, shuffling through the kitchen door followed by Thea, whose light footsteps jingled with each step. "Easy enough to make for two experienced cooks like ourselves."

Logan looked up from the newspaper he'd picked up in town after he registered the girls in school. "You're up again," he said to his aunt. "Are you all right?"

Aunt Glen hadn't gotten out of bed for more than bathroom trips in months, claiming to be too dizzy to get up anymore. When Doc Johnson hadn't identified anything to treat, Logan had figured Aunt Glen was as heartbroken over Deb as he was. For several months he'd been bringing dinner to her bedroom on a tray rather than encouraging her to get up. He'd assumed Lexie, Jackson's wife, did the same when Logan was gone.

Heck, he didn't want to get out of bed every morning, why should Glen?

"Logan, you're wound up tighter than an eight-day clock." Aunt Glen sounded offended. Her chin-length hair floated in wild, dry wisps around her face. "I won't be lazing about with company around. We're going to bake some cookies."

Thea tilted her chin, seeming to dare him to challenge

the activity. All traces of joy were absent from her demeanor this morning.

"We don't need any cookies," Logan said firmly. What he really meant was that they didn't need any of Thea's smiles. Or the cheerful blue vase on the kitchen table or the red-and-white-checked wool blanket she'd lain over the back of the couch.

"Nonsense. We haven't had any sweets around here in ages." Glen shuffled past Logan, bringing a strong aroma of urine. Her knit pants were wet.

Thea met his questioning stare with an I-told-you-so look.

Logan's stomach knotted, with guilt this time, not helpless anger.

"Now, when Deb ran the kitchen, we had sunshine and baked goods and music and…" Aunt Glen trailed off, her expression lost.

Logan was at his aunt's side immediately. "It's all right. Come sit down."

"Deb?" Aunt Glen asked in her tremulous voice as she gazed around the kitchen as if searching for Logan's sister. "Did she go for a walk?"

"It's okay." Logan helped Glen into a chair.

"What's wrong?" Thea asked softly.

Logan ignored her, focusing instead on Aunt Glen.

"When was the last time I saw Deb?" Glen mused. "I can't seem to remember."

The memory of Deb's pale, drawn face as she lay on her deathbed upstairs floated to the forefront of Logan's consciousness. He struggled to draw in air. He fought the memory as hard as he'd fought any fire. Against his will, his gaze met Thea's.

Concern filled her brown eyes. And something else, too.

Understanding.

"Glen, did you and Deb ever bake cookies together?" Thea asked.

Logan stared at Thea in amazement. Half the time he didn't know what to say to Aunt Glen, and here Thea had chosen just the right words. Thea could have been rubbing Logan's incorrect assumptions like egg all over his face, yet she chose to help him instead.

Glen repeated Thea's question as if she needed the extra time to process her words. Then her misty eyes cleared. "We did. Every year at Christmas, we'd bake cookies and frost them as pretty as you'd ever see in one of those...those..."

"Magazines." Thea supplied the word smoothly, sparing Logan a compelling glance that seemed to encourage him to join the conversation. "I bet Deb and her friends ate them right up."

Don't talk about Deb. Don't think about Deb. Keep the outside world and their probing questions out and you'll be okay.

But still he wondered, why had he survived numerous brushes with death and Deb had succumbed to this illness without much warning or fight?

"No. Deb's friends were always on diets. Logan and Jackson ate most of them." Glen had returned far back into the past, to a time when Logan was a teenager.

"They ate them by the handfuls, didn't they?" Thea was seemingly unconcerned that Glen had slipped further from the present.

Logan couldn't find enough air to say a word.

"Those boys had stomachs like bottomless pits." Glen chuckled.

"Would you like to make cookies with me today?" Thea asked.

"I'd love to." Glen frowned. "I'm sorry, what was your name?"

"Thea. We played cards last night at the pizza parlor."

"Ah, one of Logan's girls," Glen surmised with a wink at Logan. "The first time I met Eldred, I asked him if he played cards. He said he didn't. It wasn't until later that I learned what a shark he was. Now, my Logan, he's a different sort. A handful, to be sure, but you can trust him as long as you stay out of the back seat of my Buick."

Thea's cool stare over Aunt Glen's head indicated she'd trust him about as much as she would a used-car salesman peddling Buicks.

Logan almost missed Thea's smile now that it was gone. Even her bells were silent.

"Where has that book gone to? Logan, you know the one I mean?" Aunt Glen craned her neck to and fro. "It's pink-and-white-checked. It used to sit on the counter. And it has recipes in it."

"The cookbook," Logan translated as he retrieved it from a cupboard, admitting, "I don't think we have any eggs. I may have to go to the store." He doubted Glen would remember she wanted to make cookies in fifteen minutes, so he probably wouldn't have to go or have Thea entertain his aunt while he did so. He knew Thea needed to study.

"Did you post the job when you were in town?" Thea asked, hands on hips. Amazingly, she'd managed to move without making a sound.

"Yeah."

Thea gave him a chilly look, her lips firmly pressed together. In the dimly lit kitchen, Logan couldn't make out her freckles. Undoubtedly, she wanted to take the job posting for a live-in nanny down.

The phone trilled as he shook his head, sparing him the need to defend himself.

"Mr. McCall? This is Miss Kalidah from the elementary school."

The girls. Logan sucked on his cheek. "Are they okay?" he managed to ask, imagining all sorts of mishaps.

"They're fine, Mr. McCall." The cool way Miss Kalidah said it, Logan knew that the twins were in trouble. He washed a hand over his face in an effort to suppress his frustration.

"Mr. McCall, I'm afraid there's been an...*event*. The girls won't be spending the rest of the day in class. I'm sure you understand protocol. When can you pick them up?"

"I'll be at school in less than thirty minutes," Logan said. The girls had never been in trouble when Deb was alive.

Glen stood at the kitchen counter assembling flour and sugar canisters. Logan felt Thea's eyes upon him.

"I need to pick up the twins from school."

"So soon? It's not even lunchtime yet." Glen turned to study the clock.

"There's been an *event*." Logan used Miss Kalidah's word.

"Well, in that case, run along and bring home some eggs," Glen said, as if the girls came home early from school every day.

"But—"

"I said run along." Glen glared at him.

Logan reached for his jacket, still hanging on the kitchen chair where he'd left it earlier. He glanced at Thea. He didn't want to leave her here alone with Glen, but what choice did he have now? "I'm sorry. Could you... Would you mind...?"

"We'll be fine." There was no trace of a smile in Thea's voice. No dimples. No eyes creased in welcome. Just a hint of sadness as her gaze flickered over Glen. She'd be the one cleaning Glen up, not Logan.

Humbled, because he'd just proved Thea had been right when she'd said Glen couldn't take care of the twins, Logan couldn't take his eyes off Thea's red sneakers.

"HOW DID YOU KNOW how to handle Glen?" Logan asked when Thea followed him out the door.

She shrugged, watching the little terrier dash gleefully around the yard, as if he was in a race with some unseen opponent. "When I was a kid, our downstairs neighbor was the same before she moved into a home. I watched out for her sometimes."

Her fists were propped on her hips again. He was coming to recognize it as a barometer of her temper, yet her next words came out softly. "I can't believe you've been leaving her alone."

"She's been fine so far." Logan realized what a fool he'd been. Every aspect of his life was imploding and he'd practically begged Thea, a cross between Mary Poppins and Martha Stewart, to leave.

"Don't do it again," Thea commanded a little too forcefully for Logan's taste.

"I didn't ask for your help." Logan's temper had resurfaced. The sadness over his sister, his frustration about the girls, his desire to return to his normal life— to sex and travel and little responsibility. It all blossomed into one nasty-tasting foul state of mind.

Thea raised her eyebrows.

"You know what I meant." Needing an outlet for his anger, Logan thrust his finger at Thea. "I didn't ask you to poke your nose in my business. I didn't ask for your advice. I've been doing fine without anyone else's help for a long time." That was a lie. He was so far from fine it was scary. Adding the twins to his life seemed beyond comprehension.

Thea was unfazed by his outburst. If anything, her voice softened. "Logan, you don't have to do this alone. I can help. And there are people…agencies," she corrected herself.

Logan sucked in a deep breath and prepared to tell her it was none of her concern, when his brain registered the freckles dusting Thea's nose. Then he opened his mouth and uttered the words he hadn't said out loud. Ever. "My sister is dead. I'll always be alone."

Thea's lips formed a little, round *oh*.

Logan began to shake.

All these months spent grieving over another loved one being sent to heaven before their time. Months of having to watch Aunt Glen drift as miserably through her daily existence as he went through his. The pain of letting the girls go. And he couldn't do anything to fix anything, because in a few days, he was due for daily training in town and soon he'd be sent out to fight fires in any one of the western states for weeks at a time.

Firefighting was his life. Being a Hot Shot was who he was. Logan wasn't cut out to be a stay-at-home substitute dad. He didn't know the first thing about caring for little girls and elderly women. Not to mention his temper wasn't housebroken. Look how he'd practically taken Spider out the other day. Logan wasn't the right person for the job of Tess and Hannah's guardian in more ways than he could count. He let out a groan of frustration. What was he supposed to do?

Standing in front of Sister Mary Sunshine, Logan reached his limit.

He knew, in that moment, what it felt like to want to rant and rave and punch and throw things at the injustice of it all as his father had done. And why not do it? Logan could drive like a bat out of hell down the mountain and find trouble in any roadside bar.

Twenty-four hours and a jail stay later, he'd be bruised, scruffy and smelly, and he'd feel better, except…

Logan found himself staring into Thea's dark brown eyes. Found himself noticing her freckles and bright orange T-shirt.

Except he would have let down the people he cared for most.

THE HEAVY OFFICE DOOR swung open and Uncle Logan stepped in. He had that look on his face, the one that Tess had never seen before last summer. His expression was about as far from welcoming as it could possibly be.

Uncle Logan gave the girls a quick, cold nod, before being whisked away to the Tiger Lady's office. With a swish of her long black skirt, Miss Kalidah closed the door behind him with a decisive click.

"He's not going to keep us," Tess whispered to Hannah without moving her head to look at her. Instead, Tess stared at a poster for special classes in Emmett. All she had to do to qualify was take some test after Easter.

Hannah shook her long, blond hair. "Don't say that. Don't even think it. We're family."

"He didn't keep us last time." That's what Tess was

afraid of. She was almost more scared of him letting them go again than of being sent to foster care. Tess didn't want to become used to playing with her toys again, only to be whisked away by her dad, leaving everything behind.

"Tess, please," Hannah sniffed. "I'm not listening to you. I did what you wanted earlier. To Aaron."

Tess didn't want to think about Aaron and his hurtful words, even though she'd just delivered much the same message to Hannah.

Hannah wouldn't shut up, "And now the Tiger Lady is kicking us out of school and Uncle Logan's mad."

Tess shrugged. "Don't think he's mad because he loves us. He's mad because he doesn't want us." Uncle Logan had barely spoken to them since Mom had died. She'd counted the number of words he'd said to her yesterday. Fifteen. Fifteen lousy words. If he cared about them or planned to be their guardian, he'd say more than fifteen words a day to them.

"Besides," Tess reasoned, looking out the small tinted office window. "His rules suck. It's like we're in the army or something. Shower by eight? Rooms picked up by eight-thirty? Lights out at nine? He doesn't even read to us. What kind of father is that?"

"Let's go, ladies." Uncle Logan's chill tone cut through Tess's stomach sharper than any knife.

She'd blown it for sure this time. He'd probably get home and start trying to find her dad, if he hadn't already.

Tess peeked up at Uncle Logan, but he'd already slipped his sunglasses on, so she couldn't see his eyes. She did, however, recognize the hard jaw.

Hannah sniffed and followed Uncle Logan out the door. Pausing in the doorway, Tess couldn't resist glancing back at the Tiger Lady, who looked pleased to see them go. At least they wouldn't have to come back until after Easter break.

Tess dragged her feet. Her days with Uncle Logan were numbered. It would be easier if he would just get it over with quickly, rather than drawing it out.

"I DON'T KNOW who any of these people on TV are." A freshly bathed Glen sat on the couch, reacquainting herself with a soap opera while they waited for Logan to return with the eggs. "And why are the windows open? Logan wants it dark in here."

"I need to keep an eye on Whizzer," Thea said, keeping her words upbeat, despite her frustration over her untouched study plan. She'd decided when Logan left that the windows were opening, and that there was more cleaning to be done.

There was a load of linens in the washer. She'd flung open the front door and pulled back the blinds before she dusted. Sunlight streamed in, brightening the brown that was everywhere, bringing the fresh chill of spring air. Pausing between the freshly polished coffee tables, Thea watched the dust dance on rays filtering through the window.

Logan had seemed almost at the breaking point before he left, but she wouldn't regret pushing him. His distress had been palpable when he'd asked the school if the twins were okay. And the pain in his eyes had been heartbreaking when he admitted his sister was dead.

A vehicle pulled up the driveway with a crunch of gravel.

Thea poked her head out the front door to find three

muscular men in shorts and tennis shoes climbing out of a big black truck. Each man seemed burlier than the next. The fire logos on their shirts identified them as Hot Shots. A beautiful chocolate Labrador bounded happily ahead of them.

"Hello," she called, scanning the area for Whizzer, wondering how he'd react to the bigger dog or if the Lab would consider Whizzer a snack.

As the Lab pranced around Thea, the men slowed their approach and exchanged glances. She thought she heard one man, the one dressed all in black, say, "So this is what you meant."

"Is Logan home?" asked the driver. He was the tallest of the men, with dark hair and bright green eyes.

"He'll be back soon," Thea answered, still looking for Whizzer as the Lab raced off, nose to the ground. "Can I help you?"

"Is that my boys?" Glen shuffled next to Thea.

"Glen? I haven't seen you up and about in ages." The tall driver ran up the steps and encompassed Glen in a crushing embrace. When he released the older woman, he turned to Thea and offered his hand while Glen was passed around for more hugs. "I'm Jackson Garrett. And these two troublemakers are Cole Hudson and Aiden Rodas. We work with Logan."

"You're Lexie's husband." Thea recognized the resemblance between little Henry and his dad—something about the shape of their bright green eyes.

Jackson nodded. "And you're the woman the whole town has decided will be Logan's nanny."

Thea was pleased even as she knew Logan wouldn't be. Someday he'd realize how much he needed her.

"How do I get a nanny?" Aiden said with a suggest-ively playful wink. He seemed charmingly harmless.

"Will you grow up?" Cole shook his head and glared at his friend before turning to Thea. "Since you're going to be around, no one except my mom calls me Cole," drawled the broadest of the bunch with a southern accent as he gave her hand a firm shake. "Call me Chainsaw."

"Likewise. They call me Spider." The wiry man in black shook her hand. He wasn't as large as the other two men, but his grip was just as strong. Thea thought she detected a slight Hispanic accent.

"Chainsaw? Spider? Should I be scared?" They were horror-movie names.

They all chuckled politely, giving Thea the feeling that she'd just delivered a very worn joke.

"Not to worry. We're harmless. They call me Chain-saw because I'm a Class A faller." His grin was about as wide as his shoulders. "Translation—I operate a chainsaw."

"And I was named after my passion," the sinewy man explained.

"Spider-Man?" Thea guessed.

Clutching his chest, Spider staggered backward in mock pain.

Thea found herself smiling at them. All three men were decidedly handsome—Jackson with his strong chin, dark hair and bright green eyes; Chainsaw with his dirty-blond hair and broad shoulders; Spider with his long black hair and swarthy complexion. There was something, how-ever, in Logan's appearance that Thea preferred.

"He's a little more gothic than that," Jackson allowed, gesturing to Spider's black garb.

"I'm a fan of giant-bug movies—*Spiders*, *Arachno-*

phobia, Eight Legged Freaks. You know the story. Aliens visit or toxic experiment goes bad and super-strength, super-large bugs try to take over the world." Grinning, he waited expectantly for Thea to share his excitement.

Chainsaw rolled his eyes. "Stop, man. I can't sleep with the lights off anymore after so many creepy movies."

Glen looked around nervously. "Where's the spider?"

"There aren't any spiders out here," Thea said in a soothing voice, patting Glen's shoulder.

"I don't kill spiders," Glen announced. "They're good bugs. They just give me the creeps." Glen shuffled back to the couch and her soap opera.

Whizzer ran up from the opposite side of the yard from where the Lab had disappeared and began sniffing feet. Thea snatched Whizzer up before he got any ideas, and then introduced herself, relieved that he hadn't gotten into a pissing match with the Lab.

Thea looked questioningly at Jackson. "No nickname? No story?"

"Jackson is fine with me." He leaned against the porch railing.

"Have you worked with Logan long?" Thea asked with an encouraging smile. Maybe these men could help get Logan on track. They seemed responsible, not fitting the somewhat flaky impression she'd received from Lexie.

Spider laughed. "It seems like forever."

"Logan and I started together. We've been friends since high school." Jackson's smile was so easygoing that Thea felt some of the tension inside her ease.

"So you knew Deb, his sister?"

All three men immediately sobered and Thea sensed she'd crossed some unforeseen line.

Before Thea could regroup and try to put the men at ease, the Lab leaped onto the porch and loped toward Thea. Whizzer trembled at the sight of the bigger dog.

"Rufus, behave," Jackson commanded, his words slowing the dog, who skidded to a stop in front of Thea and began sniffing again, his brown nose inches from Whizzer. Thea took a step back, fully anticipating two dogs in her arms at any moment.

"Put him down. He'll be fine. Rufus is just an overgrown pussycat," Jackson said. "Here," and he took Whizzer gently from Thea. "He's not a chew toy, Ruf."

Thea gasped but nothing happened except the two dogs sniffed every inch of each other before scampering down the steps and into the yard.

"Let them go," Jackson suggested.

"Okay, but you'll be carrying Rufus home when he craps out on our run today," Spider groused.

Jackson shook his head. "That dog is like the Energizer Bunny. We'll poop out before he does."

Cole, or Chainsaw as he wanted to be called, ran a hand over his crew-cut blond hair and gave her a sweet grin. "Don't take this wrong, but I hope you'll be around for a few days. We don't often have beautiful women in town."

Although his manner was endearing, Chainsaw's grin only made Thea wish she'd seen Logan's smile. The thought startled her.

Spider punched Chainsaw's shoulder. "Don't be shy, dude. Ask her out. If you don't, I will."

Despite herself, Thea blushed. She knew she was passably pretty, but not with a face absent of makeup. Self-consciously, she ran a hand over her own hair. There must be a shortage of women up here for them to be so forward with her.

Thea redirected the conversation to safer ground. "So, what's with all the nicknames?"

"We're Hot Shots," Jackson said with a shrug, as if that said it all.

"We get nicknames like spies get code names. We're the best wildland firefighters around," Spider added, the pride evident in his tone. "They send us to the hottest, wildest part of the fire because we know how to battle the dragon."

"Dragon?" Thea repeated.

"Yep, dragon chasers go out naked," Spider continued.

"Naked?" Thea echoed, eyeing Spider—the man in black—totally mystified.

"That's right." Spider beamed. "It's man against nature out there."

"Enough, Spider. You've confused her totally." Chainsaw pushed his friend aside. "You see, we hike for miles up steep ridges, where fire trucks can't reach, to make firebreaks in the wilderness—cut down trees, chop away brush, sometimes even set a controlled burn so that when the main fire reaches us there's no fuel left. We wear what looks like khakis and button-down shirts, but they're fire resistant. It's *naked* compared to the turnout gear a city firefighter wears."

Thea nodded, worried about Logan despite herself. "And the dragon?"

"Just a nickname for the fire," Jackson explained.

"So, you have nicknames for everything, even yourselves?" Thea teased.

"Everybody out on the line has a nickname. Some of us prefer our given names when we're not on duty." Jackson sent the other two men a look that seemed to say they were a bit extreme for his taste.

"Others live with it, *Golden*," qualified Spider, revealing Jackson's nickname. He ruffled Jackson's hair before Jackson swatted him away. "Our fearless leader is our own good-luck charm."

Intrigued, Thea asked, "What's Logan's nickname?" She'd sensed Logan had one even though he'd denied it.

"Oh, uh…" Jackson hesitated, spinning his wedding ring, immediately piquing Thea's interest. Logan's nickname must be a doozy.

"He didn't tell you?" Chainsaw asked.

"This is priceless." Spider chuckled. "Are you going to save McCall's butt and take charge for the next six months or so?"

"Logan's going to be gone six months?" Thea squeaked in surprise. How were Logan and the girls supposed to start healing in four days? She'd listened to what everyone had said about Hot Shot schedules, but it was barely April, not the drought of late summer. She hadn't truly believed the season would start so soon. What had she gotten herself into?

The men looked uncomfortable.

"Don't get us wrong." Chainsaw tried quickly to allay her concerns. "We come home a couple of times a month."

"Unless it's a really brutal season," Spider added. "There have been droughts in six western states."

Chainsaw pushed his friend back down the steps with a quiet, "You're not helping."

The men studied their running shoes for a moment, before Spider finally met her inquisitive gaze and said, "Speak of the devil." Spider nodded toward the driveway and Logan's approaching truck.

"Go straight to your room," Logan commanded as he noticed the girls brightening at the sight of Jackson, Cole and Aiden.

Tess dug in her heels. "What's Spider doing? Is he asking Thea out?"

"No." Logan bristled at the idea. Thea was too colorful for the likes of Spider. His friend preferred his women to be sleek, moody, sophisticated and oozing sexuality. Although, Thea didn't look her chipper, happy self. She looked…pissed off.

"Then what's Spider doing here? He shouldn't be talking to Thea. You should be." Tess turned accusing blue eyes his way.

"We're training today." Logan sensed the territorial undertone to Tess's question, and wanted to squash it quickly. "Don't get any ideas about Thea and me." He may need a surrogate mother more than a nanny, but marriage was out of the question, not even on his horizon.

"They brought Rufus," Hannah breathed, spotting Whizzer and Rufus racing to the porch. The little girl loved animals of all kinds.

"Okay," Logan said. "Play with the dogs first and then go to your room."

With a gasp, Hannah hurried toward the group on the front steps, attention locked on the dogs. Jackson tugged a tennis ball out of his pocket and gave it to Hannah, who threw it out into the bushes without getting either dog's attention. The girl jogged out to get the ball, attracting Rufus's eye, who caught on that there was a ball on the loose.

Rufus found the ball first, knocking Hannah on her butt in his rush to get it. Logan held his breath as the little girl blinked back the tears. Luckily, Whizzer climbed into her lap and began licking her face. Hannah giggled, trying unsuccessfully to hold the dog at bay. Logan couldn't remember the last time he'd heard one of the twins laugh. The sound warmed his heart until Hannah's laughter died away, leaving only one thought.

His sister would never see the twins smile again, never hear their laughter.

Then Thea gave Hannah that smile of hers that invited you to join in the delight of the moment.

How he resented all that Thea's smile represented. Joy. Laughter. The desire to see what the next day would bring other than a heavy, unbearable silence.

Tess crossed her arms over her thin chest, drawing Logan's attention back to his cantankerous niece. "When are they leaving?" she asked, pointing at the men.

Logan bent at the knees until he was nose to nose with Tess. "It's not hard to be on your best behavior when you're in your room, is it?"

"You wouldn't talk to me like that if Mom was alive."

Logan closed his eyes for a second and sucked on his cheek so that he wouldn't snap at a ten-year-old who didn't know any better than to mess with an ill-tempered Hot Shot.

"I used to think you were so cool until Mom got sick. I know you can't wait to get rid of us again." Tess turned on her heel and left him standing alone. She stalked into the house without acknowledging Thea or the Hot Shots.

What did you say to something like that? Logan straightened on shaky knees and tried to ignore the icy ache in his chest. He was damned if he took the twins and damned if he didn't. He'd disappoint Deb either way.

Thea told Hannah she could play with Whizzer in her room. Hannah knelt down and whistled for the pup. He came running right to her and they both bounded into the house. Hannah had withdrawn so much, it was painful to watch her sometimes and remember the outgoing girl she'd once been.

With a resigned sigh, Logan grabbed the carton of eggs he'd bought in town and walked to the porch, mumbling a greeting to his friends.

"Are you ready to run?" Jackson asked him.

"In a minute." During their off time, the men ran the mountain trails in the area, training for their annual physical certification. Most of the team had already passed, but that didn't mean keeping in shape was any less important. The ability to scale a mountain trail full speed carrying a fifty-pound pack could mean the difference between life and death. Today, they planned on running the ridges above Logan's house. "I see you've met Thea."

Thea raised her eyebrows. The bells on her feet sounded ever so softly, as if she had flexed her foot or shifted her weight.

"She's your nanny, right?" Spider's smile countered what Logan had just told Tess, indicating that sweet, neighborly, colorful women were also on Spider's menu choice. "Where's she staying?"

"Here." Logan was quick to qualify, even as he wanted to say, "Not with you." That seemed territorial, and Logan had no claim to Thea.

Thea's eyes didn't crease as she smiled, and Logan noticed her bells were silent.

In that moment she seemed more like the dour Mr. Banks than Mary Poppins.

"If she needs a tour guide, I'd volunteer…" Spider began.

"Thea's going to be pretty busy. She may not have

mentioned this, but she's working on her Ph.D.," Logan explained, needing to regain the miles of emotional separateness from everyone he'd had as recently as a few days ago.

Logan stepped past Thea into the living room. "Why is it so bright in here?"

Thea leaned around the door frame. "I was dusting."

"So? Close the blinds," he growled. He could tell she'd cleaned the room. Everything was brighter, brimming with life. The room smelled of lemon. The coffee tabled gleamed. The mantel looked empty.

She'd bring out the family pictures next if he didn't say anything. Logan couldn't bear to look at Deb. Not yet. It was too soon.

"I couldn't see a thing in here. I might have scrubbed the finish off the wood, it was that dark." Thea followed Logan into the room.

"Close the blinds," Logan repeated, then went to do it himself.

"I knew a guy once who had eye surgery." Thea's words stopped him. "They claimed it corrected his vision, and he didn't have to wear glasses anymore, but he hated sunlight after that. He wore his sunglasses everywhere, even in the house. He got a job working nights at a drive-in movie theater, then he started delivering newspapers early in the morning." She sighed. "Of course, he didn't tell his wife any of this. He let her think one thing while something else entirely was going on."

Logan turned to stare at Thea. If Aunt Glen wasn't crazy, Thea most certainly was. Only, that last piece had been delivered more like a dig at him than a ditzy story.

"Wait, wait. I've heard this one." Spider crowed with a grin until Chainsaw and Jackson tried to hustle him out the door.

"I was wondering if you had the same challenge. You know, aversion to the light, avoiding his hang-ups, not coming clean about what's going on." Thea smiled sweetly, as if she was the answer to all his problems instead of the cause of several.

How dare she challenge him? He ignored the fact that he'd been feeling bad about her being unable to study just an hour before. Logan had more problems than he wanted to admit and wasn't about to let Thea bully or embarrass him into fixing them. He'd straighten out his life in his own way and time, thank you.

"I love this woman," Spider chuckled.

Chainsaw shushed him.

Logan drew a deep, controlling breath. He would not give Spider a pounding. He would not snap at Thea.

Hannah stood cradling Whizzer in her arms. "Did you have eye surgery, Uncle Logan?"

Tess was staring at Logan, too. And now his friends were smiling at him through the doorway, waiting, no doubt, to see just how much more of a fool he'd make of himself.

Thea's sneakers jingled as Logan's temper boiled and threatened to surface.

"No, I have not had surgery. I just don't like the sun." Logan sounded like a whiny ten-year-old.

No one said a word.

Angling away from the twins, Logan sighed. "Would you girls prefer the windows open?" When they didn't immediately answer, he glanced over at them. And repeated a bit testily, "Would you?"

Tess gave a noncommittal shrug, already withdrawing into her shell.

After a moment of hesitation, Hannah nodded. "Mom always had the windows open."

Logan remembered. Deb's house had been filled with light and laughter back then, unlike their house growing up. Then they'd all moved into his house the last few months of Deb's life and nothing seemed light again.

"And Logan likes the windows closed." Aunt Glen shrugged, eyes still on the television, oblivious to the struggle in the room.

"He's getting as bad as me," Spider ribbed, poking his dark head in the door. "A creature of the night."

"Spider." Chainsaw elbowed his friend. "Leave it alone."

Choking back a bitter reply, Logan thrust the eggs at Thea. "There's something for Glen in the truck," he said softly without looking at her. Logan had also bought adult diapers at Birdie's, but hadn't wanted to embarrass Glen by bringing them inside. He retreated to the shadowy hallway leading to the back of the house to change into his running clothes.

"DO THEY ALWAYS JOKE like that?" Thea asked after Uncle Logan and the other Hot Shots had left for their run. She smiled, even though Uncle Logan was mad at her. Tess thought Thea was pretty brave.

"They used to joke more," Hannah said, petting the dog. "Before."

"Hannah." Tess didn't want her twin to explain about *before*.

Hannah looked up at Tess, tears filling her eyes.

Tess wanted to swear, but she didn't want to get in

trouble. Not that Aunt Glen would remember, but Thea was pretty strict about bad language and might tattle to Uncle Logan.

"Those are pretty jeans, Tess."

"Thanks," Tess mumbled, looking down at her faded blue jeans. She knew they were too short, but she'd found them in her closet and was wearing them because her mom had embroidered the butterflies on the leg. She didn't care what Aaron Fischer said about her *floods*. She was wearing the jeans until she couldn't button them anymore. And if her dad showed up to get her, Tess was taking the jeans this time.

Tess glanced guiltily at Hannah. Her mom had made a pair for Hannah as well, but they didn't fit her anymore since she'd gained weight. Tess had considered taking the jeans out of Hannah's drawer in Seattle a couple of times, but she didn't want to hurt Hannah's feelings, so Tess was glad she'd found her pair.

"Aunt Glen and I are going to make cookies. Would you like to help? Or would you prefer to be a cookie tester when they're done?"

"We made cookies here last summer," Hannah sniffed. "With Mom."

Any mention of their mom and Hannah became such a crybaby. A knot formed in Tess's stomach. She really hated it when Hannah cried, because it made Tess want to cry, too.

"I'd like a cookie," Aunt Glen said, turning from her spot on the couch to look at them all and saving Tess from committing herself.

Somehow, the thought of admitting out loud that she wanted a cookie made Tess want to cry even harder than seeing Hannah cry.

CHAPTER FIVE

"WHAT ARE YOU GOING to do with your *nanny*?" Jackson asked after they'd run a good mile up the mountain. Rufus could be heard crashing through the brush ahead of them.

"She's only temporary." Logan ignored the twinge in his leg where it had been broken last year and continued pounding up the steep terrain. He had to be more careful what he wished for. He'd been regretting letting Wes take the twins, and then they'd showed up on his doorstep, creating a whole new set of problems. One of them a leggy, meddlesome woman who made him feel things he didn't want to.

"Thea's a cute little thing," Chainsaw noted from behind them.

"Adorable," Spider agreed, much to Logan's chagrin.

"She's not a puppy, guys, and I'm not in the market for one in any case." Logan tried to focus on his feet, not his leg. *Up, up, up. Don't feel. Think of how Thea tried to embarrass you in front of your friends.*

"Wow, she is definitely not a dog. If she doesn't work out, I can make more room for her at my place," Spider added his two cents' worth. "I think I might need a nanny."

"I can't picture her color and noise being all that appealing to you," Logan retorted. Spider didn't have kids. He was just after Thea as another easy piece of ass. Only, nothing about Thea was easy. "With your dark nature, you tend more toward the tall, silent type." With hearts hardened to things like hope and dreams.

Spider scoffed. "Watch who you're calling dark, Tin Man. Your place is looking more like the abode of the Prince of Darkness every day."

"Or a hotel," Jackson added.

"What noise? How do you know she makes noise?" Chainsaw asked, dodging a big bush to keep up. "Like bed noise?"

"No! Those bells. That laugh. There's no thinking straight around her." Just remembering Thea's crinkly-eyed smile had him feeling tense. Thea was everything he'd shut himself away from, everything he felt guilty about remembering.

The twinge in his leg was becoming an ache. He couldn't ignore it. The break should have been healed by now—nearly eight months after it had snapped.

"Ah, so you are interested." Jackson smiled next to him.

"I'm not. I've got too much on my mind." Like finding a nanny to replace Thea quickly, because he didn't want to come home to a reminder of what he and the twins had lost. Deb had been there every day of his life through the nightmare that had been their childhood. She'd been optimistic in the face of it all. She'd been his conscience. And now he had all of her responsibilities and no one to turn to. His stomach churned.

"I think she and the twins are just what the doctor ordered. You've been moping around for far too long," Jackson commented. "Why are they home from school early?"

"It's nothing. A misunderstanding." He'd be lucky if Aaron's dad, Jerry Fischer, town pain-in-the-ass, didn't call tonight, demanding an apology. The man loved to see Logan crawl. The only bright spot was that Hannah had mopped the floor with the little bully. Logan would have paid to see that.

As usual, Jackson didn't let up. "What happened to Deb…it sucked. But the rest of you are still alive. And now you're together."

Having the twins back just caused more grief, not less. "That's enough advice for one day, Golden," Logan grumbled.

"Only if what he said penetrated that thick noggin of yours," Spider retorted.

They were all breathing deeply now. The mountain-side steepened.

"Clamp it, Spider." Logan ground to a halt. His lungs were protesting more than they had on any previous run and his leg was demanding a break. He blamed it on Thea. Or maybe Spider.

Laughing, Spider stopped several feet up the slope. "Funny thing about advice. It doesn't make any sense until it's almost too late."

Logan took a step up the trail, intent upon showing Spider just how funny his advice really was.

Jackson held him back. "That's enough," he said. Jackson looked at all of them. "Time for a change of subject."

"Shall we talk about the weather?" Spider asked. He was barely breaking a sweat while Logan was dripping.

Logan bit back a curse.

"No. Let's take care of business." Jackson began running up the mountain again and the others followed without question.

Jackson picked up the pace and started talking. The rest had no choice but to shut up and keep up. "I'm not sure that Rookie's coming back. He fought those fires in Southern California last fall and rumor has it he met some girl. And Stork isn't coming back for sure. He's retired. What about Kookaroo?"

Kookaroo was from Australia—a hell-bent-for-leather guy who frequently outdrank everyone on the crew.

"I heard he went home to fight fires this year," Logan put in. "What's the deal? So we have a few more open slots than normal."

"The deal is that the bureaucrats are looking to cut fire crews," Jackson said. "We need to fill the roster with quality people and return to bulletproof status this year."

"Why?" Chainsaw pulled up even with Logan. "We've had the best record around for years. The most fire lines cut, the most days in service on a fire, the team with the most years of service and the least injuries…oh, hell."

"That's right, Chainsaw. If we look like trouble—injuries, open slots, mistakes—we'll look like a good candidate for the cut." Jackson wasn't even breathing hard. "The Department of Forestry is looking to cut a few more teams."

"I should have told Socrates he couldn't go up on the mountain last year." Guilt propelled Logan forward, until he passed Jackson, ignoring his aching leg and burning lungs. "I knew he didn't have the proper gear, but hell, Golden, he trained us."

"Yeah, it was stupid, Tin Man." Spider accelerated up the trail right on Logan's heels. He'd pass Logan the moment there was enough room to do so.

"I've been through too much with the Forest Service

to be asked to *retire* because some politician from Pod-unk, Iowa, decides he can divert the money from my salary to help pave a road to his golf course," Jackson griped from behind them.

First Thea and her unbearably sunny smiles, then the girls being sent home from school. Now the job he loved and wouldn't give up was being threatened—not just because of budget cuts, but because Logan's temper could impede his team's performance if he and Spider couldn't find a way to work better together. What was next? Celibacy forever?

Fueled by irritation at himself, the world and Spider, Logan ran faster. His heart pounded and his lungs struggled to capture enough of the thin mountain air to keep him going. Every bit of speed he forced out of his weary limbs, Spider matched—taunting him, testing him, wanting to know which of them was better. The coals of anger flamed inside Logan, hot and unbearable. Who in the hell did Spider think he was? Why didn't he hang back and give Logan room?

At the top of a rise, Rufus sprang out from behind a bush in front of Logan. Leaping over the mutt, Logan spun and unleashed his anger, shoving Spider to the ground. His wiry, black-clad friend bounced right back up without much more than a shouted curse of surprise. Logan raised his fists, more than ready to release his burning rage on somebody who could take it. Rufus sprang around them like a referee, flinging drool onto everyone.

Jackson stepped between them, his face as red as Logan's felt. "What's going on?"

With a look that promised payback, Spider took another step forward, only to have Chainsaw shoulder him back. Jackson put a hand on Logan's arm, presumably in case he decided to do something rash like smash his fist into Spider's face.

Wouldn't the twins love it if Logan returned from the run broken and bleeding? And what about Thea? If she left, he wouldn't be able to be a Hot Shot. Aunt Glen couldn't save him this time. Thea was the only solution until he found someone else.

Suddenly, the heat of his anger cooled.

"You win, all right." Logan forced the words out with what little air he could pull into his lungs. "You win."

"It's not a race," Chainsaw said.

"Yeah? Well, nobody told that to Spider." Logan's chest still heaved.

Spider spread his hands. "We're just out for a run, man."

"No, you're out for something more and on any other day, I would've given it to you."

"I OWE YOU an apology." Logan marched into the kitchen and closed the curtains over the sink. "You were right about what I need around here. Mostly anyway," he added a bit petulantly.

Calmly, as if she witnessed such outbursts often, Glen turned in her chair to study her nephew.

As Thea handed Logan a water bottle, she gave Logan the once-over as well—sweat soaked his T-shirt and the waistband of his shorts, mud splattered up his shins, and his cheeks were flushed, but his eyes flashed with that energy he tapped when he became irritated. She knew that getting Logan to help the twins heal would be an uphill battle. She'd be crazy to stay here with such a hardheaded, moody man, especially when her heart raced when their eyes connected.

Before Thea could form an intelligent reply to Logan's apology, Glen rattled off a couple of questions.

"Have a good run? Did you see Deb out and about? I haven't seen her in a while."

Logan closed his eyes. His lips moved as if he was counting to ten.

Outside, Thea heard doors slam and an engine start. The rest of the Hot Shots were leaving.

"People come and go so quickly nowadays." Glen looked up from the table where she'd been cutting out cookies in the shape of bunnies, ducks and Easter eggs. "What was your name, dear?"

"I'm Thea. I'm going to make lunch. Why don't you go rest a bit?"

Glen's expression fell. She darted a glance at Logan and then looked back to Thea. "Have you been here long? I'm sorry, dear, but I don't remember."

"Don't worry about it." Thea smiled. "I'm watching Tess and Hannah for Logan."

"How nice," Glen said as she pushed herself out of the kitchen chair. Thea steadied Glen until the older woman seemed able to make it on her own.

"I do remember how Eldred hated kids. He was such a disappointment. It's nice to have someone around who enjoys them. Logan might say he doesn't, but he does." Glen winked. "Consider yourself lucky."

Despite herself, Thea grinned. "Thank you Glen. I am feeling lucky."

Glen paused and looked at Thea with a slight frown. "Why?"

Poor thing. Thea reached out and patted her cheek. "Because we're having grilled-cheese sandwiches for lunch today."

"Those are yummy." Glen wandered out of the kitchen.

When Thea turned around, Logan had his back to her, his arms propped wide on either side of the kitchen sink and his head hanging down as if in defeat. She wanted to offer him words of comfort, but she knew anything she said wouldn't be welcome. The distance between them and their goals suddenly seemed insurmountable. She and Logan operated on two different planes. He guarded himself from others with invisible plates of armor and wanted to be alone. She called people to her with color and sound.

"I caught her wandering at the edge of the woods looking for Deb. I hope my being here hasn't upset her. She seems really confused."

"I guess she misses her," Logan mumbled.

Not wanting to think about Glen lost in the woods, Thea returned to the kitchen table to finish cutting out the cookies. "I told the girls I'd take them into town later if they read for an hour first."

Logan made a sound, half between a grunt and an assent, as if his voice had rusted in his throat.

"Whether Hannah gets any reading done or not with Whizzer around is another story." Thea had never seen two little things move so quickly. In a snap, they'd been down the hall, with Whizzer happily trotting after them. Even Tess hadn't complained.

"Glen is pretty far gone, isn't she?" Logan asked, pushing his fingers into his hair as he turned to face Thea, his expression anguished.

Thea's heart went out to him. If he didn't live in such an isolated area, he would have so many resources available to help him—counseling, home nursing, support groups.

"There are some great medicines out there. Ones that I'm sure could clear Glen's head a bit." Although she wasn't a doctor, Thea suspected Glen showed early signs of Alzheimer's.

"She's been to the doctor in town, but he didn't think it was anything serious."

"Maybe you should get a second opinion," Thea answered patiently as she sprinkled the cookies with sugar and slid the tray into the oven. To ease his suffering just a bit, she offered Logan a sugar cookie shaped like an Easter egg and covered in pink frosting. "My grandmother used to say everybody needs a good dose of sugar now and then to increase the circulation and lift the spirits."

Logan cocked his head to the side as he studied her. "Was she right?" He took the cookie, careful, it seemed, that his large fingers didn't touch her smaller ones.

"For anybody under ten, yes. Life seems to get more complicated at that age." Thea's certainly had.

"Tell me about it," Logan replied softly, before taking a bite of the cookie.

"Spider mentioned something about you going back to work soon. Do you suppose you could give me an idea about your schedule so I can plan ahead?"

Logan's expression relaxed as he chewed. "I wish I could tell you. All I can say is that we'll be on call after testing concludes on Monday. I told Birdie about the nanny job when I was in town earlier. She said she'd post it for me. Hopefully, I'll find somebody else quickly and you can get back to your life."

Reading his urgency to get rid of her, Thea turned back to the table so that he couldn't see she was hurt. She'd assumed from his apology that he was hiring her.

She wasn't ready to leave Tess and Hannah. Even Glen had grown on her.

"Are you really going to be gone for six months? The girls need you here."

"It's my job." Some of the edge returned to his voice.

"Even Wes managed to make it home a few days a month," Thea murmured.

"Sure, until he dropped off the face of the planet."

With a sigh of defeat, Thea told herself that leaving was for the best. She rolled out the dough for one more batch of cookies. If Logan didn't want her to help, there was nothing Thea could do about it. She was going to return to Seattle, get her Ph.D., find new advances in the textile industry and be respected in her field. She was going to fulfill the promise she'd made to her mother. That was important…wasn't it?

The phone rang. Logan's words brought Thea back to the present.

"Birdie, you know someone that's looking for work? Someone perfect for the nanny job?"

Thea stopped her hands midair as they carried a cookie from the cutting board to the cookie sheet.

"Oh, sure. I'll talk to her tomorrow."

The cookie plopped onto the floor. Thea found herself imagining someone else taking care of Tess and Hannah, someone who wouldn't know how to deal with Hannah's fragile moods and Tess's silences.

"Why don't we do that." Logan said good-bye and hung up.

"Do what?" Thea asked, mildly frustrated that she couldn't hear what had been said on the other end of the line.

"There's someone down the mountain looking for

work. She's got a six-month-old baby that she'd bring along, but no boyfriend or husband. It's perfect." Logan leaned against the wall and crossed his arms over his chest, looking pleased with himself.

For no reason whatsoever. That woman was far from perfect. Caring for a baby was a full-jtime job in itself. *Men just didn't get it.*

"Logan, that's no good. Taking care of babies is hard work. She won't have any extra energy for the girls. And the baby will keep everyone up all night or wake them up early." Thea was unreasonably relieved that the woman Birdie found might not be qualified. "And let's not talk about her single status. If she's young, she'll want to date." She'd probably want to date Logan. Thea picked up the cookie dough she'd dropped, balled it in her fist. With a sigh, she tossed it into the sink. "Do you know how she feels about taking care of Glen? You can't just take the first person who comes along just because they're available."

He chewed his cheek through her assessment. "Technically, you're the first person to come along. But you're right." He picked up the receiver, mumbling, "At this rate, I'll never find a nanny."

"That's why I'm staying to help you. The girls deserve the right person." Thea patted Logan on the arm, leaving a smattering of flour and dough on his tan skin. She studied his face—his blue eyes filled with sorrow, his mouth that seemed made for wicked smiles. If only he was taking his sister's death better there was hope…for the twins' sake, of course.

"WHAT DO YOU usually eat? There's not even a frozen vegetable in here. There's nothing nutritious to cook now that the casseroles are gone." Thea paused in her outburst to glance over her shoulder at Logan sitting at the kitchen table. If she felt awkward about the situation they were in, she didn't show it. She'd made herself completely at home, from the study planner on the wall to the guest towels she'd put in the bathroom to the attack she was making on his conscience. "Look. Your ice cubes look like they have dust on them."

"We eat a lot of frozen dinners and takeout." Logan sat rigidly in a chair in the face of her unvoiced accusation—that he wasn't suited for parenthood. He knew that. Then and there, Logan made himself a promise that he'd get laid if the chance presented itself on the next fire. He shouldn't have argued with Spider about the ski bunnies in Sun Valley.

Thea closed the freezer door with a crisp snap.

When he'd first asked Thea about staying, there had been a moment when he'd been relieved. Few people knew how to deal with Glen's foggy mind or the twins' silence, and Thea needed the money. She had dangled a sliver of hope at him.

Now she was just blindsiding him with conversation, and noise, and parenting decisions. He just wanted to move through life at minimum effort, and that wasn't good enough for her.

With a sideways glance at him, Thea tugged the kitchen curtains open, bringing in late-afternoon sunlight. He would have been happy to never hear her bells again, except that her being here ensured the twins were going to be well cared for and he could return to his job.

She bent to examine the contents under the sink, flashing him a good look at her toned thighs beneath the hem of her khaki shorts.

Not wanting to stare, Logan put his elbow on the

table and covered his eyes with his hand as he reminded himself she wasn't his type.

"Can we go into town to get some real food? Fresh vegetables? Chicken?" Thea's bells heralded her changing position as the cabinet clicked closed.

Logan risked looking at her. She moved to investigate the other cupboards, humming and looking happy as a clam.

He sucked on his cheek, reining in his frustration. He remembered how his father had picked on him, digging at him again and again until Logan talked back and got the beating his father had wanted to give him. If Logan was going to be a better parent, he couldn't go around exploding all the time. Only problem was, he felt like exploding all the time.

With a ringing of bells, Thea crossed the room and touched Logan's cheek, soft and featherlight, before stepping back. "Your temper is showing. What's wrong?"

"You're imagining things," Logan growled.

"If you're mad at me, tell me."

"I'm furious." He bared his teeth at her. "Happy?"

Her bells made a small noise. "I will be once you tell me what's wrong."

"Would that make you happy?"

"No, but it might lower your blood pressure."

When he opened his mouth to argue, she shook her finger at him. What the—

"You've got to take care of yourself if you want to be a parent."

"And chewing out a stranger is good for me?" This close, he could see her freckles.

"It's called venting. Think of yourself as a teapot. If you let yourself get steamed, you'll really blow."

He kicked the chair out from under him and yelled, "That theory really blows!"

She *smiled*. "That's better."

Logan's jaw gaped open. Why did she think shouting at her was a good thing?

To hell with it. "Let's load everybody up." Logan gave in. He needed to go into town and see if Birdie had found him a nanny who could mind her own business.

"LOGAN MCCALL? Twice in one day?" Birdie Lowell, the town mayor and Silver Bend Grocery proprietor, poked her head up from behind the counter where she'd been studying the *National Enquirer*.

Logan dreaded coming to town anymore. Birdie, Mary and the others meant well, but they poked and snooped into his life in the most obnoxious way. Logan braced himself for the latest onslaught.

Birdie straightened the pages of the *Enquirer* and set it back in the newsstand rack. "Why, Glenda, it's good to see you, too."

Aunt Glen beamed. "Birdie, how is that husband of yours?"

Birdie's penciled eyebrows shot up. "He's…ah…" She cast a quick glance at Logan. "He's resting."

Logan frowned. Birdie's husband had been dead for two years now.

Unaware of Glen's error, Thea grabbed a small red shopping basket and approached Birdie, shoes jingling. She greeted Birdie as if they were old friends. "Looks like I'll be here longer than I planned. I'm going to be staying to take care of the girls."

Logan hadn't thought Birdie's eyebrows could go any higher. Their penciled shape almost disappeared beneath her sparse fringe of gray bangs. Birdie had barely recovered when Thea asked if she had any strawberry Quik in stock.

"Strawberry milk?" Having only tried the chocolate-sugar version of Quik with milk, Logan imagined his expression mirrored the surprise in Birdie's face.

Thea's smile was bright. "You like strawberry milk shakes, don't you?"

"Well, I suppose if you're going to be Logan's nanny I could order some," Birdie allowed.

"Did I hear right? Logan has a nanny?" Smiley Peterson shuffled in the door, with his characteristic grin. Smiley may have owned the barbershop, but no one let him touch their hair anymore—not after he almost took off some poor kid's ear. "Those little angels need some stability."

Logan had been afraid this might happen. The town's elderly do-gooders were descending upon him like locusts. Soon, he'd be inundated with a new way to remove grass stains from Tess's jeans and be asked to fix something.

"Seems Smiley did hear right." Glen nodded with a frown, staring at Thea as she whispered to Logan, "Is Deb going to be able to afford a nanny?"

Wincing, Logan reassured Glen that the nanny was fine with Deb.

"I saw you pull up, Logan. I missed you earlier." Jackson's mom, Mary, entered the store. "I just stopped by to say hello to Thea and the girls before the Pony's after-school rush."

All they were missing to complete their fearsome foursome was Marguerite, the town's most flamboyant widow.

"I'm so glad Logan convinced you to stay," Mary was

saying to Thea. "Why don't you bring the twins and Glenda by on Saturday afternoon for ice cream."

"Do you still have chocolate?" Hannah asked.

"Always." Mary gave Hannah a squeeze.

"I've got some fantastic recipes that I just know Logan will love," Birdie cut in. "They're in the meat section. Oh, and with Easter just a few days away, you'll need supplies."

Logan started chewing on the side of his cheek, feeling as if he had no control of his life. If he said anything, they'd take it as an invitation to fill him with more suggestions, with more unwanted advice.

"Haven't seen the twins in my shop for months. I'm open on Saturday this weekend if you want to come in for a trim," Smiley offered, rubbing his bulbous nose self-consciously.

"No!" Birdie and Mary exclaimed simultaneously.

Smiley's grin dimmed. Logan almost felt sorry for the old coot.

"He could trim my hair," Hannah offered.

Tess shushed Han from the section of videos and DVDs. Trust Tess to know what was good for her.

"We've been worried about Logan for so long." Mary covered the awkward moment with a smile.

"You come to us for any advice that you might need," Birdie added. "We know what he likes. Ham on Easter, ribs on Memorial Day, hot wings if he's home on Labor Day."

"Of course, I'd love any advice you can give me," Thea said, looking at Logan expectantly, waiting, he realized, for him to straighten things out.

Logan suppressed a groan. Okay, he was a coward. Thea was taking the heat and he was letting her.

"Oh, this is priceless, Tin Man." Spider had entered

the store and soaked in the chaos with an ear-splitting grin. Since he lived in an apartment over Smiley's barbershop, it was impossible to get anything that happened in town past Spider.

Even the merry widow, Marguerite, was preferable to Spider.

"Just when we were starting to worry about the twins, they're back and Logan's being so responsible," Birdie cooed, as if Logan had done something totally out of character. "Wait until we tell Marguerite that Logan is on track."

"Maybe we can have you over for dinner this week," Thea suggested sweetly. "You can write down all your suggestions and bring them over then."

This was too much.

"If you'll excuse us." Logan swept Thea away toward the only place he knew well in Birdie's store— the frozen-food section. "What do you think you're doing?"

"I'm trying to fit in. Isn't that what you want?"

Yes. "No."

"Well then, when were you planning on telling them I'm only staying until you find someone else? I kept waiting." With her hands on her hips, her bells silent and her brown eyes blazing, Logan got the message—put up or shut up. Either she was his nanny or she wasn't.

He stared at Birdie's faded linoleum. "Who could get a word in edgewise?"

"Can we rent a movie?" Hannah asked from three aisles away.

"I'll have to know what it is first," Thea replied.

"We don't need your job posting anymore, do we, Logan?" Birdie called from across the store.

The sound of crumpling paper made Logan's ears burn with frustration. If he didn't say anything now—

"So much for the heartless Tin Man," Spider sighed dramatically. "He'll never get a date again with a babe like Thea for a nanny."

Swearing under his breath, Logan had to agree. Not that he was ready to date. He was just ready for mindless sex with a stranger.

Mary gave Spider a sharp reply that Logan couldn't quite hear, then addressed the twins. "Aren't you glad Thea decided to stay?"

Logan turned back to Thea. "You did notice they swarmed around you before I had a chance to say a word?"

"You're still free to say something now. How do you expect to raise these girls if you can't even set a couple of sweet seniors straight?"

Logan heaved a sigh. "Look, you don't know this town. It's small and people meddle, give unwanted advice and drop by with overcooked casseroles loaded with unidentifiable vegetables at the first sign of trouble. Well, that part you do know," he allowed. "It's brutal. Nothing is private. If I say you're temporary, they'll want to know why." Because Thea seemed perfect for the job.

At least if you were anyone other than Logan.

"This is totally different," Thea sputtered in a low voice punctuated by a desperate gesture of hands. "I agreed to stay until you found someone. I did *not* agree to be your nanny forever."

"Thank God."

"That's the thanks I get for trying to help you?" Thea's face paled. "Every Hot Shot has a reason for their nickname, right? That means you don't have a heart. Heroes have hearts. Heroes wouldn't continue to kick someone who was trying to help them." She poked him in the chest.

"I'm *not* apologizing for my nickname," Logan said through gritted teeth, batting her hand away. He actually liked his nickname. It was a whole lot better than Skunk, who couldn't control his farts, or Dinky, who was abnormally small below the waist. Tin Man was who he was. "I *will* apologize for my behavior. I'm just…this is…not how I expected things to be last week."

Thea left him in front of the frozen peas. He caught up to her in front of the ham hocks.

"Not those." He turned up his nose.

"It would serve you right if I bought liver," Thea said, then whispered, "*Tin Man*."

"Hang on a second. Are you mad because of my nickname? What does it matter what they call me? Once fire season kicks off, you'll rarely see me." He barely knew this woman. She was ruining his life. The disappointment in her eyes shouldn't matter. Somehow, someway, Thea had managed what other women had not—to make him care about how she felt. He pressed his lips together and glared at her.

"And your reputation will be intact if I keep my mouth shut? Is that it?"

"My rep… Hey, get off that track. This nanny business has nothing to do with my rep. It's about my peace of mind." This was why he kept women at arm's length. They tended to get upset over things that were none of their concern.

The bell on the door and the *click-click-click* of high heels heralded the presence of another woman.

"Oh, baby, even my tongue is hard," Spider crooned, followed by an, "Ow! Mary, you pinched my arm."

"Show some respect," Birdie chastised Spider from the door. "Smiley, close your mouth."

Logan couldn't keep himself from turning around to see which of Spider's babes had walked in.

"Hey, Tin Man." A cool blonde in skintight jeans and an even tighter sweater brushed past him, trailing an abundance of musky perfume. "Who's this?"

"She's our nanny." Hannah had come around the corner with her movie.

For the life of him, Logan couldn't remember the woman's name. Nina...Nancy...Noelle or something. He knew he'd slept with her at some point or another. He just couldn't remember when.

"Finally worked your way through all the locals, did you?" The blonde smiled knowingly first at him and then at Thea. Whatever her name was, her smile didn't put him at ease. In fact, it gave him a feeling of impending doom. She turned to Thea. "If you're the nanny, make sure he pays you in advance. If you fall prey to that charm—and you will—he'll be looking for a new nanny by morning."

And now Logan knew why he'd sensed doom.

Thea blanched, bells still on strike.

"Girls, why don't you pick out another video?" Mary asked.

"Naomi," Birdie warned, peeking from behind the bread display. "Behave."

"Don't worry about me, Birdie. I'm long over this Casanova, just like every woman from here to Boise. Because once he's gone, he ain't coming back."

Logan assumed the strangled sound coming from somewhere over by the videos was made by Tess because it was high and thin, but it was hard to tell over Spider's laughter.

"CAN I HELP?" Logan paused awkwardly at the refrigerator. Thea could feel his eyes upon her.

Thea's hands hesitated as she coated the chicken in a bowl of herbs. "You don't have to help me. I'm just the *nanny*." Thea shouldn't let what happened at the store upset her.

Tin Man. His nickname was *Tin Man*—a man without a heart. And that woman in the grocery store had added insult to injury when she'd insinuated Thea would sleep with him and then he'd dump her.

As if Thea hadn't been used and dumped by those who she hadn't slept with. She was tired of being the girl everyone relied on but no one needed. Just once, she wanted to be appreciated for who she was, not what she could do for someone. Was that too much to ask?

"Chopped or torn?"

Thea looked up from her chicken in surprise.

"Do you like your lettuce chopped or torn?" Logan picked up the head of lettuce from where she'd left it to dry on the counter.

"Torn," she admitted reluctantly.

Thea put the chicken in the oven and turned her attention to the cauliflower. The only sounds in the kitchen for the next few minutes were the ripping of lettuce and the slicing of cauliflower. Thea's mind wandered to Tess and Hannah, who hadn't seemed to take their uncle's run-in with the insensitive woman at the grocery store well. Tess had been rigidly indignant since they'd come home. Where had Tess learned to be so cool? From Logan? Or had Deb been like that?

"Your sister was very pretty." Thea had never been

good at keeping silent, even in school, even when she was sure talking might make things worse.

Logan continued tearing lettuce, giving no indication that he'd heard her.

"The girls look just like her," Thea added, then bit her lip in an effort to shut up.

She sighed. Two little blond beauties with broken hearts.

When Logan didn't say a word—surprise, surprise—Thea's mouth continued to run unchecked. "Were they this quiet before?"

The need to roll her eyes was overwhelming. When would she learn to keep control of her tongue? Especially when Logan didn't want anything to do with her and her unending curiosity.

"It used to be…I couldn't get them to shut up," Logan spoke so quietly that Thea almost missed it.

Thea stopped chopping to stare at him.

"Have you ever talked about Deb? All three of you together?"

"No!" He looked stunned, as if she'd asked him if he wore panty hose under his jeans.

Thea knew, in that instant, what it would be like to live in Logan's house. The silence. Blocking out the sunlight. Shunning the joy that life still had to offer. Her hand went involuntarily to her stomach.

"Have you talked to anyone? You know, a priest? A counselor? A close friend?" Anyone to help give relief to the myriad emotions he and the girls must be carrying around.

"A counselor at school spoke to the girls once. And then Wes took them away."

Once. Rather than answer, Thea set the water on the

stove to boil. She opened the refrigerator, staring blindly at its contents. He thought having them talk to a counselor once was enough?

Logan practically threw the bowl of lettuce across the kitchen counter. "What?"

"I didn't say anything."

"That's just it. You always say something." Thea sensed the fire in him before she turned to meet the accusation in his blazing eyes. "It's easy to judge when you haven't lost someone. It's easy to say I'm going to *suck* as their guardian."

"I never—"

"That's right. You've never lost a sister or a niece or a mother." He leaned threateningly into her space.

"—thought you'd suck…" But in the face of Logan's wrath, Thea could no longer keep her temper. She knew being angry with him when he was grieving wasn't right, but the anger didn't care about what was right or fair. Thea wanted to be easygoing and happy, damn it. Someone everyone liked and respected. She didn't want to be stoic, silent or angry just because a guy who turned her on felt nothing—not even respect—for her. "You're right. I haven't lost a sister or a niece. I lost my mom."

"I'M AN ASS. I'm sorry." The fire that had coursed so fiercely through Logan's veins came almost to a stop, squeezing his heart painfully in the process. Thea had been trying to help them because she understood what they were going through, and he'd abused her help by unleashing his temper on her.

Just now, she looked shell-shocked. Probably because he'd almost forced the admission out of her. "It's not—"

"Easy, I know." Logan rushed over Thea's explanation. "It's not something you're taught to deal with. And I am *not* going to press you for more. I mean, I have things I don't want to talk about and I'm not ready to talk about." There. Awkward discussion over. He wouldn't have to talk about Deb again. "What else do I need to do for dinner?"

CHAPTER SIX

THE MOMENT OF TRUTH slipped past. Logan assumed that Thea's mother was dead. As they sat down to eat dinner, Thea vowed to clear up that misperception.

Just as soon as the time was right.

Which was right after Thea broke the silence that had such a fierce hold on this house. Otherwise, the twins would have little chance of recovering. If Logan was leaving—perhaps as soon as next week—she better start right away.

"Glen, earlier today, you told me a story about Deb and her cookie-making ability," Thea began.

"I did?" Glen's eyebrows puckered with concern.

"You certainly did." Thea spread her napkin in her lap and avoided looking at Logan. "I was wondering if anyone else wanted to share a story about Deb."

The girls seemed to slouch in their seats. Thea didn't dare check the expression on Logan's face. She could feel the heat coming out of his ears from two chairs away.

Glen chewed thoughtfully. "Deb was always so active in sports. What did she do in high school? Track or volleyball or something?" Glen tilted her head at Logan.

Thea could have kissed the older woman.

"She ran cross-country," he admitted gruffly.

"Whatever it was, she wore those short shorts. Said

it gave her legs more freedom." Glen snorted. "Gave people full view of her gams is what it did." Glen went back to her food.

Logan choked on his bread.

"I think Heidi's mom was a runner, too." Hannah spoke in hushed tones after a moment, gazing tentatively at Tess and Logan, as if seeking their approval. "Didn't Heidi…um…tell us about some medal she won that her dad used to carry with him?"

Logan grunted and continued to shovel food in his mouth as if he hadn't eaten in days. Hannah sighed and stared down at her plate.

"How about you, Hannah? Do you have a favorite memory?" Thea encouraged the girl, trying to keep an eye on Tess, Glen and Logan all at the same time.

Tess was picking at her food with her fork. Logan shredded a roll as if it deserved punishment. Glen stared at the open window.

"We all used to lie in bed at night—Tess on one side, me on the other—while Mom read us stories," Hannah said softly. "*The Wizard of Oz* was her favorite."

"What a wonderful memory." Thea smiled at the little girl.

"Why don't you share one of your own?" Logan challenged. "About the mother you lost."

Tess's fork clattered to her plate. The table fell silent as all eyes turned to Thea.

Here was her chance to come clean. Only if she did, Logan would never speak, and the girls would never use their mother's memory to heal their hearts and rediscover what life still had to offer.

Thea pasted a smile on her face. "Of course." She cleared her throat, hearing her father's voice reprimanding her, "A lie of omission is still a lie." And yet, he was a police detective, trained and paid to dissemble. If it helped to lie a little, she'd swallow her qualms.

"My mom loved to sing. Only, she had the worst voice I've ever heard. And she would belt out these show tunes as if she were Bette Midler. God, it was awful." Thea's eyes welled with tears. Stupid. She would not cry over something that had happened seventeen years ago. She'd rediscovered sunshine and flowers and music, even if she hadn't discovered a home filled with love.

Hannah allowed herself a small smile. Glen looked endearingly oblivious. Logan and Tess stared hard at their plates. Silence encompassed the table.

Logan cleared his throat. "Deb used to interview all my dates, as if she were my older brother instead of my twin sister. She always watched out for everyone." Logan gripped his water glass, staring into its depths instead of at his family.

Thea hadn't been lucky enough to have a sibling. She'd always envied the kids with brothers and sisters, even as she listened to them gripe about them.

"Tess?" Thea prompted gently.

Tess's chest heaved. "May I be excused?"

"You've barely eaten," Logan protested.

"I'm not hungry."

"Tess—" Logan began.

"It's all those cookies. It's my fault." Thea stared at Logan, hoping he'd realize that if Tess wasn't ready to open up, she shouldn't be pushed.

"I don't like chicken, okay?" Tess said angrily. Without waiting for the permission she'd asked for, Tess shoved her chair back and carried her dishes to the sink.

"I'm sorry," Thea said when Tess had left the kitchen. "It helps to talk about it."

"It might have helped you, but *we* don't need to talk about it." Logan stood and took his plate to the counter.

But Thea wasn't convinced.

LOGAN SAT IN THE DARK, shadowed living room, trying to clear his mind of emotion.

And not succeeding.

Thea and the twins had been with him only a few days. He should be relaxing. He had a big week ahead of him, months of hard work to follow. Yet, he couldn't sleep.

He walked quickly down the hall. The four downstairs bedrooms had been empty until Deb got sick. When she'd sold off her house and moved into Logan's, he'd insisted on giving her the master bedroom upstairs so that she could have some privacy.

Logan stopped at the first open door and looked inside. Glen dozed in her bed, yarn in a heap on her lap. The door to the girls' room was shut. It was early, but the house was quiet. He liked the quiet. He looked forward to the quiet. After several long, emotional roller coaster days, Logan was tired. His leg was starting to ache. He just wanted to collapse on his own bed in the darkness of his room, sink into sleep and forget. If he could only sleep.

Thea breezed past him and through the door to her room with a soft tinkle of bells, leaving the barest scent of perfume as she passed. She must have been in the kitchen studying. She sank onto the quilt that covered the small twin bed and flipped open a tattered notebook. A blue suitcase sat in the corner. A knee-high stack of books was piled on the floor next to the bed.

And her window blinds were open.

Logan sucked on his cheek. He supposed Thea could do whatever she wanted with her door closed. He reached for the doorknob so that he could shut her in, giving himself some much-needed privacy.

"Would you…come outside with me?" she asked suddenly, looking at him.

"What?"

"I need to take Whizzer out one more time before bed." She bit her bottom lip.

"What? The nanny of steel is afraid of the dark?"

Thea blushed.

Logan's bed would have to wait. "It's okay. I'll go."

"Thanks. I wasn't looking forward to taking Whizzer outside alone, what with lions and tigers and bears around."

"Coyotes, wolves and bears." Logan couldn't resist correcting her, but he carefully kept his tone detached.

"Whatever. Anything with sharp teeth." She made fangs with her fingers.

Her pantomime was so unexpected, he almost smiled.

"Sorry, I'm a city girl. We're afraid of rats, but we live with them. Anything larger than a rat is considered dangerous."

Logan rolled his eyes. "You have terrorists, carjackers and muggers. That's ten times as dangerous as what you'll encounter out here."

"Spoken like a man who's never been to the city."

He refused to look at her crinkly-eyed smile, especially when he felt the upward tug of his lips.

They retraced their steps back to the kitchen, donning their jackets—his sensible one and her lightweight jacket that wouldn't be warm enough on the Washington coast, much less the Idaho mountains in springtime.

Whizzer scampered around the yard as soon as Thea opened the door.

Preferring to control the conversation rather than have Thea ask her painful questions, he asked, "What are you going to do with Whizzer?"

"You should be asking yourself that. Hannah's become quite attached to him."

"It's only been a few days."

"After the first hour, I'd already fallen in love."

Too quickly, Logan decided. She was exactly the type of woman he wouldn't touch with a ten-foot pole.

Whizzer raced from bush to bush.

"Maybe the yard will lose its appeal after another day or so," he said. Maybe Thea would lose appeal to Logan after a day or so. Logan nearly had a heart attack at the thought. He found Thea appealing? It had to be because he hadn't been with a woman in eight months.

"As long as no new lions or tigers or bears pass through, I'm sure he'll be fine." He could tell Thea was smiling without looking at her by the sound of her voice accented by those bells.

What on earth did he like about her?

Her legs. Even if the bells were annoyingly distracting.

Her smile. She had an okay smile, he allowed. Still, she was resistible and not sexy as all get-out. He went for women who were open for a good time, who advertised their availability in low-cut blouses and sultry looks.

What was wrong with him?

Nothing. Not a damn thing. She was a woman and he was a man. His reaction to her just proved he was ready to date again.

Satisfied with his logic, Logan leaned against the house. "He's got to be nearly empty."

She shook her head.

"He's not that big."

"But he only goes a little each time." She beamed at him, bright despite the darkness. "The first thing those girls are going to teach you is patience."

"Who taught you patience? I can't see you standing still for long."

"I've got experience. In standing still." Her smile lacked worry and practically begged him to share in the joke. "I've been a bridesmaid. Three times."

"Wow. Do you think that's bad luck or something?"

She shrugged, the smile long gone. "It's not a bad thing. I can't see myself getting married. Guys don't seem to want what I have to give."

Her words didn't fit with her appearance, with her now-familiar smile, with the promise of welcome in her warm brown eyes. "Who are you?"

"I would suppose some would say I'm your nanny." She didn't smile.

Whizzer hopped up to the porch, panting from his efforts.

"And you?" Thea asked when he held open the kitchen door for her.

"Huh?"

"What are your views on marriage?"

Logan recoiled. "That word is not in my vocabulary."

Squeak. Squeak. Squeak. Squeak.

"What the…" Logan heard the sound even before he entered the kitchen the next morning. But when he opened the kitchen door, the room was still. Which was even stranger, because Thea stood there without making noise. He eyed her suspiciously.

Dressed in navy sweats with a racing stripe down each slender leg, a plain blue T-shirt and red-and-white slippers, Thea just stared back at him. Her notes were stacked on the kitchen counter. The dark oak table was livened up with blue gingham place mats and a sunflower napkin holder. They were Deb's. Logan had stored those things in his linen closet. Thea had placed steaming bowls of oatmeal at several places around the table, as if she owned the place. The curtains were pulled back, spilling sunlight onto her brown hair.

"Good morning." His houseguest greeted Logan with too much color and a smile.

Logan grunted, assuming Thea expected him to actually eat oatmeal. As if he wanted to keep his broken heart healthy with a bowl of tasteless oats cooked into paste. He supposed he'd have to sit down and push the stuff around his bowl a little before he left, just like whipped husbands everywhere. The idea of breakfast at the Painted Pony beckoned—pancakes, bacon, homemade jam—and the freedom to choose what he wanted when he wanted it.

Squeak. Squeak. Squeak. Squeak.

Logan couldn't believe his eyes.

Her red-and-white fluffy slippers made that *noise* every time she took a step.

Thea poured orange juice into plastic Disney-cartoon glasses that Logan hadn't seen or used since last summer. Deb had brought them when she moved in. Thea set one in front of him.

Squeak. Squeak. Squeak. Squeak.

Logan sank into his chair, glaring at Goofy in a sailor

suit on his juice glass, silently cursing Wes for hiring Thea. Couldn't Wes have hired someone dour and dowdy? Someone silent? Someone like Lurch on *The Addams Family*? "Do you have any shoes that *don't* make noise?"

Feminine laughter cascaded over him like a warm and steamy shower. "Of course I do." She made it sound as if the notion of her *not* having quiet shoes was impossible.

The sweet aroma of the oatmeal in front of him momentarily caught Logan's attention. This wasn't base-camp lumpy oatmeal. It looked good. But before Logan could even pick up his spoon for a taste…

Squeak. Squeak. Squeak. Squeak.

Thea set a Ziploc bag of raisins and two bananas in front of him. "Makes the oatmeal more interesting."

"You're wearing your cool slippers," Hannah commented as she entered with a yawn. "Where's Whizzer?"

"Outside," Thea said. "I think he's decided to stay."

Tess trailed in after her sister, wearing a scowl so deep it seemed to be permanently etched in her face. Logan braced himself for the almost certain storm.

"My goodness, everyone is in here early. I was going to call you as soon as the oatmeal cooled off. Is Glen up?" Thea grinned as easily as if all was right with the world, as if she was unaware that the sight of her alternately turned him on and irritated the hell out of him.

"Glen's still asleep," Hannah offered.

"Oatmeal? Maybe for Aunt Glen but not for me." Tess slid into her chair and pushed the bowl away. "If you're going to make breakfast, I'd rather have pancakes."

Tess's dig didn't faze Thea a bit. "I thought maybe we'd try something different today. My dad never began his day without oatmeal. I learned to make it, oh, about twenty different ways. Give it a try. I think you'll like it."

"Prove it," Tess countered.

"Tess…" Logan warned. Just the enticing smell of his oatmeal had his stomach rumbling. He was ready to try it, foul mood or not.

So far, no one had touched their breakfast or even picked up their spoons.

"Thea said she knew about twenty different ways to make oatmeal. I want to hear all twenty," Tess challenged.

"You'll try the oatmeal if I can?" Thea asked.

"She'll try the oatmeal regardless." Logan gave Tess a look he hoped conveyed the fact that he wasn't standing for any of her nonsense.

Thea winked at Hannah. "Will you count for me?"

With a quick glance at Tess, Hannah nodded.

"Okay." Thea's slippers squeaked as she spread her feet shoulder width apart and leaned her hands on the oak table. "Let's start with the basics. Plain. Brown sugar with cinnamon. Apples and cinnamon. Strawberries and marshmallows. Peaches and cream. How many is that?"

"Five." Hannah held up one hand.

"And then there's brown spice. Banana nut. Pumpkin. Zucchini. Hazelnut."

"Ten." Hannah had been ticking the flavors off with each finger.

Thea didn't look at all worried. But frankly, Logan had his money on Tess. How many ways could you cook oatmeal?

"Those were certainly the most popular ones. Let's see." She tapped her finger on her chin. "There are the healthier ones, like orange Julius, and the tropical one with pineapple and kiwi. And I used to make one with blueberries in the summer. I tried watermelon once, but melon doesn't do well in hot cereal."

"Ick." Hannah pulled a face. "Fourteen."

"If it didn't work, it doesn't count." Tess raised her chin. "You can't count watermelon."

Thea shrugged. "Not a problem."

Hannah curled up a finger. "Thirteen."

"There are some that are more fattening. Like cream cheese. M&Ms. Crunch. Oreo. And Butterfinger."

"Eighteen."

"This was breakfast? What kind of a house did you grow up in?" Logan grimaced. It sounded more like an ice-cream parlor.

"I'd do anything to get my dad to eat. He lost a lot of weight for a while after..." Thea caught herself before she finished her sentence, but Logan could just bet that she'd been about to say after her mother died.

"Peanut butter tasted really good, except it took a bit more time to get it to melt and mix well."

"Nineteen." Logan could hear the excitement in Hannah's voice. She was pulling for Thea.

"How could I forget? Chocolate-chip cookie!" Thea cocked one fist on her waist, raised the other to punch the air and swiveled her hips. The action was punctuated by her squeaky slippers and a singsong chant. "Oh, yeah, oh, yeah. She's good. She's good." She offered her palms to Hannah, who gave her an enthusiastic, two-handed high five.

For a moment, Logan was reminded of his sister's enthusiasm and joy for life. The feeling was bittersweet. Deb was gone, but a part of her lived on in the rare smiles of the twins.

Tess frowned into her bowl. "You've been watching too much TV."

Tending to agree, Logan picked up his spoon. His porridge was no longer steaming. He'd waited long enough—for smiles, for food, for something resembling normal, even if it came from a ditzy stranger.

Flopping into a chair, which groaned from all her enthusiasm, Thea announced, "Let's eat! We'll need lots of energy so we can clean house today."

"THIS WASN'T HOW my mom used to clean house," Tess complained. "And you never did this at our apartment."

"We had carpet." Thea ignored Tess and led the girls into the living room. "Sit on the couch, please."

Hannah sat right down. Tess took a little longer.

"Do you girls know how to skate?"

They shook their blond heads slowly.

"There aren't any flat parts around here," Hannah explained.

"Well, I suppose it doesn't matter. Feet up, please."

Hannah's feet went right up. Her little feet were draped in a pair of Logan's large socks, as were Tess's feet. Thea had found them in the laundry room off the kitchen.

Without hesitation, Thea sprayed the soles of Hannah's socks with furniture polish. "Hannah, I want you to skate around the living room and down the hall. Let me know when your feet don't glide very well anymore."

"But my feet will be slippery," the quieter twin protested.

Thea reached out to cradle the girl's chin, then she grinned. "That's the point. Skating, remember?"

Hannah's smile was tentative, but she'd smiled! Thea

considered that a triumph in itself. Despite Logan's withdrawn nature, the girls were more open now than they'd been in Seattle, Hannah more so than Tess.

Hannah stood carefully and began taking small, shuffling steps across the hardwood floor. She bobbled once, made a sound suspiciously like a giggle, and headed around the couch. When Thea turned back to Tess, she had one foot extended in the air.

"If we've got to do it, let's get it over with."

Thea suppressed a sad smile. She could almost feel Tess's desire to join in on the fun with her sister. A few squirts from the can and Tess was up and skating along with Hannah. Sunlight streamed in through the blinds and glinted off the golden hair of the two girls.

Thea sprayed the bottom of her stocking feet and began her own round of exhibition skating, complete with turns, little leaps and small lunges. Tess wasn't giving in to the fun easily, but she didn't look like the keeper of the keys to doom, either. It helped Thea's spirits immensely.

"Look, Uncle Logan, look at me! I'm skating!" Hannah cried out happily as she nearly slid into him when he appeared at the end of the hallway.

Logan didn't look very happy. He held Whizzer firmly against his chest and glanced around at them.

Tess hopped onto a chair. "She made us do it." She pointed at Thea.

"We were just polishing the floor." Thea infused her statement with lightness. "And we're not done yet. Why don't we race up and down the hallway."

But the damage was done. Hannah, taking a cue from her sister, sat down on the sofa. Thea looked at Logan imploringly. He had to understand what his silence was doing to his nieces. He had to give them permission to live again.

Logan took his time assessing the situation before him. Then he strode across the room in his socks and handed Whizzer to Thea. He picked up the can of furniture polish and examined the label as if seeing it for the first time. Then he looked down at Thea, his blue eyes carefully expressionless.

Shocking them all, Logan shook the can, sprayed the bottom of his socks one foot at a time and said, "Last one to the bathroom is a rotten egg."

Hannah squealed as she raced after Logan with Tess trailing silently, but quickly, behind her. Thea dropped an excited Whizzer to the floor, almost unable to believe what had just happened. Eyes welling with tears, she skated after them.

Amidst a jumble of limbs and after several "crashes" with their uncle, Hannah won the race.

Thea caught Logan's eye and mouthed, "Good job."

He looked away without acknowledging her compliment, but then Hannah hugged him.

"I'll never complain about cleaning house again," Hannah said. Then she released him and held up a hand to Tess. "Don't even say it."

Tess froze, mouth open, sending Hannah and Thea into a second round of giggles. Tess and Logan looked at each other but didn't even crack a smile.

"What's up here?" Thea paused at the foot of the stairs on her way back to the living room.

Everyone froze so quickly that Thea couldn't miss the significance of the moment. Deb's room must be upstairs.

Hannah's eyes were as big as saucers. Tess glanced quickly at Logan and then back to Thea, for once without a suspicious remark. Something teased Thea's memory, something Tess had said in Seattle about a perfect room. No. Stairs leading to a *magic* room.

"We don't go up there anymore," Logan said, removing his socks.

Trying to recapture some of the lightness of the moment, Thea joked. "What? There's no dust upstairs?"

"I don't care if there is dust upstairs," Logan snapped, then walked out of the room.

Hannah touched Thea's arm. "It's okay. Nobody goes in there."

"Nobody," Tess emphasized, jutting her chin.

"I CAUGHT YOUR little rodent chewing my boots," Logan complained to Thea a few minutes later as she watched Whizzer take his hourly mandatory break.

She wrinkled her nose but didn't look at him. "He didn't do much damage, did he?"

"Just several teeth impressions. They were old boots." Logan had picked up the dog a little too quickly, and rubbed his black nose on the boots. The boots could withstand one hundred-plus degrees, but not a terrier's little teeth. Go figure. The anger Logan felt at finding that bit of destruction had been smothered by the delighted faces of his nieces as he watched them skate around the living room.

"Sorry about the boots. You can add the cost to my tab."

"What tab? I told you the boots were old." Just last week he didn't have to worry about where he put his stuff, because no one messed with it no matter where he put it.

"You didn't say you never wore them, though. Are you running with the Hot Shots today?"

"Yeah."

She did look at him then, taking in his running shoes and T-shirt. "Should I plan on you for lunch?" There was nothing cheerful or chipper about her. He'd squelched that when she'd suggested they go clean upstairs and he'd gone ballistic.

"Yeah, sure." Logan resisted rolling his eyes. He sounded like a domesticated animal.

Thea half sat on the porch railing and crossed one leg over the other. That's when he noticed her shoes. Red. Of course, she didn't seem to wear any other color on her feet. These were the new canvas tennis shoes, the ones without the heel that you didn't have to lace, decorated with lightning bolts.

"These would be your quiet shoes?" He didn't know what possessed him to tease her. Her shoes were an irritation, something he didn't want to encourage.

Holding out her arms for balance, she flexed her foot this way and that, making the lightning bolts glimmer and shine. "The one and only pair. Like them?"

"I prefer the bells," he grumbled, because she had two silver bracelets on her wrist that tinkled softly when she moved her hands.

"Why don't you want to go upstairs?"

Immediately, he felt as if a five-hundred-pound gorilla had leaped onto his chest. "It was her room," he managed to say.

"There might be things up there that the girls would cherish, that Deb would have wanted them to have."

Logan shook his head. He did not want to go back up there. He'd shut the door tight the day Deb had died. He didn't want to go back up there and relive finding her not breathing.

He dragged in a lungful of air. "There's nothing left upstairs."

"But—"

"Leave it." Logan barely kept from shouting the bitter command. "She's gone. No one wants to be reminded of that."

"You can't shut out the importance of Deb from those two girls. You can't flip a switch and stop missing her."

"Oh, yes I can." Deb had betrayed him that last day. He couldn't believe it himself.

Stop thinking about Deb.

"But the girls can't. They need to come to terms with this or they'll go through life with a gaping hole in their heart that no one will ever be able to mend."

"You're not a psychologist."

"What are you afraid of, Logan? These girls need you to be strong."

Instead of answering, Logan nearly ran out to his truck. Thea was right. He was afraid. He was afraid of facing the truth of the last day of Deb's life.

"LIKE THIS, Thea?" Hannah showed Thea the daisies she was embroidering on a pillowcase.

Thea put her arm around Hannah and drew her closer. Her little body leaned into Thea's until she could smell the fruity shampoo Hannah used on her thick mane of blond hair.

Thea carefully examined the little girl's stitches. "Very good, sweet cheeks." She stroked the girl's hair.

Slowly, as if afraid to do it, Hannah hugged Thea. Then Hannah returned to her chair by the window. Thea clung to the feeling of Hannah's little arms wrapped around her in something as simple and meaningful as a hug, because the gesture indicated Thea was helping at least one of her little charges cope with the loss of her mother.

"I'm doing an orange flower next," Tess said in a small voice from where she sat on the couch. "Mom liked them."

"I know that flower." Glen smiled at everyone. "It's orange. You find it in California. It's…it's a…"

"Poppy," Thea supplied the word.

"Yes," Glen agreed, settling back in her chair with a yawn. "Poppies."

Thea stared out the window at the empty driveway. Logan was perplexing. He was obviously still hurting from the loss of his sister. Yet, he could still surprise her with something as joyous as skating through the house with the girls. Thea sighed and picked up a small pair of denim pants.

It was as her grandmother used to say. Some things take more time than others.

"Shouldn't you be studying, Thea?" Hannah said.

"I thought Tess's jeans could use a bit of length to them first." She'd let down the hem earlier and was adding a decorative ribbon to give Tess an extra inch.

Tess had dropped her sewing at Hannah's observation and came to stand in front of Thea. Her small hand fingered the embroidery on one pant leg.

"My mom did this," Tess said softly.

"They're so beautiful that I thought they might be special." Once Thea had seen the too-short pants on Tess, she'd suspected the jeans must hold some special memory for the girl. "I hope I haven't ruined them. I can always hem them up again." That had been Thea's biggest fear—that Tess wouldn't like what she'd done.

"It's okay," Tess whispered. Then she ran out of the room.

Hannah followed her.

"Am I missing out on something?" Glen asked.

"No." But Thea realized *she* had been missing out, and when she left, she would be again.

When Logan made her leave.

THE RUMBLE STARTED OUT small, and quickly turned into something as loud as an avalanche. At the kitchen table, Thea finished making a notation in her notebook and paused as the floor of the house began to shake.

Hannah, playing on the floor with Whizzer, looked toward the window, her eyes as watery and round as saucers.

Tess ran into the room and grabbed Hannah's hand. "Hurry, for cryin' out loud. Before he gets here," Tess urged, pulling her twin up and leading her out of the kitchen.

Thea heard their footsteps retreating down the hallway and then a door slam. There was no mistaking the fact the girls wanted to avoid what was coming.

They wanted to avoid Wes.

A huge, black semi truck pulled up next to the garage. The rumble of its engine vibrated through the soles of Thea's socks. She moved into the living room, where she'd left Logan, Glen and her shoes.

Logan stood looking out the window with a grim expression on his face.

"When will we ever be free of that man?" Glen drew herself to her feet and shuffled away. "I'll be in my room."

"Better see what he wants," Logan said as he moved with deliberate, almost reluctant, steps to the door.

Thea scrambled to put on her shoes and scurried after Logan with Whizzer at her heels. Twenty feet from the truck, she stopped just behind Logan.

Once outside, she could read the logo on the side of the black truck—Flying Monkey Trucking, Wes Delaney, Boise. Almost as an afterthought, Seattle was printed in smaller red letters. A winged monkey was painted on the door of the truck, his expression mocking. The huge back tires sported mud flaps with the silver silhouette of a naked, buxom woman.

If Thea had seen his truck before Wes Delaney hired her, she never would have come to work for him.

Whizzer apparently felt the same way, because he just stood staring at the behemoth parked in front of them with his head down and a low growl in his throat.

Wes climbed out of his cab, exposing the world to his white underwear and unpleasant indentation on his backside. He dropped the last two feet and hitched up his pants. Thankfully. Then he nodded a cool greeting in Logan's direction.

"I see you made it here safe, Thea," Wes said, then spit.

The sun seemed to hide behind a cloud as the wind picked up. Thea felt the joy being sucked right out of her.

"What do you want?" Logan demanded. If Thea had thought he'd been cold and standoffish with her, she'd been wrong. His words were delivered on a gauntlet of steel that sent a shiver down Thea's spine.

It didn't seem to have the same effect on Wes.

"I want my girls."

"You signed away that right last year, Delaney."

"I was grief-stricken. I didn't know what I was doing at the time." His grin was lopsided from the wad of chewing tobacco stuffed in his cheek.

Logan clenched his fists. "You'd better climb into that truck and head it as far from here as you can. You're not getting the girls."

Wes frowned at Logan's words. "Don't matter what you say, McCall. I'm taking you to court. I've had the girls for months now. Possession is nine-tenths of the law."

"She wanted me to have them. You signed the papers." With his fists clenched and his chin jutted out, Logan looked ready to pound Wes.

"Are you saying that *you* have custody and you gave the twins to *him*?" Thea couldn't believe it.

Logan's gaze dropped briefly to his feet. "He caught me at a bad time."

Wes snorted. "Yeah, he was drunk as a skunk. From the smell of him, he had been for days."

Logan took a quick step forward, only stopping when Thea grabbed his arm.

"Why don't you go get the girls, Thea. I brought them gifts." He reached into his truck and pulled out two baby dolls dressed in clothes so worn, Thea knew they were used. Wes was always bringing the girls something questionable and not appropriate for their ages.

"Gifts?" Thea echoed, affronted. "You couldn't have sent us money for food, or to pay the rent or to pay *me*?"

"I wasn't exactly in a place I could send you money." Wes adjusted his pants and looked down his nose around the yard and at the house, as if the fairy-tale house and everything it represented was repugnant to him, as if where he'd been was infinitely better.

Thea was struck dumb. She looked at Logan.

"Prison," Logan clarified.

"I know what he meant," Thea snapped. She just

couldn't believe it. She turned to Wes. "I reported you missing. I was worried something had happened to you."

"Something did happen," Wes grumbled. "But I've done my time and now I need those girls."

"I know why you want Tess and Hannah. You're not coming near them," Logan said, taking another stiff step forward. "Get off our property."

Fully expecting Wes to answer Logan's challenge with blows, Thea jumped when Wes shrieked and kicked out, sending a little ball of brown and white fur flying across the yard.

CHAPTER SEVEN

"HE LAUGHED," Thea ranted, storming across the kitchen. She paced back and forth, finally stopping in front of Logan. "I can't believe he laughed!"

Logan sat at the table cradling a whimpering Whizzer in his arms, running his hands over the little trooper in an effort to discover any broken bones. It was only about the fifth time he'd checked Thea's pooch. Logan was pretty sure nothing was wrong. The dog didn't yelp at anything, just sat whimpering, as shell-shocked as his owner. He was a brave dog to have attempted peeing on Wes.

Thea opened her mouth as if to say something else, glanced over at the twins sharing a seat at the kitchen table and began pacing again. "And he kicked Whizzer. Not just a light get-off-my-foot kind of kick. He really kicked him."

The twins huddled together in silence, blue eyes wide. From their vantage point in the kitchen, they'd both shrieked almost as loud as Thea when Wes had booted Whizzer. Hannah had run down the steps and kicked her father in the shin before racing to the tiny dog's side.

"What does Wes want?" Glen asked. "Didn't he sign the…the…*papers*?"

"The divorce papers? No, he never signed them,"

Logan confirmed. "He signed over custody of the girls to me, but he didn't sign the divorce papers."

"What does that mean?" Thea stopped pacing and studied Logan.

Logan glanced quickly at the twins and then back to Thea, weighing what he should say in front of them. He didn't want to hurt Tess and Hannah's feelings. "Girls, why don't you help Glen back to her room."

"He wants money," Logan said with words devoid of emotion once the girls and Glen had gone. "Deb's life insurance policy will be paid out soon, to whoever has custody of the girls." Logan didn't care about the money. He cared about Tess and Hannah's well-being. Seeing Wes again—through sober eyes—only made him realize there was no way he could let Wes take care of them.

"So that's what this is about," Thea said, half to herself. She rubbed her forehead and walked back to the door. She stood facing it an awfully long time.

Whizzer shuddered and sighed, closing his eyes as if shutting out his run-in with the devil.

"You probably did him a favor by bringing the twins here instead of turning them over to the authorities," Logan surmised. "He had a point about the possession thing."

Thea spun around, bracelets banging together. "He never seemed to care about the girls. It was like he didn't want to be at home, like he could barely stand to be a father. The last time he was home he slapped Tess when she said something he didn't like. I told him never to do that again."

Logan bet she had. Still, the fact that Wes was capable of hitting his daughters left a sick taste in Logan's mouth. He'd be damned if he let the man have the girls again.

But could *he* really take care of them?

As if reading his thoughts, Thea's gaze was painfully scrutinizing. "Are you sure you want the girls? You had them before and let Wes take them."

Logan's gut churned but he still managed to say, "I had a broken leg. It wasn't as if I could fight him for Tess and Hannah."

"How long had you been drinking?" She gave him the once-over, along with an unwelcome dose of guilt.

Logan considered not answering. It was none of her business. But she kept staring at him. "A couple of days," he admitted finally.

"If you're an unfit guardian, he'll challenge you on it. If you have a drinking problem, sooner or later, someone will come knocking on your door and take the girls."

Logan bristled. "I am not a drunk. I had a lapse in judgment. Look at you. You took a job from Wes. I mean, *from Wes*, of all people." That was almost as hard to comprehend as thinking Thea could ever be Wes's girlfriend.

"It's hardly the same thing." Thea raised one eyebrow as if to confirm what Logan knew in his heart. He wasn't cut out to be responsible for Tess and Hannah. What if Logan sunk to his father's level again and lost himself in the booze?

Logan hated that idea as much as he loved his nieces. He just didn't want to be responsible for them. He wanted his old life back. A life where he was able to laugh without feeling guilty that Deb would never laugh again. A life with few responsibilities.

"Uncle Logan is great," Hannah said with a weak smile as she came through the kitchen door. It was obvious she'd been listening. Tess stood silently behind her.

Logan was ashamed. He was so far from great, it was

sad. He was a selfish bastard. Even when he knew Wes sucked at fatherhood, Logan couldn't help wishing, just a bit, that he was a different man and could take the twins. The reality was, Wes could never be a good parent—not after leaving Deb when she and the twins needed him most.

"You won't let him take us back, will you, Uncle Logan?" Hannah pleaded.

Tess just stared at him with a lifted chin and accusing eyes. How could he tell them how wrong he was for them, how his blood ran hot when he got angry, then cold when he realized how angry he was? But he was coming to realize it wasn't just the fact that he had a temper, or even that he didn't know what to do as the guardian of two girls. It was that he didn't want to take responsibility for them and he didn't want to feel guilty about not wanting to take it.

"You'll get married, of course," Glen said simply, having come back into the room. "Thea will do."

"Like hell she will." Once the words were out of his mouth, Logan felt his face go red. Marriage? To Mary Poppins? Not in this lifetime.

Thea stood stock-still, her gaze slipping away from his, her reaction indecipherable. The twins looked back and forth between the two of them as if watching a close tennis match.

"There are other ways to deal with this," Thea said finally, breaking the awkward silence.

"But none as sensible as this," Glen surmised. "Two parents are better than one. Otherwise, it's just the two of you men, his word against yours."

"Don't listen to her," Logan mumbled, more to himself than Thea.

Glen smacked Logan's shoulder none too gently. "You better listen to me, boy. I've kept you in line more years than I care to count. We have to stay together. You, me, the twins and Deb…" Her eyes glazed.

Logan was immediately out of his chair, placing an arm around Glen's thin shoulders, hoping to distract her. "Sorry, old girl, your idea took us by surprise, is all."

Thea was oddly quiet.

Glen blinked, then seemed to come around a bit. "Were we arguing? Because when I'm right, I'm right. Your mother used to say I was a bit stubborn." Glen patted Logan's hand.

"She said you could talk the back leg off a donkey," Logan corrected, unable to keep his eyes from Thea anymore.

She stood apart from the rest of them, her hands gripping the chair back, her gaze fixed on Tess standing next to Hannah.

MARRIAGE.

Thea couldn't get the word out of her head as she folded laundry. That was what she wanted. It was clear to her now. She longed for a family she could call her own.

After her mother left, Thea had stopped playing with dolls because she'd had a real role to fill, meals to plan, toilets to clean. Her father, lost in his own world, had let Thea grow up too soon. Thea could easily imagine Tess and Hannah ending up in much the same place with Logan. She shuddered to think where they'd end up if Wes took the girls back permanently. Would she go back with them?

Thea wandered into the kitchen, stopping to stare out the window at the pines towering thirty feet away. It really was a perfect house.

Except that everyone in it suffered from a broken heart.

Thea will do. Glen's words came back. The old woman had sounded so confident that Thea was the answer to their problems.

She wouldn't do, of course. Logan would end up with Malibu Barbie—a woman who was the envy of every Hot Shot. She'd give him another set of picture-perfect blond twins—boys—and she'd never question his silences unless he forgot to compliment her on her new haircut. He'd remain the way he was now—withdrawn, despondent and reluctant to smile.

Thea sighed, suddenly sad as she gathered the cleaning supplies to tackle yet another room in the house. She wasn't the answer to their problems. She had her own dreams to pursue. Years from now, when she'd made something of herself, she'd get married, have kids and live in a perfect house. Logan was right, her judgment had been lacking when she'd taken the job with Wes. She couldn't afford to be sidetracked again. She'd had her doubts about him, but the position had seemed too good to pass up.

Like this house.

Thea gave her wrist a slight shake, sending her bracelets jingling.

Malibu Barbie was the kind of wife Logan wanted.

Too bad that it wasn't the kind of wife he needed.

"HELLO, LADIES."

Logan looked up from stretching out his calves to see Spider walking toward the Silver Bend Hot Shot crew, gym bag slung over his shoulder. Several crew members called back a greeting even though only two of their members were women. Gym bags and water bottles littered the Silver Bend High School football field. Everything was normal and yet, Logan's life was in an uproar.

"Tin Man, I want you to pair up with Spider," Jackson said, not looking up from his clipboard filled with scribbled training notes.

Logan suppressed a groan. He hadn't talked to Spider since he flattened him days ago. "Why?"

"Because I'm working with a rookie today. Unless you'd rather take on the new guy?" Jackson lowered his voice and gestured with his head in the direction of the newbie.

Rufus squeaked as he danced at Logan's feet. The chocolate Lab had a ball in his mouth with a noisemaker. He dropped it on Logan's foot.

No one ever willingly took on a new guy as a training partner. Rookies weren't in good enough shape to push the veterans into peak condition. They lagged. They complained. They smelled of Ben-Gay and raw nerves.

Logan would rather deal with his guilt over his temper and Spider's biting sarcasm than the timid and unpleasant aroma of a rookie. Logan shook his head, picking up Rufus's drooly ball and heaving it across the field. Rufus streaked away to retrieve his toy.

"Okay, everyone. Two days left after today. Our next test for red cards is on Monday." Jackson surveyed the group. "Who's ready?"

A series of shouts rang out across the football field and into the pines lining the opposite end of the track. No one could keep their job or be hired onto a Hot Shot team without passing the firefighters' annual strenuous physical exams, earning a red card certification. Today they were conducting a mock physical test. Monday afternoon, those who hadn't yet passed would take the test for real.

"Slow jog, once around the track," Jackson called out, leading the team, with the new guy falling into place next to him. Rufus bounded beside them, then stopped right in front of the rookie and dropped the ball at his feet. The would-be Hot Shot tumbled over Rufus, which earned him a rousing round of applause. Red-faced, he picked himself up and sprinted to catch up with Jackson.

Unconcerned, Rufus shook himself once, snatched his ball back and trotted after him.

"Spider, you're with me," Logan called as he jogged past him, the memory of their altercation on the mountain burning in his mind.

"My pleasure."

Logan swore as Spider fell into step with him. "We look like salt and pepper." Logan wore gray sweats cut off at the knee and a white T-shirt. Spider wore his usual black T-shirt, black shorts and black tennis shoes.

"Good and evil." Spider grinned. "Yin and yang. Both sides of the force."

They rounded the first bend in the track. Watching Rufus harass the rest of the team to throw his ball, Logan waited for the stabbing pain in his leg to begin.

"Loosen up, Tin Man. You're tense. You need to get laid or your leg's not going to make it through fire season."

"Damn it, Spider." Logan felt his leg twinge.

"I'm serious. You're living up to your nickname. I mean, look at you, even your arms are swinging like you have armor on. Shake it off, will you?"

Logan took a deep breath.

"Why so grouchy, Tin Man? Trouble with the nanny?"

"No!" Unless you counted his aunt offering Thea a marriage proposal trouble.

"Trouble with the angel twins then?"

"No." It was trouble with himself. He wanted what was best for the twins, but how could he fit them into his lifestyle? Thea was really the more qualified parent. She seemed to care about Tess and Hannah. But she had dreams of her own, dreams that would take her away from Silver Bend.

Marriage. The concept kept taunting him, a crazy, yet almost plausible way to ensure Wes wouldn't bother the twins again. And with a wife at home, Logan could continue his Hot Shot career while honoring his promise to Deb. Logan shook his head. He was definitely losing it if he thought marriage could solve his problems. It would only create a dozen more. Like losing his sanity.

Spider jogged on in silence, leaving Logan to his tumultuous thoughts. They were bringing up the rear of the group, but Logan didn't mind because they were only warming up.

"Is that The Queen up there with Chainsaw? I swear that boy can't take a hint." Spider snorted in apparent disbelief. "He follows her around like a puppy dog, doing whatever she wants done. Do you know that last night at the Pony he let her take his turn at pool?"

"What's wrong with that?"

"*I* had to play with her. That's what's wrong with that. She was wearing nail polish, for cryin' out loud. Let's get serious here. She's going for her certification on Monday and she's wearing nail polish."

"Spider—"

"Red is one thing," Spider cut him off. "But pink with little flowers painted on? No way. Not in the team."

· "I'm sure the nails will be gone by May." When the fire season hit its stride. "Besides, she's in my half of the crew, not yours." And she could hike faster than any man on the team.

"Thank heavens for small favors." Spider laughed. "If I had to watch the way she put Chainsaw through his paces every day, I might just tell him to track down that woman who broke his heart."

Rufus decided it was Logan's turn to throw his ball, dropping the squeaky toy a few feet ahead of him. Without breaking stride, Logan scooped up the toy and tossed it onto the football field. Rufus chased it down happily.

"That was years ago, Spider. He's over her." Chainsaw had tried to stop his high-school sweetheart from getting married to someone else—on her wedding day.

"No, he's not." Spider turned and jogged backward. "You'd tell me, as a friend, if I was making an ass of myself, wouldn't you, Tin Man? I mean, if I went overboard like The Queen and got on everybody's nerves."

"You always get on people's nerves."

"Well, yeah, but not on the nerves of our team, right?"

Just as Logan realized how relaxed his stride had become, they rounded the last curve. Jackson started setting up the crews for sprints.

Logan stopped Spider with a hand on his arm before they caught up with the others. Spider's babbling had given Logan back something he hadn't had in a long time—comfort in his own skin. "About the other day and getting on somebody's nerves—"

"Forget about it. That's what friends are for, right?"

"Right." Grinning, because that's what he and Spider were, despite their recent troubles, Logan jogged on. He'd blown everything with Spider these past few months way out of proportion.

Spider matched him step for step. "But next time, can I push you on your ass?"

CURLED UP ON one corner of the couch, Tess watched cartoons with Hannah and Aunt Glen. It was the first time she'd sat and watched television in ages. Thea was down the hall cleaning the bathroom, something Tess wasn't about to help her with, no matter what kind of game she made out of it.

Tess hadn't decided if Uncle Logan marrying Thea was a bad idea or not. If it meant not having to live with her dad, it was probably a good idea. But the way Logan had said no to Aunt Glen's marriage idea meant she and Hannah would probably have to go to foster care. It wasn't as if Uncle Logan was retiring from the Hot Shots. And Thea had no reason to stay.

What was worse? Living with the uncle who used to love her or living with a father who never had? Her heart hurt when she remembered how fun Uncle Logan used to be. Her cheek tingled at the memory of her father's punishments.

Whizzer hopped up onto the couch next to her with a grunt, then he curled into a tight ball on her feet. Tess resisted reaching down to pet him. He was cute and all, but she didn't feel as if she could touch him or anyone else without crying, and that scared her.

A cartoon penguin appeared on TV asking the rabbit where his mother was. Tess blinked hard and tipped her head back so that she could look up to the ceiling. Heaven. How did she know heaven was real? For all she knew, her mother was down the hill in the cemetery where they'd buried her.

Something creaked upstairs.

Tess might have thought she imagined it, except that Whizzer looked up, too.

There it was again.

Whizzer leaped off the couch and ran toward the stairs.

The stairs. Mom's room.

Sitting up, Tess almost cried out, "Mama!" Only her mother was dead and no one was allowed upstairs. She rubbed her hands over the soft denim jeans her mother had embroidered and Thea had fixed.

With a small *woof,* Whizzer raced up the steps.

"What's happening?" Hannah looked worried.

"That stupid dog ran upstairs," Tess answered. "Now he's probably going to pee up there and Uncle Logan will be mad." At the dog. At Tess for not catching the dog.

Dragging her feet, Tess walked toward the stairs. She did not want to go up there. As long as she didn't see the room was empty, part of her could believe her mother was still there.

"What if *she's* upstairs?" Hannah asked, right behind her. "What if Mom's an angel visiting us or something. I told you it was a magic room."

Tess and Hannah exchanged looks. Then, as one, they sped up the stairs after the dog, only slowing on the top step. Their mom's bedroom door was open, the doorway bright, as if an angel *was* inside the room.

Hannah reached for Tess's hand. Together they walked the last few feet to the place where they'd last seen their mother alive.

Whizzer poked his head out at them, making them both jump back and scream. He trotted around their feet, then went back inside the room with a wag of his tail.

Tess looked at Han. "Angels are supposed to like dogs, aren't they?"

"You look." Hannah held back.

Holding her breath, Tess peeked around the door frame. What she saw had her dropping Hannah's hand and charging into the room. "What are you doing in here?"

"Dusting," Thea said, not startled in the least by the appearance of Tess. The windows were wide open and the blinds up all the way. The curtains danced gently in the breeze.

"Uncle Logan said you weren't supposed to come up here. None of us are." Stupid lady. It wasn't hard to understand Uncle Logan when he said no.

Thea smiled just a little. "I'm cleaning house. That includes this room."

"No one… It's not like… You don't need to clean in here," Tess sputtered furiously. "Get out!"

Ignoring Tess, Hannah picked up a framed photo from the chest of drawers. "This is where all the pictures are. Do you think Uncle Logan put them up here?"

Despite the feeling that they shouldn't be in the room, Tess stepped closer to look at the picture.

"That was the day Uncle Logan took us all rafting," Hannah whispered.

Long blond hair sopping wet, life vest on, their mother's smile almost made Tess cry.

"Put that away, Han." Tess struggled with the words. She didn't want to see Mom's face. "Let's go."

Hannah put the frame down but didn't turn to the door. Instead, she looked around the room. "I can smell her." Hannah opened a drawer and shook out a T-shirt that read, With a Body Like This, Who Needs Hair?

Uncle Logan had bought the shirt for Mom when the medicines made her hair fall out. Mom's face swam into Tess's memory. She'd lost weight and her bald head was pale and shiny, but she still laughed as if she wasn't dying when Uncle Logan gave the shirt to her.

Tess couldn't fill her lungs with air.

Han brought the shirt up to her face. "This is a magic room. I can smell her," she repeated softly.

"So what? She's not *here*," Tess shouted.

Thea was by her side in two seconds. "It's all right, Tess."

"No, it's not." Nothing was right now and nothing would ever be right again. Mom was dead.

Aunt Glen stepped into the room with a frown on her face. "Is Deb here?"

"Ai-yeeee!" Trembling, Tess shrieked in pain and frustration. Instead of everyone leaving her alone, Thea, Aunt Glen and Hannah circled her until she was suffocating in the middle of a group hug.

"What the hell is going on here?" Uncle Logan's voice boomed over Tess.

Everyone turned.

"I was cleaning and the girls came up," Thea explained. Her cheeks were white, as if she knew she'd broken the rules.

Uncle Logan tossed his hands into the air. "What do we need to clean up here for? You see how it upsets the girls. Is this your idea of helping?"

Crossing the room to Tess, Uncle Logan lifted her up in his arms. He'd been training with the Hot Shots and smelled stinky, but his arms felt good. Strong. Safe.

"Everyone out. Now." Uncle Logan was mad.

Tess wrapped her arms around him and buried her face in his neck. No one had held her this way since her mom had died. Her dad hadn't even come back for the funeral.

"I'm taking this T-shirt," Hannah said, stubborn all of a sudden. "And this picture." Tess looked up to see Han grab a photo of them with their mom on their ninth birthday.

"Fine. Downstairs," Uncle Logan snapped.

"Why are you so mad?" Aunt Glen asked. "Deb won't mind if we're in her room while she's out walking."

Uncle Logan sighed and headed through the door. Tess heard Thea encourage Aunt Glen out of the room, and then Glen asked her usual question of Thea.

"Do I know you, dear?"

TESS MUST HAVE WEIGHED less than fifty pounds. Logan had felt helpless when he'd discovered everyone in Deb's room. But not now. Not as he cradled Tess in his arms and carried her downstairs and into her bedroom. His niece had been a trembling bundle of nerves when he picked her up. By the time he tried to set Tess down, she was no longer shaking.

"Don't let me go," Tess begged, her face tucked into his neck.

Logan sat down with Tess on her bed, turning her in his arms so that he could see her face before she buried her little nose in his chest and used his T-shirt as a tissue.

"Hey, now. It's over." What in the hell had possessed Thea to clean Deb's room, much less let the girls in? Logan could feel the slow burn of anger in his gut. He'd have words with Thea again later as soon as Tess was okay.

All these months, Tess had been such a trooper—a bitter trooper, but a trooper nonetheless. He hadn't seen her cry once since September, not once until today. Even though she'd spent months with Wes, Logan was willing to bet she hadn't cried there, either.

After several minutes, Tess's sobs turned into hiccups.

"I think we should agree not to go in there anymore."

Tess sucked air in ragged gasps. "I thought Mom was upstairs."

Logan bit off the oath he wanted to spit out.

"I heard a noise and I thought she was upstairs."

He didn't want to listen anymore. He did *not* want to talk about Deb.

"The door was open…and…and…there was light coming through. Hannah thought it was an angel."

More like the devil's spawn in rainbow gear.

"And then we were in there and there were so many pictures of her everywhere. I'd almost forgotten what she looked like, but I couldn't look at the pictures because she wasn't *there*." This last word spiraled into a wail and Tess dissolved into tears again.

Logan wondered how he was going to turn his niece's anguish into something that didn't hurt quite so bad. All he could think of to say was, "I know, kidlet. I miss her, too."

"And sometimes," she gasped, "in the middle of the night, I can't remember what her voice sounds like."

Oh, God.

"What if someday I don't remember her? What if—"

"Hold on, hold on a second." Logan had to stop Tess before this runaway train took down all the protective walls he'd erected around his heart. "We have pictures and video somewhere. You'll always have that." He'd taken those mementos away from her and Hannah because he thought it would help them deal with their grief. It had made his pain more bearable. He hadn't realized it would only make Tess's pain that much worse.

Tess was silent for a few moments. Her breathing grew steadier. Then she whispered, "Sometimes I hate her for dying."

Logan's body stiffened. He'd harbored the same resentment, not quite hate, but something harsh and uncalled for, feelings he felt guilty carrying around.

"She should have known she was sick earlier," his niece continued in that small voice, raspy from crying. "Or she should have found a better doctor. One who could keep her alive."

In the end, all he could say was, "We did the best we could. All of us."

In the end, it was Deb's choice.

"I WANT TO GO to the cemetery," Hannah announced at dinner. She was wearing Deb's T-shirt, which was long enough on her to be a dress.

Logan kept his eyes on his plate of lasagna. This was all he needed to add to the heap of problems he already faced.

"I want us all to go," Hannah clarified. "But if you don't want to come visit Mom…" Her words trailed off and she shrugged. "I guess you can drop me at the gate or something."

Logan sucked on his cheek and shot a glance at Thea. This was all her fault.

"Is Deb working at the cemetery?" Aunt Glen gazed around the table, her faded blue eyes clouded with concern.

"Glen, would you like some more garlic bread?" Thea asked, attempting to distract the old woman.

"Will you take me, Uncle Logan?" Hannah prompted.

I'm not ready for this.

Say no. Just say no and change the subject. It shouldn't be that hard. Hannah was ten and used to doing what Logan told her to.

Just. Say. No.

Logan looked down into the clear blue eyes of his sister's baby and couldn't find the words. Instead of refusing her, he nodded curtly and shoved a bite of lasagna in his mouth.

Tess kept casting him sideways glances, but said nothing.

"You don't have to go, Tess," he told her.

"I'd like to," she said in a small voice.

Damn.

"If you don't mind, I'd like to go as well," Thea added.

Well, hell's bells. He didn't want Sister Mary Sunshine going with them, too, and he opened his mouth to say so.

"Okay." Hannah beat him to the punch. "We'll all go tomorrow."

Logan's appetite disappeared. "We had some day today. Are you sure you want to go so soon?"

"But we haven't been to see her at all. What if she's lonely?" Hannah's face clouded with concern.

"You've been thinking about her, haven't you?" Thea asked.

Hannah nodded.

Tess listened intently to the conversation but said nothing.

"She knows you've been thinking about her," Thea said.

"How does she know?" Hannah asked, eyes wide.

Logan was just as interested in Thea's answer as Hannah seemed to be.

"She hears you with her heart, sweetie."

"I want her to talk back to me. I want to hear her say she loves me." Hannah's voice cracked on this last part.

Logan's throat closed on the same wish. He wanted to talk to Deb, too.

Hannah lifted the neck of the T-shirt and put it over her mouth so that she could breathe in Deb's smell. She'd been doing that all afternoon.

"You'll have to listen with your heart," Thea advised.

Logan wasn't sure if that was true or not. It sounded like a lot of bullshit. But it seemed to comfort Hannah, and that was the important thing, he supposed. Maybe having Thea around wasn't such a bad thing after all. Maybe...

He'd marry her.

It was the logical solution. Thea could study as much as she needed to without worrying about money. They'd sign a prenup, agree to be married through the fire season and divorce in October or November when he came home for the winter. Wes couldn't contest that. Who would doubt Thea's ability to nurture the twins? And he'd have plenty of time to find a nanny for next season.

LOGAN STUDIED THEA as she began cleaning up the dinner dishes.

Was he crazy? They had nothing in common.

But it wouldn't be a real marriage.

Thea leaned down to retrieve the dish soap from under the sink. Unexpectedly, she turned and cooed at

Whizzer. The neck of her red T-shirt hung open and exposed small breasts encased in a polka-dot bra with white lace trim.

Parts of Logan that he hadn't remembered existed for several months sprang to life.

Sex. They may have to talk about sex when they made this marriage arrangement. Thea's polka dots taunted him more than any black-and-red lace ever had.

Make that, definitely talk about sex.

Logan had needs. The fire community was a small one and Silver Bend even smaller. And if Logan satisfied himself outside of his marriage, even if that marriage was only on paper, the twins might suffer from the rumor mill. He'd marry Thea and honor the bonds of the marriage bed for the girls.

If Jackson could make a marriage work, Logan ought to be able to.

Thea straightened with a tinkle of bracelets and smiled at him briefly before looking away. It was that same crinkly-eyed smile that she'd given him the first day they'd met.

Only this time, Logan couldn't bring himself to look away.

CHAPTER EIGHT

"Hey…uh…Thea?"

Thea turned from her spot on the porch. Soft light spilled through the open kitchen window behind Logan. She'd been enjoying the way the stars seemed so much closer here than in Seattle, while she waited for Whizzer to finish his end-of-the-day rounds, while she tried to forget about the horrified look on Tess's face when she'd discovered Thea in Deb's room, while she struggled to find the words to apologize to Logan for the day's debacle.

"I…uh… Did the girls get to bed?" Logan sat down on the porch just outside the beam of the kitchen light. He propped his elbows on his knees and clasped his hands before him, his hunched silhouette the epitome of a man overwhelmed.

Thea's heart went out to him. She was proud of the way he was adjusting to the unfolding emotions of the girls. He'd known exactly what to do with Tess. He could have refused Hannah's request to visit the cemetery, but he hadn't. "We read a bit first and then they got ready for bed without a fuss. They're very well behaved."

"Deb was a stickler with rules."

Thea chuckled. "She wasn't the only one."

"I guess I deserve that." He clasped and unclasped his

hands. Even though she couldn't see his face clearly, she could sense his discomfort. He wasn't at ease with his role as Tess and Hannah's guardian, but he was trying.

Whizzer snuffled in the bushes across the yard.

"About today…I've been thinking."

"I'm sorry. I was out of line," Thea interrupted.

"Ah…"

Thea pushed on. "I know you told me to stay out of Deb's room and I should have listened."

"Well…" Logan blinked, gazing at her oddly, making Thea wonder again if she was pushing Logan too far, too soon.

"Whizzer!" Thea looked around the yard for Whizzer, hoping for a reason to go back inside. It was bad enough she'd made Tess cry. When she didn't see Whizzer, she said quickly, "It's awfully late. I better get back to my notes."

"Of course," Logan said, his words a huge relief to Thea.

"Could you bring Whizzer in?"

"Yeah, sure, no problem." Logan had a bad case of the fidgets. "Hey, um, can I ask you something first?"

Did he have something more to say about this afternoon? With a nod, Thea waited for him to continue.

He drew a deep breath. "Will you…will you marry me?"

Thea sat back in surprise, bumping her head against the porch railing, suddenly wishing she was the one sitting in the shadows instead of in the light.

Logan hurried to explain. "It would only be temporary. I've been fooling myself into believing that I'd find someone to run things here before I have to leave. And I don't want to leave the girls with a stranger. We can have a prenuptial agreement drawn up and we can set up some ground rules. You can run the house and take care of the girls and Aunt Glen during the fire season. You'll have plenty of time to study. It'll be as if I wasn't even here. And then sometime in the fall when things slow down for me, we'll get a divorce."

My first marriage proposal.

Thea couldn't breathe.

It sucked.

Logan was proposing using her to care for the twins and Glen. The stars might be shining in the sky above, but romance was not in the air. He wasn't going to slip a ring on her finger or kiss her tenderly as if she were the most important thing in the world to him. Thea could probably tally the number of dates she'd been asked out for on two hands, and most of those invitations had been delivered with more sensitivity and sentiment than Logan's marriage proposal.

"Oh, damn. I totally forgot that you have a life." He swore softly.

"Yeah," Thea mumbled. She had some life, all right. She'd been studying for months—or she should have been studying—to take her Ph.D. exams. Only now she was realizing she might not want to give up on having time for a family. Sure, she was young and there was plenty of time to finish her Ph.D. and meet someone. But that someone wouldn't be Logan.

Oh, boy. Her instincts must be kaput. She'd practically forced him to take her on as his nanny. She'd let Logan believe her mother was dead, and hurt Tess by pushing too hard too soon. And now, he'd proposed.

Rather than a paycheck, Thea would get a band of gold. And, most likely, a broken heart.

She should walk away. This was ludicrous. She had plans for the next year. Pass her exams, finally settle on a topic for her dissertation, write the proposal and get it approved. Then work on her dissertation until it was perfection, until it ensured her a position at a top university or lab. This was all wrong. Her mother would never approve. Forget walking.

Run! Hide!

Except Thea couldn't move her legs as she realized Logan seemed to be waiting for her answer, as if this marriage idea was the only hope he had left. And she knew that couldn't be right. There was someone in the state of Idaho who was perfect for this job. He just wasn't going to find them in less than a week.

"Say something," he prompted.

"You just can't ask a girl to marry you and make it sound like contract negotiations," Thea blurted.

"You, of all people, should understand the situation I'm in. You saw Wes. You know he only wants custody to claim the money from Deb's life insurance policy. You know how he treats Tess and Hannah. If I have to fight fires, who would stop Wes from taking the girls? A baby-sitter or a wife?"

He made sense. If Thea wanted to protect Tess and Hannah, she should do the right thing. Which was what? Marry the man?

Marry the hunk with the sorrowful eyes?

She imagined there were many women who would kill for the deal Logan was offering her now. He was hot, sexy and employed. So what was her problem? Here was her chance at a home, at a family. Only, she didn't know diddly about him.

Just one kiss.

That's all she needed to determine the kind of man Logan was. Her grandmother used to say a kiss told all. Of course, he might kiss like her seventh-grade boy-friend—a cool, formal peck on the cheek—which wouldn't be so bad because she'd finally be able to squelch the flutter Logan created in the pit of her stomach every time he looked at her. Harrison Ford was rumored to be a second-rate kisser, yet he looked first-rate and was her ideal action hero. If Logan was an A-list kisser, she'd run as fast as she could in the other direction because he'd break her heart. She was already half in love with him.

"All right, forget it. It was just an idea." He stood up.

Thea stood, too. She couldn't believe what she was about to suggest. Where were her instincts for self-pres-ervation? Where was that detachment her mother had had in spades?

Oh, yeah. Thea had never been the detached one in the family.

Right now, the longing in her heart could not be ig-nored. From the beginning, she'd wanted Logan to be a knight in shining armor, even if he wasn't hers. From the moment she'd seen Logan, all of her usual caution had gone right out the window, replaced by a wistful-ness she couldn't begin to understand.

"Could you…would you…would you kiss me first?" she asked.

Logan towered over Thea and she wished the light wasn't behind him, glinting off his short blond hair, wished that she could see the blue of his eyes and know if hope had replaced some of the sorrow there.

"Why?"

She couldn't very well tell him she was giving him a road test, now, could she?

Without stopping to think about it, Thea wrapped her arms around Logan's neck and tugged him to her, as she realized she'd been wanting to do since she met him. His lips were warm and gentle against her own, tender and nonthreatening.

Perhaps it was the surprise attack, perhaps it was just the way he kissed—like a fish. Thea pulled back in disappointment. And relief.

Only to find Logan's arms drawing her back.

And then he was kissing her, really kissing her, with a masterful dance of tongues and the exchange of warm, minty breath. He kissed her as if he were a man deprived of sweets and she was his first taste of chocolate, something to be savored, something to be lingered over—until the last morsel was gone.

Thea could go on kissing him forever. Her fingers crept up into the short fringe of hair at the nape of his neck.

And suddenly the night air replaced the feel of Logan against her. She was breathing deeply and she felt oh so warm inside. Reluctantly, she opened her eyes to find Logan staring down at her, his hands steady on her arms.

"Well, that might have replaced the sex talk I was going to have with you."

Meaning he wanted to have sex if they got married? Or he didn't?

And how was she supposed to answer? Women like Thea didn't sleep with a guy they'd just met. There were coffee dates, dinner dates, movie dates and then maybe sex. Not, will you marry me and, oh, yeah, we will have sex at some date to be determined later.

Or not.

Thea's body hummed with desire while her brain issued red-alert, panic warnings.

And what about his word choice? *Sex?* Not *make*

love. Not *I want to make love with you under the fountain at the Louvre.* There was nothing romantic or passionate about anything he said. Logan might just as well have been talking to her about the laundry.

Now that she'd discovered he was an A-List kisser, she'd be unable to resist making love to him if the opportunity presented itself. She respected him. She longed to ease his suffering. And he was hot.

She was no good at resisting temptation. And what would happen to her in the fall? Her heart would be crushed when he asked for a divorce and she'd most likely be ruined for any other man.

No way could she marry him. She'd have to chalk this up to the biggest missed opportunity of her life. Marriage. Hot sex. Helping his family heal in this picture-perfect house.

The one spoiler was the fact that he didn't love her, and certainly didn't have her best interest at heart.

"I don't think I can do this." She said it more to convince herself than to convince him.

He cupped her chin, stroking her cheek with his thumb, sending warm shivers down her spine. "You don't have to make up your mind tonight. I can't get a lawyer or a justice of the peace until Monday regardless of what you decide."

Thea was still standing on the porch, swaying slightly from the shock of his touch when Whizzer scampered up the steps and scratched at the kitchen door, ready to be let inside.

Logan hadn't accepted her half-hearted rejection. He was sleeping in the room next to hers. And she knew how he tasted, how his arms felt wrapped around her.

Oh, my.

THEA HEARD the kitchen door swing open at three in the morning and whirled, trying to hide the Easter eggs she'd been dyeing. She'd had Birdie sneak an egg dye kit into her purchases a few days before. Whizzer lifted his head sleepily from his spot in the corner.

"Aha! It's taken me thirty-one years, but I've finally cornered the Easter Bunny." Logan walked over to the kitchen counter in a pair of flannel pants and a gray T-shirt. He checked out her handiwork with a frown, as somber as the stranger he'd been three days ago, as somber as he'd been last night when he'd asked her to marry him.

Thea's skin prickled with awareness of him. She wiped her hands on the sides of her sweats. "I thought you were one of the girls."

"Why are you going to all this trouble?"

"Because it's Easter. Because it's the first Easter they'll have without their mother." Thea wanted to give the little girls asleep down the hall something to smile about, especially before they went to visit their mom in the cemetery.

"They're ten, not six." Logan stared at her in a way that made Thea uncomfortable, as if he didn't know whether he wanted to kiss her or send her on her way.

Blast.

"You're never too old to enjoy a special holiday." She gently stirred an egg in a cup of green dye. "I once met a woman who was convinced every day was Christmas. She carried a supply of gifts in her purse. Even if you thought she was crazy, she made you smile and feel good about the world."

"The woman who lived upstairs from you?"

"Yes." Thea was impressed that he'd remembered.

Logan looked out the open kitchen window into the night. "I was just coming to get something to drink before going back to bed."

"And now?" He was going to help her? Thea didn't know if that was good or bad. That kiss…it was unforgettable. And then there was the whole sex issue. She risked a quick glance at his lips before sending her gaze firmly back to the eggs on the counter. It would be better if he went off to bed.

"Now you've reminded me of something. I'll be right back."

All-righty, then. He wasn't going to help her. Thea watched Logan's retreating back before returning to her eggs. Perhaps she'd reminded him of something that had sent him back into his grief for his sister.

The door swung open behind her, and Thea whirled once again.

"It's just me," Logan said wearily, as if her theatrics were too much for him at this hour.

"I don't have X-ray vision. It could have been the girls," Thea answered grumpily.

Logan rolled his eyes as he carried a box to the kitchen table. "Here. Deb picked up some things for the twins last summer. She knew I'd suck at this stuff." He pulled two stuffed bunnies out of the box, then two kits with what looked like play makeup and two porcelain teacups. "I forgot to buy the chocolates," he admitted dourly.

"But you remembered these." Thea was so touched, she rose up on her toes and kissed his cheek before she knew what she was doing. He'd probably never realize what a wonderful man he was.

"Only because I couldn't sleep." Logan passed his

palm over his skin where Thea's lips had touched him. Then he moved his hand and rubbed the back of his neck.

"The subconscious works in mysterious ways." Thea backed away, but she couldn't stop smiling at him. "They have Easter baskets somewhere, don't they?"

"In the hall closet."

"Good. I was worried." She couldn't pull her gaze away from his. She couldn't get over how pleased she was with what he'd done. "You know, Deb was really special to buy this stuff in advance. I don't know if I would have been strong enough to do it, knowing the end was near."

Logan made to leave, then said without turning, "You could have done it."

Thea breathed a sigh of relief that he was leaving, only she couldn't let him go back to bed just yet. "You'll help me hide the eggs, won't you?"

He did face her then, with a shake of his head, and with what Thea swore was almost a smile. "Don't tell me, you're afraid to go out there."

"Remember me? City girl?" Thea pointed out the window. "Lions and tigers and bears."

"Like I told you, it's more like raccoons, coyotes and bears."

"Same difference." And she meant it. Anything with teeth and claws gave her the heebie-jeebies. Some people had dreams of falling off cliffs. Some people had dreams of car crashes. Thea had dreams of being trapped somewhere and being eaten alive by some sharp-toothed animal.

"You've got a lot to learn about the mountains." Logan rummaged through a kitchen drawer until he found a flashlight. He checked to make sure the beam was working.

Thea opened her mouth without filtering her thoughts. "Good thing I have someone like you to teach me."

"HOW MANY EGGS did you dye?" The sky was still inky black and Logan was longing to return to his bed, which was most likely cold by now. He looked across the yard to see what Thea was doing. She'd accepted the offer of his jacket to keep warm, which she wore over her sweats and T-shirt.

"Too many eggs, according to you," Thea retorted, trying to balance an egg in the crook of a tree branch. It fell to the ground with a disappointing crack.

"Leave it for the raccoons. I got new bearproof trash cans this year and they've been unable to mooch any trash from me. They deserve a little Easter treat."

She smiled approvingly at him, just as he knew she would. It warmed him in just the right way. His mind started anticipating moves, what he'd say, what her response would be and how best to approach her. He was rusty when it came to women. But not *that* out of practice.

Logan moved closer to her. "Have you thought more about my proposal?"

"No," she answered too quickly, dropping her eyes.

"You're lying. I bet you can't stop thinking about it, especially not after that kiss." He was having trouble not thinking about it. That's why he'd gotten up in the middle of the night. He couldn't sleep without dreaming about Thea and that polka-dot bra, about the way her hands cooled him down and heated him up at the same time.

"The trouble with you is—" Thea tilted her head up at him "—you think too much of yourself."

"Guilty as charged." He laughed. She was smart. Logan didn't normally appreciate that in a woman, but he did in Thea. She wasn't just intelligent, she had a generous heart. And legs that just wouldn't quit.

Her body language said she wanted him. Logan could see that it would be easy to get what he wanted—to touch her body until she burned for him, then bury himself deep inside her and let her warmth envelop him as they reached for the ultimate heat. The need to have her pressed on him until he had to gulp for air.

Submitting to temptation, Logan leaned down and pressed his lips ever so gently onto hers before pulling away.

Thea took a step back—not quite the reaction he was looking for. "What was that for?"

"I had to touch you, even if it was only for a second." He smiled.

Before he realized what was happening, Thea was heading for the house.

"Hey, hey, wait up. What's your hurry?" He trotted after her, boots crunching over the frosty ground.

But she didn't wait. "You must think I'm so stupid."

"I don't—"

"You say those lines as if you'd rehearsed them." She flew up the steps. "The Tin Man probably does."

"Hey, whoa, wait a minute." He caught her arm, stopping her a step above him so that they were eye to eye. "You think I practiced saying those lines?"

"I know you did. *I had to touch you.* Oh, puh-lease. Is that how you get women?" She jerked her arm away.

Yeah. "Of course not."

She scoffed at him. "I have news for you, Tin Man.

You may think you've been seducing women all these years, but you've been the one that's been seduced."

"You are so full of it."

"Am I? I bet Naomi had you trembling in your boots the other day."

"Naomi?"

"The woman we saw at the grocery store? The one overflowing—" she made a round gesture in front of her breasts "—with advice for me."

Naomi had made Logan nervous, all right. But only because he'd sensed she was going to take a shot at him. He narrowed his eyes at Thea. "What's your point?"

"Do you really like women like her or is it that they're easier to deal with? Ugh, forget I asked." Closing her eyes, Thea blew out a breath, and then opened her eyes to return his stare. This time, she spoke softly. "The point is that you can have any woman you want if you speak from your heart."

"Any woman I want?" Oh, he had her now.

"Yes." Her eyes were like liquid pools of chocolate, melting just for him.

"What if I said I want you?"

She cupped his cheek with her hand. It felt cool and soft on his skin.

It was going to happen. Logan could feel her resistance crumbling away.

"Like I said, you can have any woman you want if you speak from your heart." And then she walked inside the kitchen, leaving the Tin Man out in the cold.

IT TOOK LOGAN nearly a half hour to work up the courage to knock on Thea's bedroom door. She knew, because she lay in bed watching the clock and listening to him moving around in the kitchen.

Her door didn't have a lock and he opened it after rapping on it a second time.

"Thea, are you awake?"

"No." Not only was Thea awake, her blood was humming through her veins, driven by want, while her brain was sending out emergency warnings that sleeping with Logan was the last thing she needed right now.

But maybe, just maybe, making love with her was what Logan needed.

He stepped inside and closed the door. Moonlight cast deep shadows over the room. She couldn't see his face, but she could imagine what he looked like—sorrowful blue eyes, a mouth set firmly against any reason to smile. If only her heart wasn't hanging in the balance, she'd toss back the covers and welcome him into her bed. She could offer him comfort, and take some as well, but her heart needed some bit of protection.

It was too late to prevent her from suffering. She'd fallen in love with him—this aloof man who skated in his socks and hid Easter eggs. And she was certain that he'd never accept her love, not the way she needed to be accepted. He'd take her physical gift and she'd create a memory to fill the lonely nights that were sure to be in her future.

He sat on the bed next to her. "I don't think I've ever met anyone like you."

Huddled under the covers, wearing only her bra and panties, Thea kept silent.

"You piss me off and make me want to laugh. You drive me nuts with the way you look at life. And yet, from the moment I laid eyes on you, I couldn't stop looking."

Thea held her breath.

"I wasn't lying out in the yard. I want you so much I ache." He rubbed the back of his neck. "I did approach you in a calculated, planned way. But that doesn't mean I don't respect you."

Ee-ew. This sounded nothing like a pass.

"I guess it's just been so long since I've been around a regular woman—"

He was getting colder. Thea wished she'd kept her clothes on and maybe kept a book in her hand to thunk the idiot on the head with.

"—that I've lost touch with what really matters. You're right. I can have any woman I want—"

She was going to kill him.

"—but the fact remains, I only want you."

She was going to kiss him.

And without waiting for him to say more, she did.

"You don't really think you're heartless, do you?"

Thea's hand skimmed over Logan's chest, leaving a trail of heat in its wake. She had one of her glorious legs draped across him as they snuggled in her narrow twin bed.

Logan's eyes were closed and his body was settling into the zone of deep satiation when Thea's question finally penetrated his thick skull. He'd asked her to marry him. They'd just shared some bone-melting sex. Of course, a woman like Thea expected to hear words of commitment.

He could spout some smooth lines. "That was really special." Or, "Did the earth move for you, too?" Anything to distract her from the truth.

Only, Thea shifted her hips—she had the most incredibly limber back—and he remembered how close he'd come to sleeping alone tonight because Thea seemed to be able to read him like a road sign. She valued honesty.

He thrust his hips against her thigh. "You know who I am." And she did. Somehow, in just a few brief days, he felt as if someone else in the world knew him.

The tightness in his chest eased.

Thea slid up on top of him, pressing her body hungrily against his, finding his lips with hers and giving them a bath, like a cat delicately licking up cream.

He wanted her again. It wasn't like the raging fire she'd lit in him before. It was a slow-burning need that made him pull her even closer, guiding her over him until he filled her.

"Come closer," he murmured against her lips. Even though there wasn't a millimeter of space between their bodies, he needed her closer. Maybe if he closed the gap between them, he could understand why she knew him so well. Maybe—

Her hips undulated against his and she contracted around him.

"Oh, yeah." That brought him closer. Logan's palms pressed down the length of her back, pressed her round cheeks against him. He could feel her smile in her kiss. She was so warm, so open.

Warmth. Cripes, she was oozing warmth all over him, not just down there—down there! But against his mouth, through his chest. Hell, he melted from the touch of her toes on the tops of his feet. It was as if she'd been made for him, as if she knew exactly what he needed, exactly when.

He was going to burst into flames with her if he could just fill his lungs with enough air to pulse upward. Only, he wasn't ready for their connection to end.

Thea shifted, straddling him with those delicious legs and holding him down with her hands on his shoulders.

"You don't want it that easy." Her voice brought home that this was Thea, the woman sporting too much color and noise. She had to realize who he was and that he'd hurt her at some point, not physically, but emotionally. Forget this crazy marriage scheme. He was using her with that. He was the Tin Man. She'd held that up as a shield often enough. She had to know this wasn't forever.

For one moment, Logan hesitated to take what she offered. Thea was freckles and sunshine, not the slick heat of the night. "Do you know who I am?" he asked almost desperately.

She moved, bringing him into motion with her. He couldn't resist.

"You're the Tin Man."

And she brought him home.

"COME ON, TESS. Wake up. It's Easter Sunday. Let's go see what the Easter Bunny left us."

"Stop bouncing the bed, Han, and I'll get up." Tess blinked her sleepy eyes open.

The sun was out and shining on her face. She yawned and squinted.

"Come on," Hannah repeated. She always waited for Tess to wake up before going out to see what Santa and the Easter Bunny had left them.

"I don't know why you're in such a rush. The Easter Bunny probably doesn't know where we're living now." Santa hadn't been able to keep up.

"Remember what Mom said," Hannah pulled on her jacket over her pajamas. "You have to believe or the magic doesn't work."

Tess lay on her back with her hand over her eyes, trying to decide if she believed or not. She wanted to believe.

She swung her legs out from under the covers. "Okay. I believe." But if the Easter Bunny didn't deliver, she wasn't going to anymore.

"Did you hear Whizzer barking earlier?" Thea asked when they got to the kitchen.

Tess shook her head.

"Do you think he heard the Easter Bunny?" Hannah ran over to the corner to pet Whizzer. "Did you, boy?"

Tess could almost feel Hannah's excitement. If that Easter Bunny disappointed Hannah, Tess was going to get mad.

"First the dog wakes me up, and now you two are makin' all this noise." Uncle Logan sipped his coffee while he flipped through one of Thea's textbooks. "The neighborhood's going downhill."

"Well?" Thea said.

"Well, what?" Tess and Hannah both asked at the same time.

Tess looked at Hannah. They hadn't said things together like that—in unison, their mom used to say—in a long time.

Thea pinched her nose as if she had a headache. "—Aren't you going to go look?"

With a giggle, Hannah ran to the kitchen door and slipped into her boots. Tess hurried after her. She wanted to see, but she didn't.

What if there was nothing out there? What if the Easter Bunny was like Santa and had decided they were too hard to find or hadn't been good enough this year?

"Hannah, wait." Tess wanted to stop her sister from getting hurt, but it was too late.

Before she could stop her, Hannah threw the kitchen door open and raced across the porch and down the steps.

Tess couldn't look. *Please don't let it be bad. Please don't let it be bad.*

And then Hannah called to her. "Tess! Tess! Come quick!"

With slow steps, Tess moved into the kitchen doorway and looked out. Everything had a layer of frost. It had to have been too cold for that stupid bunny to make his rounds.

"Tess," Hannah cried from across the yard. "I found an egg."

THE NEW SILVER BEND CEMETERY was carved out of the mountainside with green flowing lawn broken only by the occasional headstone. The cemetery hadn't been established long—only a few years, long enough to open its gates for the likes of Birdie Lowell's husband, Deb and a dozen or so others. The true old-timers, settlers, prospectors and the like, were buried up the hill in the historic cemetery.

This cemetery was a peaceful place.

A place that weighed heavily on Logan's soul.

At dawn, he'd returned to his own bedroom, reluctantly leaving Thea before the kids or Aunt Glen discovered them together, hoping to save her any embarrassment. Later, the wondrous morning had continued with the twins giggling as they searched for Easter eggs in their pj's, jackets and mud boots. With the help of Deb, Thea had created a special memory for them, and to Thea's delight, most of the eggs had survived the night.

For a few hours, Logan had started to feel, well, almost like his old self. And then came the time to go to the cemetery.

Logan drove slowly through the arched gates out of respect for those whose time had passed, but also because he dreaded going to his twin's grave site. Thea took his hand as they entered the gates, letting him know she was there if he needed her. He was grateful for the contact.

When had he become such a wuss?

He parked near Deb's final resting place and climbed out of the truck slowly, helping Aunt Glen and the girls out the back door. The girls wore jean jackets over the velvet dresses he'd bought them last year when Jackson and Lexie had remarried. Their skirts ruffled in the brisk spring breeze. Thea had braided their hair in two pigtails, each hanging over one ear. Deb had always liked it kept neat.

Aunt Glen wore an ankle-length jean skirt and a pale pink sweater that Thea had found somewhere. The colors made Glen's skin look that much healthier. Or perhaps it was because Glen was cleaner than she'd been in a long time.

Logan cursed silently. He'd really screwed things up for all of them.

Thea came around the other side of the truck. She'd insisted on purchasing carnations at Birdie's store. And, of course, she hadn't chosen just one color. There was a pink one, a yellow one, an orange one and a red one. The various colors complemented Thea's dark blue jeans and purple suede jacket. Logan realized he'd never seen Thea wear black. Other women couldn't stay away from basic black. She shunned it for brighter, more cheerful colors.

She gave Tess, Hannah and Glen each a kiss on the

cheek and a carnation. Logan wrapped his arms around her when she handed him his flower, hugging her tight, trying to recapture that special feeling from the night before.

"You're doing a good job," Thea said as she backed out of his embrace. Her gaze sent him strength. "She's been waiting a long time to see you."

They walked forward in a procession that seemed to move more slowly than the day the pallbearers had carried Deb to her plot. Logan kept his eyes on the tree-filled horizon beyond his sister's grave, oddly comforted by the soft jingle of bells from Thea's shoes. If not for that, the stillness would have been too ominous to bear.

"I'll wait for you over here," Thea said softly, breaking away from the group and sitting on a bench beneath a pine tree.

Logan remembered that this must be tough on Thea as well, being reminded of her own loss. And then they were standing next to Deb's grave marker. Logan's eyes scanned the headstone.

Deborah Kaylie McCall. Beloved Mother. Cherished Sister. Treasured Niece. The sun is shining on your side of the mountain.

Logan would be damned before anything about that lowlife husband of Deb's went on the headstone, including his name. Wes had been gone for half a year when Deb died. Deb hadn't seemed to care too much that he'd left. She had always been good about picking herself up and moving on. Logan wasn't so levelheaded. Perhaps that was why he couldn't move past her death. *God, he missed her.*

Deb had always seemed to sense when Logan was feeling lost, or reliving the chaos that was their childhood. No matter where he was, she'd find him, get a hold of him on his cell phone or sweet-talk a fire dispatcher into relaying him a message.

"Hey, you. Put your boots on." Or, *"Hey, you. Sun's shining on this side of the mountain."* It was their code for keepin' on.

Logan clenched his eyes shut, angling his head away from the rest of the family.

He would not cry out here. But the pain of her loss was so intense that he almost couldn't breathe. Deb was the one person in the world who had known the hell of his childhood, that could communicate to him with just a look. He missed that.

Someone sniffed next to him. Logan opened his eyes and gazed down on his nieces. Hannah had tears streaming down her face. Tess held herself in such a tense way that she looked as if she'd shatter at any moment. Her arms couldn't wrap any tighter around her thin frame. She blinked back tears defiantly.

Hannah knelt next to her mother's headstone with a whisper of velvet. Very carefully, she laid her flower at its base. "I miss you, Mommy. I miss listening to you read to me at night. I miss sitting on your lap." She gave a big juicy sniff. "Thea reads to us at night. You'd like her a lot. She's opened the windows and cleaned Uncle Logan's house."

How was Logan supposed to know how to be a good parent? The closest he'd come to a real father was Sirus Socrath, the Hot Shot who trained him and was now married to Mary, Jackson's mom. Sirus would just as quickly cuss you out as slap you on the back for a job well done. Not exactly the role model Logan needed to raise two little girls.

Humbled by his failure to care for his nieces properly, Logan bowed his head. What had Deb been thinking to leave him in charge of her two kids? He and Deb had both been beaten regularly by their dad. Deb may not have inherited Eldred McCall's hot temper, but Logan sure had and he feared what he might do if the pressure of parenthood became too much. Even now, Logan could feel the heat of frustration winding its way through his blood—a heat so undeniable that he could barely keep himself from shouting at the heavens, at God himself, for taking the one thing that had been decent about his childhood.

"I don't…I can't… Where is Deb?" Aunt Glen's eyes darted about the area, a worried frown gracing her features. "Is this a joke?"

It wasn't a joke. It was his own personal hell.

Logan moved next to Glen, drawing her away from the grave. "She's gone, Glen. She's been gone awhile now."

Glen shrugged off his arm. "How dare you! She's not gone. Why, just this morning…" Her words faltered and her gaze drifted back to the headstone. "She went for a walk up the mountain," she added stubbornly.

Sparing a glance to the twins, Logan put his arm around his aunt once more. Hannah watched them with luminous, tear-filled eyes. Tess kept her back to them, eyes on her mother's headstone.

"It's okay, Glen. Why don't you go sit over here with Thea." Logan wished he believed his own words, wished he had someone to blame for his sister's death. At least then, he could channel all his frustration and pain at someone.

Glen's face was pale. She looked up to where Logan

pointed. "Is she one of your girlfriends? Have I met her before?"

"She's a friend of the family. She's your cookie-making buddy." Thea was his rock. He wasn't alone anymore. For now, that was enough.

"I'm quite good at making sugar cookies, you know," Glen announced.

"The best in Silver Bend." They stopped in front of the bench and Logan exchanged a glance with Thea.

"She'll be fine with me," Thea said, patting the bench beside her as if she knew exactly what Logan had been about to ask her. "Glen, have you ever made snickerdoodles?"

"Of course I have." Even as Glen sat down, Logan could tell her spirits were rising. "Did you know that snickerdoodles can be traced back to Roman times?"

Thea laughed and squeezed Glen's hand. "You're kidding?"

"Not at all. Those Pennsylvania Dutch tried to claim them as their own creation, but that's just not true."

Now that Glen was on steadier ground, Logan returned to the twins.

"Don't be mad at Mom," Hannah was saying to Tess.

"She didn't have to die." Tess was still wrapped up tight as a mummy.

"She was sick," Hannah wailed.

"But she didn't go to the doctor in the end, did she? She didn't try hard enough to stay with us."

"Tess." The word was wrung from Logan's throat as he knelt next to her and put an arm over her thin shoulders. "Don't."

Tess's blue eyes blazed with fury. "She left us. Moms aren't supposed to leave."

What could he say to that?

While he fumbled for some words of comfort, Hannah wrapped her arms around Logan's shoulders.

"She was too sick, Tess," he said, sliding an arm around Hannah as he ignored the burning in his gut that talking about Deb caused. "She was too sick for the doctors to help her."

He felt a bit of the tension leave Tess's little body as she leaned into him.

"I want her back. I'd give anything to get her back," Tess whispered.

"Me, too," Hannah added.

Logan could do nothing but silently agree.

CHAPTER NINE

"WHY DON'T YOU WAIT in the truck with your aunt Glen," Thea suggested to the twins. The wind had started to pick up, chilling the midafternoon air.

Logan stood stiff and still at his sister's grave site. He didn't seem ready to leave.

As the trio trundled off to the shelter of the truck, Thea walked slowly toward Logan. She'd made her decision. She had to tell him the truth about her mother. And then he'd never want to marry her or make love to her again.

For one heartbeat, Thea wavered. He'd seemed less the wounded soul this morning until they'd come to the cemetery. He'd stolen a sweet kiss in the kitchen while she made breakfast, and had seemed relaxed with her and the girls, easing what little awkwardness Thea had felt after making love to him. How badly did she need to tell the truth? Because it was sure to shatter their fragile relationship.

Side by side, she and Logan stood in silence. Thea read Deb's headstone and noticed immediately there was nothing there about Deb being a wife. Her maiden name was on the headstone. Thea wouldn't have known Deb was married if she hadn't known Wes.

Without thinking, Thea rubbed Logan's back ever so

gently. Logan's expression was stony, a mix of hurt, disbelief and anger. She'd avoided bringing up his proposal, hoping he'd come to his senses and tell her it had all been a foolish idea, saving her the heartbreak of turning him down.

"She and Glen were the only family I had left," Logan admitted gruffly. "We buried Deb next to my mom in the plot that was meant for Glen."

Thea's hands encased Logan's larger, cold hand. "I'm so sorry." Sure enough, the next headstone over was inscribed *Megan Marie McCall, Loving Mother, Taken Too Soon.* "Was she sick as well?"

"Never." He spat the word bitterly, seeming to struggle with his emotions before he explained further.

"My father was a dangerous drunk. He had too much whiskey one day." Logan chewed his cheek, then he added, "He shot Mom before emptying the gun into his own head."

Thea couldn't breathe. "How old were you?"

"We were ten. We came home from school and found them in the living room."

Thea buried her face in Logan's arm, clinging to his hand, now in desperate need of support herself. He'd been too young to discover such horror existed in the world. "And then Glen took you in."

"Yes."

He and his sister had lived through something horrible. No wonder he was so devastated by her loss. "And you all stayed here? In Silver Bend?"

"Yes."

Without benefit of counseling, Thea was willing to bet. Silver Bend was miles from anywhere. She could just imagine a ten-year-old Logan, chin lifted against the grief, trying to protect his sister, trying to be brave for himself. He had lived his life with more honor than Thea ever had. She'd hidden away from the pain and anyone she thought might hurt her.

"I'm still mad at my sister for dying, too."

"What do you mean? She was terminally ill, wasn't she?"

His thumb stroked hers before he squeezed her hand, making her wonder if he drew any comfort from her. She hoped he did.

"Deb was very ill. The doctors couldn't give her any hope, only a morphine drip against the ever-increasing pain. One morning, I came to check on her and her morphine dial was cranked up too high."

Logan stared down at Thea with distant eyes, no doubt recalling his sister that morning. "She'd taken herself out with a morphine overdose. After all we'd survived…" He swallowed and continued in a tight voice. "She just gave up."

"I'm so sorry." Now Thea understood. Logan had survived his father's abuse, only to be left alone. His sister had surrendered to death and his aunt couldn't stay in the present longer than a few minutes. "Her pain would have to have been very great for her to end her life that way."

Logan's gaze returned to his sister's headstone.

"My mother…" Thea began, paused to swallow. He wasn't going to like what she had to say, but Thea had to say it anyway. "My mother left us on my tenth birthday, after I blew out my candles. I can remember begging her to stay, but she wouldn't." She'd clutched her mother's flowing silk pants with one small hand. Tears had streamed down her face as she tried not to look at her father, whose unspoken anger had filled the room more so than Thea's sobs.

Logan frowned down at her but said nothing. His facial features seemed carved in stone.

Thea pressed the back of her hand to her mouth against a wave of nausea. "She was a doctor, one of the best in the field of AIDS research. And she had theories about how to develop a cure. There were new things being discovered in the farthest, most remote parts of Asia and Africa, cases that were different than the strains here in the U.S. But she couldn't take us with her. Couldn't take *me* with her," Thea clarified.

"How did she die?"

Thea stared directly into Logan's blue eyes, knowing she had to see his reaction, knowing she deserved the anger he was sure to unleash on her. "My mother didn't die. She chose the pursuit of a dream over her daughter and I haven't heard from her since. She may have died by now. She may have fallen to the very disease she tried to cure. But she's as good as dead to me."

Thea hated the fact that her eyes had filled with tears, hated the fact that being left behind hurt almost as much now as it had back then. "It's been seventeen years and there's been no cure for AIDS, no indication that she made a difference in the search for a cure. But one thing is certain." Thea's voice trembled. "She didn't make a difference in the life of a child, of *her* child. And that's why I couldn't just drop Tess and Hannah off with you and leave. I knew how much they were hurting."

Logan looked away, at the headstones of his mother and sister.

"I'm sorry if I led you to believe she was dead, but the healing process is similar. I grieved because my mother was no longer there for me. I tried to make sense of the world without her and I somehow managed to move on." Not alone, as Logan had. She'd had her father—a distant workaholic—frequent visits from her grandmother and counseling to help her overcome her pain.

"It's not the same." Logan's cold response was expected, and deserved. He shook her hands off of his.

"No," Thea admitted, struggling to mask her hurt. "It's not."

"You lied." His deep voice shook with anger.

Thea knew there was truth in his accusation, so she didn't deny it. "I should have explained myself better. I'm sorry. I let you believe it because you seemed to open up."

"All that crap you've been telling the girls and me…it's all…just crap." His words cut unexpectedly deep.

"No, what I've been saying is from years of therapy." What was it her last therapist had tried to tell her? Oh, yeah. She was responsible for letting the words and actions of others hurt her. She'd just met Logan a few days earlier and somehow his opinion mattered, and his harsh words sliced deeply.

Because he'd asked her to marry him. Because she loved him.

With a snort of disgust, Logan turned on his heel and headed for the truck, leaving Thea no choice but to follow.

"What's wrong?" Hannah asked when Logan gunned the truck out of the cemetery.

"Are your seat belts fastened?" Thea asked.

"Don't pretend to care," Logan snapped, sparing Thea a sharp glance.

Of all the things he could have accused her of, that was the one wrong thing to say. "I do care. And you know what else? I show people I care, unlike you, who has his feelings locked inside so tight even the dog thinks you're an inanimate object."

"I'm honest, which is more than I can say for you, honey."

"You might be honest, but no one would know because you won't let yourself say more than a handful of words to anyone at a time." Thea was breathing hard now. Even if Logan had started opening up, he could just as easily return to being that distant, cool man she'd first met.

He took a sharp left turn onto the road leading home and everyone was thrown to the right side of the truck.

"Logan McCall!" Glen protested from the back. "I've no idea why you're fighting with this woman, but if you don't slow down you can stop and let someone else drive."

"You have no idea how angry I am at you right now." Logan flexed his fingers on the steering wheel as he slowed down. "For your own good, when we get home, you'd better pack your things and leave."

His temper was as loud and physical as her father's. After years of weathering that particular storm on her own, Thea knew just how to react—by not backing down.

"If you can't forgive something like this, that's fine by me. I was tired of playing housemaid anyway."

"Logan, are you breaking up with one of Deb's friends?" Glen leaned forward. "If so, Deb's not going to be happy."

Logan brought the truck to an abrupt halt in front of the house, sending gravel spewing everywhere. He spun around in his seat to face Glen.

"Logan, don't," Thea cautioned, sensing he was about to let loose some of the frustration he'd kept bottled for too long.

"She's *dead*, Aunt Glen. Deb has been dead for more than six months."

Tears spilled over Hannah's cheeks. Tess looked white as a sheet.

"That…that can't be. She's just out for one of her walks up the mountain."

"We buried her in the cemetery next to my mom, Glen." His voice softened. "She's gone. She's never coming back." Logan turned narrowed eyes toward Thea. "Unlike some people's relatives who probably *will* come back someday." Then quick as lightning, he was out of the truck and storming toward the house.

Thea hopped out after him. "Now wait just one minute. You want to compare your pain to mine? Fine." When he didn't turn around she tossed up her hands and jogged after him. "You win. You've had more injustice, bad luck and hard times than I've ever had. But you know what? That doesn't mean I haven't experienced loss. That doesn't mean I don't feel empty inside, tortured by the same question you are."

"Leave it alone," he grumbled as he stopped in front of the kitchen door, flexing his fingers as if he was considering making a fist and punching something.

Thea stopped close to him, within two feet, within punching distance, confident he wouldn't hit her. "Why?"

"You're playing with fire."

"You think you're the only one with a temper? Think again, Hot Shot. I grew up with one parent who had a volcano of a temper."

"When I open this door, I want you to pack your things and get out."

Soft footsteps sounded behind her. They had an audience.

"Why?" she repeated.

"You know why." He wouldn't look at her now, only stared at the kitchen door as if he wanted to tear it to smithereens.

"I'm not asking you why. I'm saying you can't answer the question about anyone's death." She took a deep breath to control the shaking in her voice. "*Why?* You can't answer *why* your dad drank so much. You can't answer *why* your father committed the unthinkable. You can't answer *why* your sister had a terminal illness. And because you can't answer those questions, you let the why eat you up inside. And then there are the maybes. *Maybe* their time had come. *Maybe* you were meant to go through this for a reason. *Maybe* you were meant to help others because you know how much a person can suffer." Thea felt the steam run out of her. She only had enough energy left to say softly, "You just don't know why."

They were both breathing hard now. Blinking back tears, Thea willed him to look at her, willed Logan to acknowledge the truth in her words, willed him to gather her in his arms and tell her everything was going to be all right. But all he did was step back to allow her room to pass through the kitchen.

SHE'D LIED TO HIM.

Temper raging, Logan retreated to his room only to find that he couldn't stay caged in the ten-by-twelve space. He launched himself out to the garage. He was willing to stay there until Thea left, even if it took hours.

He thought they'd shared something special. He'd been drawn to her warmth and color despite his common sense. He'd thought he was no longer alone.

Why? He snorted in disgust as he found himself in

front of his workbench, welcoming the distraction of putting a wrench back in its place on the wall.

He remembered that his brother-in-law was quite a mechanic. Wes had a full set of tools at the house he and Deb had owned, as well as a garage big enough to house his rig and a couple others when he came home. Logan wondered why Wes hadn't come home for Deb's last days, for her funeral. He'd called Wes's cell phone and left a message. His absence stank of indecency.

Why?

Shit.

He'd never understood what Deb had seen in Wes. The guy was several years older than her, full of bull and slicker than an icy road. After high school, Logan and Deb had both pursued degrees at a junior college in Boise, but Deb had met Wes and that was the end of her education. She preferred to be a wife and full-time mom, and Wes had, surprisingly, gone along with it. Why was anyone's guess.

Why, again.

Damn.

Logan wandered over to the tractor in the corner that had belonged to Deb and Wes. It had an enclosed cab with a heater. It wasn't unusual for Deb to drive the kids down the snowy mountain in it to school during the brutal winter months. Her house had been situated close to one thousand feet above Silver Bend. It often snowed up there when it didn't down below in town, making the house damn inconvenient. When he'd asked Deb once why she built a house so far out of town, she'd said it was to escape the whispers, the finger-pointing and the stares.

If she wanted anonymity, she should have moved to Boise.

Why had Thea lied to him?

"Uncle Logan?"

Logan turned to find Hannah standing hesitantly in the doorway.

"We can't find Aunt Glen."

"THANKS FOR COMING SO quickly," Thea said to Jackson Garrett when he and his family arrived, glad that she'd given Hannah responsibility for Whizzer with all the volunteers she expected to be streaming into the house in the next few minutes.

"I take it that means Logan hasn't found her." Jackson steadied Lexie as she climbed up the front steps carrying Henry in her arms. Heidi had already slipped past them.

"What happened?" Lexie asked as Thea ushered them inside.

"We went to the cemetery today. I'm certain Glen hasn't accepted Deb's death. Glen said something about Deb just being out on a walk. I'm afraid Logan got a little upset. And then she disappeared." Thea stuck her hands into her pockets, feeling responsible. She should have told Logan the truth from day one. The girls wouldn't have started to heal their broken hearts, but Glen wouldn't be outside, lost in the dark on a chilly mountain, in danger from the elements and wild animals.

"I've called Chainsaw, Spider and The Queen. Did you call the sheriff?" Jackson kept his jacket on.

"Yes, but there was a bad accident down the road. As soon as they clear that up he promised to be here."

"He'd better call down to Boise for some dogs and air support," Jackson grumbled. "It's too dark now, but we'll need them by morning."

"I'm sure he knows how to do his job," Lexie said with surprising calm.

Thea felt about as wound up and helpless as the baby squirming in Lexie's arms. It was pitch-black outside, cold, and getting colder.

Chainsaw and Spider—it was oddly easier to remember them by their Hot Shot names—traipsed in without knocking, wearing boots, jeans and heavy jackets, followed by a slender woman dressed similarly.

"Did you bring the equipment?" Jackson asked.

"Yeah." Chainsaw swung a large backpack with two smaller packs attached to each side onto the coffee table, rattling its contents. He began pulling out walkie-talkies and flashlights. In his winter jacket, his broad shoulders looked huge. "It took us a bit longer because we had to stop and get batteries at Birdie's."

"Not a problem." Jackson turned on a walkie-talkie and filled the room with static.

"Hi, I'm Victoria," the woman introduced herself to Thea.

"Queen Victoria," Spider said without looking up from checking that the radio worked. His voice held more than a trace of sarcasm. Thea hadn't seen this side of Logan's wiry, swarthy friend before.

"Another Hot Shot," Thea surmised, wondering how a woman could keep up with men during all the feats they'd bragged about the other day, especially a woman sporting fake pink nails.

"You betcha." Victoria nodded proudly with a toss of her fiery red hair.

Thea wished she could be as strong and confident as Victoria.

"Don't worry, we'll find her," Victoria said, touching Thea's shoulder.

"You might want to stay here with the *women*, Queen," Spider said, not in a nice way.

"Like hell. Don't start all that chauvinistic crap on me again, Spider," Victoria snapped back.

"Let's stay on frequency two," Jackson broke in, ignoring Spider and Victoria's bickering. "Spider, you come with me. Chainsaw, you pair up with The Queen. Thea, if Logan comes back, make sure he doesn't leave without a radio. This one's for you, Lex," he added softly, handing his wife a radio.

"And don't let Tin Man leave without this backpack," Spider said, gesturing to another large lumpy backpack on the floor. "I've loaded it with blankets, food and water."

Chainsaw, Spider, Victoria and Jackson already had a similar pack slung on their backs.

"What about me? How can I help?" Thea asked.

"By staying here with the radio on and waiting for the sheriff," Jackson said before he turned to kiss Lexie and his infant son goodbye. "Runt, where are you?"

Heidi came pounding down the hallway and practically threw herself into Jackson's arms. "Love you, Dad," she said, then spun away and ran back down the hall.

"Be careful," Lexie added, worry in her eyes.

With a clatter of booted feet, the Hot Shots went out to search for Glen.

"Do they always rush in and out like that?" Thea asked.

"Pretty much." Lexie smiled down at the now contented baby in her arms. "They're used to handling emergencies. They know every second counts."

Thea sank into a brown chair across from Lexie. "So, what do we do?"

"Brew coffee, make something warm and hearty to eat, like stew or soup, and stay close to the telephone."

"That's it?"

"I'm afraid so. When they find Glen—and they will find her—they'll be cold, tired and hungry. Whether you like it or not, tonight you're part of the Hot Shot family. Big or small, everyone helps out by doing the jobs that need to be done."

"Spoken like a woman who's been around this a long time."

"Advice for a woman who wants to stick around." Lexie studied Thea with a knowing stare.

"I've got to get back to Seattle, I'm already behind on my studies," Thea protested, albeit weakly. She sounded like a broken record. She was packed and ready to go if Logan still wanted her to leave. And leaving was the right thing to do. Despite her good intentions, she'd gotten no more than she deserved for lying—a bruised and disappointed heart.

"Logan barely lets any of us up here to visit anymore, except for letting me look in on Aunt Glen. We've all been worried about him, Glen and the girls. He's nothing like he used to be before he lost Deb. If he opened up the house to you that must mean something."

"He tossed me out this afternoon." In Thea's mind, she could still see Logan's angry expression.

"At least you're making him feel again. That's more than we've been able to do."

LOGAN RAN UP the front porch, heedless of the twinge in his leg. He'd been stumbling around on the dark trail too long. With relief, he saw that Lexie had arrived and sat on the couch cradling Henry. That meant Jackson was out looking for Glen.

"Any word?"

Thea burst through the kitchen door, looking anxious. Logan quickly pulled his gaze away from her. Her deception still stung.

"None. You missed them by about an hour," Lexie said in a quiet voice, gently rocking a dozing Henry from side to side.

Logan shed his lightweight jacket and rummaged in the hall closet for a heavier one.

Behind him, he heard the rustle of the backpack and the snap of a walkie-talkie clip. Lex must be getting his backpack ready. But when he turned around, Thea was hefting his gear onto her back.

"That's not your jacket." He recognized the bright yellow coat as Deb's. "And you're not going."

"Yes, I am. If it wasn't for me, Glen wouldn't be out there now." She hooked her thumbs through the pack straps.

Sorting through the jumble of emotions—fear for Aunt Glen, anger at Thea—Logan chewed on his cheek.

He shook his head. To be honest, his own temper was to blame. If he hadn't lost his cool and yelled at Glen, she'd be in her room right now, safe and warm, crocheting something. Yet, Logan wasn't about to let a city girl out on the mountain at night. "Hand over the backpack."

"Logan, she's been going crazy here waiting," Lexie said. "She's making me nervous, which makes the baby nervous." As if on cue, little Henry whimpered.

"I'm not taking her." Logan ground his teeth. He

didn't care if it was foolish to go searching alone. He knew the country. He knew he'd be the one to find Glen. But not with Thea tagging along.

Thea plopped her hands on her hips. "If you don't take me with you, I'll just head out on my own."

That was just what he needed. "Then we'll be looking for two crazy women instead of one."

"Exactly." Thea smiled at him and her bells tinkled. "Besides, everyone else went out with a partner."

"Logan, it makes sense to take a buddy along." Lexie wasn't helping at all. Whose side was she on anyway?

Thea wasn't his buddy. "She'll just slow me down."

"If you plan on charging up the hill in the dark, yes, I can see how I'll slow you down. But somehow, I don't think that's what you had in mind."

Logan narrowed his eyes as he stared at her, assessing what he knew about Thea's stamina. She did seem fit. He supposed that she wouldn't slow him down too much...if he took her.

"All right. But give me the backpack." He reached out for the straps, but Thea danced away with that annoying jangle of bells.

"I'll take a turn carrying it first."

"You think I'm going to race out of the house and leave you here."

She nodded.

The thought had crossed his mind, had in fact lodged itself as an attractive option.

Biting back words of frustration, which would have been wasted on Thea, Logan headed for the door. He supposed it was fine that she wanted to come along, but he wasn't about to coddle her.

PLAYING THE ROLE of mountain rescuer was not one of her brighter ideas, Thea decided when she found herself huffing and puffing up the side of a mountain in near-total darkness. The pack was heavy, Logan's pace was brutal and he wasn't talking to Thea at all. Not that she deserved to be spoken to. Still…

Her lungs couldn't seem to fill adequately to make her move quickly enough to keep up with him, and her leg muscles burned from exhaustion after hours of hiking. If this was what it was like to be a Hot Shot, she wanted no part of it. Every twenty to thirty feet on the steep slope, he'd stop, call out Glen's name, listen for a response, then continue up the mountain. If it wasn't for those stops, Thea would have fallen behind long ago, so she was grateful. But, darn it, she suspected Logan was stopping occasionally for her sake, under the guise of calling for Glen. She was slowing him down and she didn't like the idea. It was getting darker and colder by the second. They needed to find her soon.

"Did you hear that?" Logan asked from twenty feet above her.

She'd fallen pretty far behind this time.

Thea paused to listen. The crisp mountain air was still, but she couldn't hear much of anything over the sound of her labored breathing, so she shook her head. "Nothing."

"Glen!" Logan called again.

Thea strained to listen. And she did hear something. "To the left," she said. "She's somewhere to the left." Her heart felt lighter as she pushed her way up the trail. They'd found her!

Rather than leap into action, Logan yelled for Glen again.

What Thea heard this time had her puzzled. "She called back her own name?"

"It's an echo. There's a small valley to our left." Logan explained coolly before spinning about, continuing to push up the slope at a breakneck pace. He must have the eyes of a cat, because Thea carried their only flashlight.

Dispirited, Thea had no choice but to follow him. Her muscles screamed in protest. If it wasn't for Glen, she'd be happy to roll back down the mountain.

Sometime later, Logan asked her once more, "Do you hear anything?"

Thea tucked her hair behind her ears and listened. There may have been something, but it was so faint. "Another echo?"

Logan doggedly called out again. Lulled by the quiet and inactivity, Thea's mind wandered to dreams of hot tubs and massages, back rubs and that lovely vibrating chair at the salon where she got pedicures a couple of times a year. Logan turned to continue his upward charge. But wait...

"I heard something."

He paused, turned. With the light beneath him, his face was an indiscernible set of shadows. "Are you sure?"

"Yes. Off to the right. Call for her again." Thea looked off in the direction she'd thought Glen's voice came from with hope in her heart.

And sure enough, when Logan called, someone answered with a faint, "Over here."

"Oh my gosh. Is she on another trail? How do we get over there?"

Logan shushed her and listened. Thea's feet were cemented in place. Without thinking, she swung the flashlight beam from the bush beside the trail to Logan's chest.

"Did you hear her?" she asked.

Nodding, Logan started up again. "We'll walk out thirty feet and call again."

Thea hesitated. She had to ask. "I don't want to be a wimp or anything, but we won't be stepping on sleeping snakes or coyotes or anything, will we?"

The growl Logan released expressed more than words could.

"Never mind," Thea mumbled, venturing off the trail and into the scrub. Immediately, she was clawed by brush. It pulled at her jacket, tugged at the backpack. And when she stubbed her toe on something unyielding, she couldn't help crying out in frustration.

Behind her, Logan made a sound suspiciously similar to a laugh. Thea couldn't turn around fast enough to see his face and give him the evil eye. Only his expression stopped her. He was smiling. At her. Something warm blossomed inside her, easing the ache in her chest.

"Sorry," he managed to say between chuckles. "It's just so comical. You've moved forward maybe a foot in two minutes."

Thea grinned back at him. She couldn't help it. Her first impression had been right. Logan's smile made him devastatingly handsome, even in the dim light of her flashlight. His earlier scorn toward her seemed forgotten, at least for now. "Why don't you lead the way, Hot Shot."

"First off, let's back you out of the brush. There's what looks like a game trail farther up. The going should be a little easier."

"You couldn't have told me that before?" Thea grumbled good-naturedly.

After a moment of hesitation, he admitted, albeit in a cool voice, "I thought you knew what you were doing."

"Hardly." Her actions over the past few days were proof of that.

"Do you think they'll find her?" Hannah asked. She was sitting on her bed, cradling Whizzer in her lap as if she owned him.

"My dad says Hot Shots don't leave anyone behind." Heidi knelt on the floor at Hannah's feet, petting the little dog.

"It's awfully cold outside, and she only had her sweater on," Hannah added.

Tess sat in the corner, clutching a pillow to her chest in the hopes that it would ease the ache that had begun when Aunt Glen had run off. Just about everyone knew that Aunt Glen had lost her marbles. But Tess had never imagined that Glen would walk away like that. Hiking alone in the mountains without a jacket was like suicide or something.

"Can we talk about something else?" Tess whined. She couldn't help it. They'd just gone to the cemetery and Tess could remember too well the time they'd gone to the cemetery before that. She didn't want to take Aunt Glen there to see her buried.

"Talk about what?" Heidi asked.

"Anything." Boys, bras, basketball. Tess wasn't particular. And Heidi was interested in all three.

"Is Logan going to marry that lady?" Heidi asked.

"Aunt Glen thinks he should," Hannah answered, as if she couldn't care either way.

"He doesn't even like her. He yelled at her a lot today." But what would happen to Tess if they didn't get married? "Can we talk about something else?" Thea really wanted to get her degree and that was in Seattle.

"If she doesn't marry Logan, maybe Spider will marry her. My grandma says he's next." Heidi didn't look up from petting Whizzer.

Tess was about ready to throw the stupid dog out. Heidi had come over to play with Tess and Hannah, hadn't she? Not play with Thea's worthless dog.

"But then, what would happen to us?" Hannah looked up. At Tess. "Would Spider adopt us?"

"Spider isn't family." Tess turned away and sealed her lips.

Heidi got huffy. "That's not true. My mom says all the Hot Shots are family."

"If that's true, maybe Thea can choose one and adopt us." Hannah's staring at Tess was becoming unbearable. It was as if she wanted Tess to agree or something.

"Who would you choose?" Heidi had stopped petting the stupid dog.

"Uncle Logan." Han's voice came out all small and hurt, because she knew Tess didn't believe in him.

Tess swore. She didn't care if Hannah tattled or not. "Don't think he's going to take us, because he's not. We'll wake up one day and he won't be here for us, just like before."

CHAPTER TEN

"WHICH WAY NOW?" Thea asked.

Logan turned slowly in a circle, listening hard for Glen's voice. "Come on, Glen," he whispered, then yelled, "Glen! Aunt Glen!"

"This way." With a total disregard for the risk she was taking, Thea half jogged, half slid down the rocky slope. Her hearing must have been attuned to Glen's tone of voice, because Logan was having a hard time distinguishing Glen's calls for help from the other sounds of the forest. But that didn't mean Thea should disregard her own safety.

He hopped down the stony mountainside after Thea, following the beam of her flashlight, hoping that she wouldn't tumble head over heels and break something, praying that he wouldn't, either.

Been there, done that.

As if on cue, Logan stumbled on a rock and his bad leg twinged in an all too familiar place. Dropping all pretense of skillful woodsman, he skidded down the rest of the way on his butt. The dust cloud Thea was making filled his nostrils, making it hard to breathe. The sharp clack and scuttle of rock on rock filled his ears. At this rate, they wouldn't hear Glen until they were at the bottom of the ridge. They'd probably have to climb back up to her.

"Thea, stop! Try to slow down!" They'd be in a world of trouble if one of them got hurt. He was supposed to be the rescuer, not the rescuee.

Logan had to yell twice more before Thea slid to a halt at the base of a tree and turned, practically blinding him with the ray from her flashlight. Realizing he was unable to dig his feet in and stop before he slammed into her, Logan grabbed onto a pine tree with one arm. The rough bark bit into the skin of his hand and wrist, bit harder as his grip slipped, causing him to swing to the side and bang his head against the trunk.

When the dust in the air and the colors blinding his eyes cleared, Logan focused on Thea's face in front of his own. She had somehow managed to scramble back up the slope to him.

"Are you okay?" she asked, placing her palm on his forehead and lifting the hair away. The gesture was surprisingly comforting. He should still be holding on to his anger, but he seemed to have left that alongside the trail that he'd just tumbled down.

"You're bleeding." Her voice was trembling. In the face of her concern, Logan couldn't seem to find his resentment. Thea cared about people. She hadn't fully explained herself because she'd thought she was helping. And maybe she was, Logan realized, recalling the way the twins were opening up, the way he was opening up.

Logan reached into Thea's backpack, turning her slightly so that he had better access to it. His hand found something thick, rectangular and familiar. He tugged it out. "Here. First-aid kit. Patch me up. Quick."

Thea stared at the white box with its big red cross. "They have instructions in here, right?"

"I'm trained in first aid. Come on. Disinfect the cut and apply a butterfly bandage."

"How do you know you'll need a butterfly bandage?" Her hands shook as she opened the kit.

"Head wounds bleed a lot then seal up pretty quickly. Don't forget to dig out an aspirin, too. My head's going to start pounding pretty soon."

"You sound like you've done this before."

"Cuts, scrapes and bruises are all part of the job." Burns and broken bones came with the territory as well, but he could tell from the shocked look on Thea's face that it wouldn't help for her to hear that. He'd scared his city girl.

Thea pressed an antiseptic wipe to Logan's forehead and he sucked in a sharp breath. The cut stung like crazy. When Thea was done tending to his temple, he took the wipe and daubed at the torn skin on his hand and wrist.

Thea stared at him, her face pale in the flashlight. "It's my fault, isn't it? I was going too fast down the hill and you crashed into that tree."

"You were going fast," he agreed. "I was worried you'd wipe out and then I'd plow right into you. When you stopped, I saw this tree and made a grab for it."

"It is my fault. I'm sorry." She peered at his forehead before placing a butterfly bandage on his temple. The bottom of the adhesive strip clung to his eyebrow. It was bound to take at least some of his eyebrow with it when he removed the bandage later.

"It's okay. I've been knocked around most of my life."

"Don't." Thea pressed her palm over his mouth. "Don't joke about it as if it doesn't still hurt."

"You don't—"

"Your father couldn't have done what he did to your mother if he wasn't abusing the rest of you." Thea wasn't trying to challenge him, or argue. She just called the facts as she saw them.

Logan didn't know what to say. She was right.

"Can I just give you a blanket apology?"

"For what? You already apologized for this." He pointed to his head. "Twice."

"I'm sorry that I lied to you. About my mom. It was one of those things where I didn't speak fast enough and then it became awkward to clarify later." She blew out a breath. "I wanted to tell you the truth, but I thought if you knew she'd left then you'd think I didn't understand your loss. And you seemed more open to letting me talk about it after we had this common bond."

"It wasn't common." Logan winced at the hurt in his words. Her timing left much to be desired, but her assessment was right on the money.

"I don't want to argue about whose loss is greater. Grief isn't a competitive sport." She propped her fists on her hips.

"If this is your idea of an apology, it's totally off base." Damn it. They needed to find Glen. He didn't want to get into a fight about this now, but he also couldn't stop himself from wanting to hear what she had to say. He'd thought he could trust her.

"I've just got one more." She met his gaze with her determined one. "I really had no right to go into Deb's room. I just thought that it would be worse if you and the girls went up there and found things covered in dust and cobwebs." She rubbed at her eyes with the back of her hand. Her brief laugh sounded suspiciously like a sob. "And we know how badly that turned out."

"Not so bad." With effort, he resisted touching her. He should be happy he had an excuse to end things and move on.

"Says the man injured while on a night rescue mission."

"Time heals all wounds."

"Do you really believe that?"

He shrugged. "Not really. Deb did." She believed in forgiveness, too. Logan knew he wasn't quite ready for that yet.

Thea wiped her nose with the back of her hand. "I couldn't hear Glen once we started down and I haven't heard her since we stopped."

Logan drew a deep breath, preparing to shout, but all that extra air gave his head a sharp throbbing pain. He blew out slowly, his breath making puffs of fog. "You'll have to call for her."

"Glen, where are you?" Thea called. "Glen?"

Logan heard a faint cry above them and experienced a rush of relief that made him feel weaker than ever, now that the adrenaline of their slide was over.

Thea's eyes held hope. "Do you think she's all right?"

"She's a tough old lady, my aunt." Logan pushed himself upright, hugging the tree for balance.

"Can you walk?"

"Ask me that after you give me an aspirin." But Logan knew they had to hurry. According to his watch, the temperature had dropped at least fifteen degrees since they'd left the house. Forty-two degrees was too cold for the light sweater Aunt Glen had worn to the cemetery earlier.

"Glen, we're coming. Hang on," Thea called into the night while Logan swallowed the chalky tablets dry. "Should we radio the others?"

"No. Not until we've found her." Logan didn't want to mention that the radios might not work. Radio signals traveled flat and sometimes didn't extend over a ridge, and several now separated Thea and Logan from the others. The higher up they climbed, the more likely they were to work. Tomorrow, if the sheriff sent a helicopter, the radios might send a signal to the sky. "I'm ready. You go first."

"Are you sure?" Even in the dim light he could see the worry in her eyes.

"Would you rather have me in front of you? That way, if I lose my balance, I can fall on you." He gave her a wry grin he was pretty sure she couldn't see well.

"I suspect that's your chivalrous streak talking." With the flashlight aimed at their feet, she grinned back at him. Her face was smudged with dirt, but she'd never seemed so attractive—out of her element and trying to be brave. "I'll go first. Do you want me to stop every few feet and call to her?"

"Yeah. I'll need to go a little slower anyway." He could already feel his pulse pounding a hearty rhythm in his temple. *Ow. Ow. Ow.* The cold air wasn't helping any.

Instead of moving, Thea said, "I'm really sorry about everything. I never meant to hurt anyone."

Logan put a hand up to his throbbing temple. "I guess things have gotten out of hand around here—both on your side and mine."

"I just want what's best for everyone."

"Me, too," he agreed. "Come on, let's move." They were close to Aunt Glen and the activity might keep his mind off the pain.

They climbed up the rocky slope, feet slipping on the shale. Logan's fingers stung from their injuries, the cold and the occasional pinch when a group of rocks shifted on top of his fingers.

Finally, they heard Glen's voice more clearly.

"Over here. Bring the light over here," she called in that endearingly shaky voice.

Logan's breath came in ragged gasps as he hurried past Thea and around a huge boulder. "Aunt Glen!"

"Logan!" Glen sat at the base of a pine tree, cradling her arm against her chest.

Drawing Glen to her feet, Logan gave her a careful, heartfelt hug.

"I knew you'd come," Glen said in her shaky voice. "I just knew it."

"Are you hurt?"

"My wrist. I think I fell on it when I came over that ridge."

Logan drew her forearm carefully forward.

Glen gasped as he straightened it.

"Sprained or broken. Either way it's painful, isn't it?" Logan shone his light back down the slope. "Thea, pull out the first-aid kit again. There should be an Ace bandage and a sling in there."

"Logan," Glen whispered urgently. "I can't remember if I came out here with Deb. Do you know where she is?"

"Yes, Aunt Glen. I know where she is." Logan's words snapped out tight as a whip. Then his voice gentled. "You came up here alone."

"Alone? I know better than to hike alone." Her voice held a trace of its usual vigor.

"You'd best remember that, old gal."

She swiped at him with her good hand. "Hey, I remembered to stay put when I realized I was lost, didn't I?"

"You sure did." Logan hugged his aunt again, careful of her arm, unbelievably relieved to have found her relatively safe. "You sure did," he repeated.

"Can we get back to the house tonight?" Thea asked.

Logan continued to bind Glen's wrist with the stretchy bandage. "We shouldn't risk it with the unsteady footing. We've got blankets, some food and water. I'll try and radio the others once Glen's fixed up. Don't worry. We should be home by lunch tomorrow."

"These blankets are a little thin," Thea observed as she shook one out.

"They're space blankets. Warm with a minimum of layers. Besides, we'll huddle together for shared warmth. Just wait and see. You'll be complaining of the heat before the night is over."

"Who's that?" Glen asked in her tremulous whisper as Logan tied her sling in place.

"That's Thea. She's a friend."

"Did you have to come to my rescue with your latest girlfriend?" Glen teased, still whispering, although Logan knew Thea could hear her.

"I came as soon as I realized you were lost. I've got Jackson, Aiden, Cole and Victoria out looking for you as well."

"I was *not* lost."

Logan grinned. "Okay, I came as soon as I realized you weren't coming home for dinner."

"Better." Glen turned to Thea. "Bust my snaps. Are you a new Hot Shot?"

"No, ma'am. I'm helping take care of Tess and Hannah."

"Eldred never lifted a hand to help. It takes a person of real character to pitch in, you know." Glen chuckled. "Most non-helpers just pitch a fit."

Thea beamed at Glen. "I'm so glad we found you."

Glen poked Logan with her elbow. "I like this one. If you've got to keep one, she just might be it. Plus, if I ever want to go night hiking, she'd come in handy." Glen grinned at Thea.

"I'm afraid I'm not much of a hiker," Thea admitted.

Logan looked away from Thea. She'd definitely experienced him at his worst today. He wouldn't be surprised or blame her if she didn't hightail it out of Silver Bend in the morning.

"Why don't we find a place to spend the night before you start planning my wedding," he said gruffly, trying to ignore his throbbing temple and the ache in his heart.

Last night he'd experienced heaven. Tonight, it seemed nothing more than a dream.

IT WAS COLD.

Huddled on the ground with Glen to her right and Logan next to Glen, Thea shifted her weight, but the chill still seeped through her jeans, right, it seemed, to her very bones. The thought of falling asleep didn't comfort her much—not with all the wild animals in the area that might want to try her for their midnight snack.

Lions. Tigers. Bears.

They had one blanket wrapped around their shoulders and one spread across the front of them. Glen's arm radiated no heat beneath Logan's jacket. Thea resisted snuggling up to the older woman just to share her warmth.

"Anybody hungry?" Logan asked. He'd been quiet ever since he tried to raise his Hot Shot friends on the radio and failed to get any answer.

Thea's stomach had been growling softly every so

often, but once Logan asked, her stomach fairly roared. Apparently, fear was not an appetite suppressant.

Glen chuckled next to her. "We're hungry gals, Logan. What do you have?"

"Beef jerky."

"That might suck my back dentures right off," Glen said.

"Raisins."

"Can't eat raisins, they give me the scoots," Glen sighed. "Anything else?"

"Apples?"

Glen stuck a hand out into the cold night air. "I'll take one of those."

"Me, too." Thea waited until Logan had an apple in hand before she stuck her fingers out from under the blanket.

While they crunched away, Thea looked out over the tops of the pine trees to the velvety sky above them. There were more stars here than she'd seen in the city. They twinkled brighter, too. Thea didn't want to say anything, but she was scared. They were out in the wilderness without even the flimsy protection of a tent against the forest's inhabitants.

A short while later, Glen's head tilted over into Logan's shoulder. He put his arm around his aunt, brushing his hand along the arm of Thea's jacket as he tried to support the older woman against him. The contact left Thea longing to have his arms around her.

"It's going to be a long night," he said. "Sleep if you can."

Thea didn't think she'd be able to sleep at all with her back against a slab of frigid rock and her butt being prickled by stones.

Lions. Tigers. Bears.

She shivered. "Will it get much colder?"

"At least ten degrees cooler. We're lucky to have these blankets. They're lightweight, but they keep out the chill."

Thea kept the fact that she was still freezing to herself. Logan only had a sweatshirt on. She felt guilty even shivering. She bit her lip.

"What?" He peered at her through the darkness. "Are you cold?"

"Yeah. I would have lugged a sleeping bag up the mountain if I'd known we'd be camping up here."

"What did you think was going to happen?"

"I don't know. We hiked up in the dark. I assumed we'd be able to hike back down. Or that we'd call backup and get a ride down the mountain in the sheriff's helicopter."

When Logan didn't say anything else, Thea ventured a guess at what he was thinking. "You think I'm stupid."

Logan grunted. "No. You're getting your Ph.D. You're going to revolutionize the clothing industry."

"Yes, I am." Only, her words felt hollow.

Something whispered above them.

"What was that?" Thea kept her voice low for fear of alerting a predator to their whereabouts.

Lions. Tigers…

"It was an owl flapping his wings."

Thea searched the sky and surrounding trees with her eyes but didn't see anything. She imagined there were more creatures out there she couldn't see and her heart raced. "So, the animals are coming out to hunt? The lions and…and…?"

"Coyotes and bears. Quit being paranoid. You're too big for a coyote to attack."

She doubted that. "They hunt in packs, don't they?"

"No. You're thinking of wolves."

"But you said there were wolves out here, too."

"We are not going to be eaten, Thea." Logan said each word slowly as if he was either about to lose his temper or laugh.

Thea gasped. "What about bears?"

Logan paused.

"They'd like our food, wouldn't they?"

"It's wrapped in plastic."

"That's good, right? They can't smell anything in plastic, right?"

She heard Logan shifting on the other side of Glen. He eased his aunt against Thea and then stood.

"I'm just going to hang the backpack from a tree. Not that I think a bear will come, but just to be on the safe side."

"One of these trees?" Too close. Way too close.

"No, a tree farther away."

Thea sank back against the rock in relief. "You won't get lost, will you?"

Logan sighed. "Not if you shine the light on me."

Thea flicked the flashlight on and, being careful to expose only one hand to the frigid air, aimed the beam at him. Logan looked back at Thea, holding up a hand against his eyes.

"Don't blind me," he protested. "Point it at the ground so I'll be able to see where I'm going."

Thea did as he asked until she could barely see him, even with the flashlight.

A branch creaked above her, making Thea's heart lurch. Cold and scared, she knew if it wasn't for Glen's reassuring weight and warmth against her, she might have bolted after Logan.

Too many minutes later, when Logan finally returned and gently pulled Glen against him, Thea rearranged the blankets over them all.

"Do you think—"

"Thea, don't start again."

"But—"

"Thea, go to sleep."

Thea drew a deep breath and pulled her feet closer to her bottom, clutching her end of the blanket tighter around her.

Visualize sunny days. Hot sunny days.

Logan sighed. "What are you thinking about? Bears? Raccoons?"

"Daffodils. I was thinking of daffodils, and how bright and sunny they are." Thea hoped that by saying it, by acting cheerful, she wouldn't be swallowed by fear. "Once, when I was in California, we took a drive to the foothills and met the most amazing woman. She grew daffodils, but not just any daffodils. She grew—"

"Don't." He cut her off.

Thea hesitated.

"Don't run on with one of your stories."

Like that didn't hurt.

"You always do that. Every time you feel uncomfortable or you want to make someone feel comfortable, you spin these tall tales."

"I do not." Thea was indignant and embarrassed at the same time. How did he know that about her?

"Tall tales. Yarns. Malarkey. Bull—"

"That's enough," she cut him off. He was right. She didn't have to hear him go on and on about it.

The cold night air did more than just nip at Thea's nose. Combined with Logan's words, it stabbed at her heart.

"So, why do you do it? Why all the dissembling?"

Thea rested her head on her knees for a long time before answering. Logan was prying into places Thea would rather not explore. Just as she'd done to him. With a sigh, she admitted, "I'm not sure." Once she'd overheard her father say that she could charm the birds from the trees.

Logan didn't say a word.

Daffodils. She had a really cool story about the daffodil lady. It was one of the last trips she'd taken with her mom and it always made those she told it to chuckle. And making people happy always made her feel better. The bright yellow color of the flower filled her mind.

"This woman had planted the hillside next to the road with daffodils and—"

"I'm not listening."

"Uh…"

"I'll have a conversation with you, but unless you tell me why you feel the need to deflect attention, I'd rather not hear a thing."

Fine. Okay. Perfectomundo.

She'd just sit silently and hope if she fell asleep that she wouldn't wake up to a bear eating her toes.

Thea shifted her shoulders against the cold stone behind her back, rocked back and forth on her bottom and wiggled her toes, trying to get warm, trying not to think about sharp white teeth and yellow eyes glowing in the dark. She closed her eyes and tried to imagine herself at home somewhere in Seattle after a successful day of studying, in a regular bed, burrowed under a stack of quilts. The thermostat would be set at seventy and she'd have her slipper socks on. And she'd be warm and safe.

And alone.

Thea frowned and tried to visualize her room again. Only she didn't have a bedroom or an apartment or even a dorm room. But she'd find one. She scrunched her eyes shut tighter and tried again. The power of positive thinking was supposed to help, right?

It didn't work. She was still cold and wide awake, in fear of being eaten by a wild animal. She could practically feel its fangs closing around her ankle.

TESS SAT at the kitchen table, writing on a blank page in one of Thea's notebooks. Hannah and Heidi had long since fallen asleep. Mrs. Garrett was out in the living room watching television. Even Whizzer left Tess alone.

Tess finished copying the letter neatly, signing her name in cursive at the bottom, just like the adults did. The only difference was that most adults didn't cry big drippy tears on their letters.

> *Dear Uncle Logan,*
>   *I know you loved my mom more than us and you love being a Hot Shot more than you love us. We'd rather find parents that are around all the time and would love us than stay here. We don't want to live with you anymore.*
>   *Tess*

Tess left the sloppy copy with all the scribbles in Thea's notebook. She tore out the good copy and put Thea's notebook back on her stack of books. Tess read her letter again as she walked down the hallway to Uncle Logan's room.

Carefully, she laid it on his bed. She wiped at her

nose with the back of her hand as she stared at the letter and wondered what Uncle Logan would do when he read it.

"WHEN MY MOTHER left I was under a microscope of attention—all the mothers of my friends, in particular, didn't seem to want to leave me alone. It was as if they were talking behind my back all the time in code, pointing fingers and listening to every word I said. So I told stories." Thea shrugged. There. Logan should be happy.

"Were they pointing at you?"

"Probably not," she allowed. "But it felt as if they were. And when they did talk to me, it was a stilted conversation, as if they didn't know what to say to the girl who'd been abandoned by her mother." The first day Thea had worked for Wes, she'd tried talking to Tess, but the girl had accused Thea of pitying her. Thea had known exactly what Tess meant, and had respected her need for silence, by not asking Tess many questions. Bit by bit, Tess had opened up.

"So you started making up tall tales."

"I did no such thing," Thea frowned. "All my stories are true…even the one about meeting Cowboy Temptation, the stripper," she added when she thought he might contradict her.

"They're based on truth," he amended. She could almost feel the grin in his voice, and wished she could see his face clearly, imprint his smiling features in her memory, knowing that she'd been the one to lighten his spirits.

"*Embellished* for listener enjoyment," she admitted. She knew how to tell a good story, but she wouldn't make one up.

"So you started *embellishing*, and then what?"

She hugged her legs tighter. "People loosened up. I didn't feel so much pressure to smile, to behave, to be the perfect specimen under the microscope." If only the stories had worked on her father. He just frowned and didn't say a word, like Tess, and the way Logan used to be.

"Ah, you were the princess that got left behind."

"No!" she almost shouted at him, causing Glen to stir beside her. She'd tried to live up to her father's expectations, tried to be no trouble at all so that he wouldn't have reason to leave her, too. She'd been anything but a princess before her mother had left, guilty of finding more pleasure in her grandmother's company than either of her parents'.

Thea put her head down on her knees again. She'd prefer the fear of feral life to this interrogation.

"Daffodils," Thea murmured under her breath. So bright. So cheerful.

Logan's hand stroked her hair. The warmth from his palm radiated into her skin. Thea couldn't remember a time prior to last night that someone had touched her so intimately, with such care.

"What were you then, if not the princess?"

If the sun had been shining and Thea had her feet firmly on the ground, she would have smiled and made a joke of it. But out here, in the wilds of Idaho, with only a thin blanket separating herself from whatever roamed in the night, she couldn't muster any words other than the truth. "I was the reason for the wedding and the only reason they stayed together so long."

Logan's hand stilled.

It was time for a change of subject. "I'm sorry to be such a drag," Thea said.

Had her mother regretted her choice?

Not enough to reclaim her daughter. Thea blinked back the sudden onslaught of tears. She hadn't been important enough for her mother to even consider compromising her dreams to fit Thea into her life. Her father had admitted once that her mother had never really wanted children.

"You're not complaining, Thea."

"No, but I'm not comfortable. My mother was the type to sit and never complain."

"Is that true or has your memory made her into a saint?"

"Saint Emiline? Hardly." But his words made Thea wonder. Had she molded her memories of her mother into a shining example of perfection? How could Thea, at ten, know what perfect was?

"I know that she was comfortable with herself, with who she was." Thea rubbed her hands down her legs, spreading warmth across her limbs. She couldn't remember having such a revealing conversation before. Perhaps it was the darkness that made this conversation seem more intimate than it was.

And then, despite her intentions to the contrary, Thea was suddenly angry. "I resent my mother. How do you like that?"

Logan's hand retreated.

"I resent my mother," she repeated firmly. "That took me years of therapy to be able to say out loud. I felt bitter toward her for leaving us, for leaving *me*."

When Logan didn't say anything, Thea continued. "But she was noble. She believed in what she was doing and that made me feel guilty for being hurt or angry at her. If she did have a shot at stopping AIDS, I was being selfish. So I decided to do what she wanted and make something of myself. I mean, really, how important is your own child when weighed against defeating such a deadly disease?" It hurt to remind herself that she was unwanted, unloved and unnecessary.

Thea will do. Glen's words resurfaced, a reminder of Thea's private desire—to put a family above all other things. Only she couldn't do that until she'd made a success of herself. She'd made a promise. Even if it was a promise to a woman who had broken a promise to her.

Silence descended around them, thick and depressing, another layer between the blanket and the stars. If there was one thing Thea could count on about Logan, it was that he was a man of few words, a man who avoided emotion and emotional displays. She bet if they weren't trapped on this mountain until morning, they wouldn't be having this conversation.

"I used to wish my mom would take us away," Logan said quietly. Thea froze in surprise. It was the first he'd spoken of his mother to Thea other than at the cemetery.

"Why didn't she?"

"Maybe she believed we'd have a better life with Dad. With her steady income and his spotty paycheck, we were able to rent a place up here in the mountains that was private, so he could beat her or smash things without anyone else around."

"Oh." Thea caught her breath. She could imagine Logan out in the woods, hiding behind a tree and watching his dad, burning with the need to do something. "How did you survive?"

"I was close to my sister. We'd hide out together when Dad was in one of his ugly moods."

"That's a terrible thing for a kid to live through."

"I always wanted to run away, but Deb said that Mom needed us." The blanket rustled on his end. "I guess I didn't realize just how much she did need us until it was too late."

"You couldn't have stopped him, Logan." She was sure of that. What could a little boy do against a grown man, made indestructible by liquor?

"You're wrong. If it wasn't for me, he wouldn't have done it."

CHAPTER ELEVEN

LOGAN WAITED for that bomb to drop.

"You were only a child."

It was just like Thea to believe the best of people. "It was my fault just the same." Logan swallowed. He'd never told this to anyone. Not Deb. Not Jackson. Not Glen. Why he felt the need to tell this woman was beyond him. But the words pressed at the back of his throat and came spilling out. "The day before my father killed her, I saw him behind the house with Deb. I saw him put his hands on her."

Thea gasped. Logan slammed his eyes shut against the memory. He'd only been ten, but he'd known what he saw was wrong.

"She swore it was the first time. I'm not even sure now that I believed her. I begged Deb to leave. I yelled at her to leave with me that night. I did everything but drag her out by the hair." He could still see Deb's young face, drawn so tight he thought she might explode into tears at any moment. But she hadn't, just as Tess had kept her anguish locked deep inside. "So instead, I went to my father. I told him what a waste of a man he was. I told him how he shouldn't be allowed to live for even thinking about touching his own daughter that way."

Thea's hand rubbed the arm she had around Glen,

came to rest on his elbow. As usual, her touch soothed the rawness inside him.

"I told my dad that if I was him, I'd kill myself." Logan drew a shuddering breath. "I didn't expect him to follow through with it. He was hungover and seemed horrified by what I'd accused him of. So I went off to school with Deb, threatening all the way to tell the principal about Dad. But Deb wasn't going anywhere without Mom. We made a pact to tell Mom that night, but we never got the chance." His head ached. Logan rubbed the skin over his butterfly bandage. "When we came home, Dad's truck was still in the driveway—which was weird for three o'clock in the afternoon because that's when Dad was either at the bar or working somewhere."

"We came through the kitchen door on tiptoe because we knew if we were quiet, we could sneak upstairs without Dad knowing we were home if he was in the living room drinking." The shades had been drawn, the house dark. "So Deb starts climbing the stairs and I'm thinking I've got her home safe, but what did safe mean anymore? I meant to follow her upstairs, I really did. But I couldn't hear the TV and God knows my old man couldn't drink a lick without the old boob tube on full volume. So I crept over to the hallway and peeked around the corner into the living room."

Logan tilted his head back and blinked up at the stars. What had possessed him to tell Thea the truth about his past? With her sunny optimism and cheerful disposition, she was the last person he should spill his horrible history to.

And yet, somehow, she seemed the perfect person. Besides, Glen was asleep. Once she was out, there was usually no waking her until morning. And Logan couldn't stop himself now.

"I saw Mom first, crumpled across the gray carpet as if she'd clutched her stomach in pain. I ran into the room and whispered her name to get her attention, thinking my dad had beat her really bad this time. Only, when I knelt next to her, she was cold to the touch and I could see the blood, the bloodstains. I stumbled back onto the coffee table. And that's when I saw him, or what was left of him, against the far wall." For a moment, Logan couldn't think beyond the horrific, full-color image of his father's demise.

"So you see, I really was responsible," he admitted with a heavy heart when Thea didn't reply. Perhaps she wasn't the right person to confess to after all. Any hope he had of Thea helping him with the twins and Aunt Glen was gone now that the truth was out.

"I don't see it that way." When Thea finally spoke, her voice sounded hoarse. "You aren't responsible for the actions of someone else, particularly an adult, and especially not when you were just a child."

Unconvinced, Logan shrugged. She should be damning him to hell for the role he'd played in his mother's death.

"Forgive me for saying this, but your father was sick. What you did may have allowed you to finally live life the way you were meant to, the way all kids were meant to—without fear. No child should have to wonder if they're going to be hit—or worse—when they get home."

Logan recognized the anger in her voice now. "You're dramatizing."

"Your life was a drama, all right. But let's be clear. You were *not* the villain."

Logan wished he could believe her. Only there'd been a string of events that had occurred after he was ten that proved he was no saint. And now she knew all of his deepest failures. Any hope he clung to that she'd stay through fire season either as his wife—as far-fetched as that sounded because he wasn't capable of the love she deserved—or as the twins' nanny, evaporated.

Thea took a deep breath. "Logan…I…I know it doesn't mean much now, but I would have been honored to be your wife. But finishing my Ph.D. is very impor-tant to me."

Logan didn't know what to say. Just when he thought he knew what to expect from her, Thea threw him a curveball. This one hit him square in the chest and hurt like hell.

If Thea wouldn't stay, if she couldn't love a guy like him, what hope did he have of raising two sweet kids? The urge to give up clawed his way into his heart.

"Maybe tomorrow we can start looking for that new nanny of yours." Thea paused. "As long as I don't get eaten by a bear tonight."

"OH, NO." It wasn't Hannah's voice that woke Tess up. And it wasn't Whizzer's low whimper, either.

Uncle Logan's house seemed to tremble and shake as the rumble of a familiar truck engine became louder.

Their father was back.

"Is Uncle Logan home?" Tess asked in a whisper with a quick glance at the window above her. Their room was closest to the front of the house, but the bushes were so tall out there, there was no way to peek out.

"I don't think so."

The digital clock read 3:00 a.m. Heidi slept on the

floor in a sleeping bag. None of them had even changed into pajamas because they'd expected the Hot Shots back before they went to bed.

The truck engine stopped and it became so quiet that Tess could almost hear her own heartbeat.

"You don't think they left us alone, do you?" Hannah asked. She was sitting up in bed with Whizzer in her lap.

"No, Heidi's still here, so her mom's gotta be here somewhere." Tess didn't think Mrs. Garrett was a match for her dad though.

"Maybe he's just going to sleep out there until morning," Hannah said.

He'd done that a couple of times at home. They'd hear his truck pull into the apartment complex parking lot and he wouldn't show up until morning. Sometimes, they'd tiptoe to the window—

The door to their room opened on its squeaky hinges.

"What are you doing?" Tess whispered, sitting up in bed.

Hannah turned around and shushed her softly. "I'm just going to go see what he's doing," she said before disappearing down the hall.

Tess flopped back onto the bed and pulled the covers up to her chin. She could just barely hear Hannah's soft footsteps and the light *clack-clack* of Whizzer's paws on the wood floor. The dog whined once. And then there was silence. Tess wished Hannah would hurry up and come back to their bedroom. With the doors all locked, her dad could drive circles around the place and they'd still be safe.

Something clicked. It sounded a lot like Uncle Logan's front-door lock. But that couldn't be.

They'd be safe unless that dumb dog wanted out and Hannah opened the door for him. She'd never do that. Hannah wasn't that stupid. Except…

It felt colder in the house all of a sudden.

Tess jumped out of bed and ran down the hallway. She skidded to a stop in the kitchen doorway. The cold air made her shiver.

There was Whizzer, hair standing on end, emitting a low growl.

Whizzer had never growled at anyone. Except her dad.

LEXIE GARRETT WOKE UP when the bedroom door opened. It took her a moment to get her bearings.

Thea's room at Logan's house.

A cold house. The temperature must have dropped a lot since last night for it to be so cold inside. That didn't bode well for the search and rescue.

Heidi stood in the doorway. She'd always been an early riser, just like her father. Right now, she didn't look so good.

"Mom?" Heidi looked scared.

Henry stirred in the port-a-crib at the sound of his sister's voice.

"Did they find Glen?" Lexie kept her voice low as she pushed herself into a sitting position. She'd turned off the portable radio around two o'clock so that it wouldn't wake Henry. And Thea's room was at the back of the house, so if anyone came in, chances were she wouldn't have heard them, except that she'd locked the doors, so they would have had to have woken her up to get in.

"I don't think so." Heidi came over to sit next to Lexie. "But Mom, Tess and Hannah are gone."

"Tin Man." The radio crackled to life as Logan, Thea and Glen reached the top of the first of many ridges they'd have to hike to get home. "Tin Man, come in."

Logan yanked the radio out of its clip holder on the front strap of his backpack and pressed the talk button. "Tin Man, here. We've got Glen." They'd been hiking since the gray light of dawn and hadn't made near as much progress as Logan would have liked.

"What's your ETA home?" It was Jackson.

"Another two hours, unless you've got the sheriff's chopper handy." They were moving at Glen's pace, which was slower than Thea's pace, which was maddeningly slow.

"Negative on the bird. Is Glen okay?"

"Yes." Logan glanced at his aunt. She was wearing his coat this morning, one arm through one sleeve and the other arm in a sling underneath the jacket. She was as well as could be expected.

"Then we need you back here ASAP." An order? It was hard to tell.

"Something's wrong," Logan muttered. His skin prickled as he pressed the talk button. "Request situation update."

"Negative. Too many ears. The girls need you. Hurry."

"Come on." Logan snapped the radio back on its strap and reached out to steady Glen as she stepped over a log.

"He didn't say what's wrong," Thea noted, bringing up the rear.

"He didn't have to." Logan knew. "The twins are gone."

"Did you have to open the door?" Tess complained for about the hundredth time as she sat on the bed in the back of their father's truck. They'd been gone for a few hours and the sun was finally coming up. Hopefully someone would discover they were missing and send out the Hot Shots to their rescue.

Unless Logan found Tess's letter and decided they'd run away.

"I told you before that Whizzer had to go out. Everything was dark and I thought Dad was sleeping," Hannah whispered back.

"Like I care if that dog had to take a leak." That wasn't totally true. But she'd rather be at home in bed at Uncle Logan's than being told to sit in the truck and shut up or else. She'd experienced her dad's "or else." She didn't want to get slapped again.

"Well, I care. I hope Thea doesn't leave when they come back and find us gone. Uncle Logan and Aunt Glen need her, too."

"You don't even know if they found Aunt Glen." Tess squeezed her eyes shut against the tears.

"They found Glen. I just know it. And Thea won't stay if we're not there. She'll want to get back and take her test."

Tess's stomach knotted at the thought of Thea leaving. She shouldn't care. She should be thinking about herself. "It doesn't matter what happens in Silver Bend," she said, to prove to herself that she was more important than Uncle Logan, Glenda and Thea, and in more trouble. "Besides, Uncle Logan and Thea don't want to take care of us." She was almost glad that Thea wouldn't stay with Uncle Logan without Tess and Hannah there. They wouldn't get married and start a family, and forget about Tess.

Beside her, Hannah sighed.

The truck slowed down.

"We're stopping," Hannah said.

"I'm gonna need a rest break," Dad called back to them. "You two are going to sit quietly up front while I take it."

He didn't have to say "or else," but Tess knew that's what he meant.

"WHAT DO YOU MEAN, the girls are gone?" Thea stumbled after Glen down the trail. Her leg muscles ached from the hours of climbing last night. Her back and neck were stiff from sleeping upright on the cold ground.

If you could call the dozing she'd done in fits and starts sleeping.

"There's no other reason for Jackson to want us to rush home."

"He could just want to see your smiling face," Glen said as he helped her down a patch where the trail seemed to have eroded.

"They wouldn't run away. They want to be with you." Thea was sure of that. "And why all the secrecy?"

Logan didn't answer. Six feet below her, he held out his hand to Thea while he sucked on his cheek.

"Unless…you don't think Wes took them?" Of course, it had to be Wes. "It's the money, isn't it?"

Thea grabbed onto a tree trunk, then slid a few feet over the rough spot until she slid right into Logan.

"Sorry," she mumbled as she pried herself off him, reminiscent of the way she'd pried herself off him the other night.

Logan had been a gentleman all morning, helping both Glen and Thea over rough spots, fallen logs and loose shale. And they'd gone very slowly. The snail's pace had to have been frustrating for Logan. And now that he was worried about Tess and Hannah—

"You go on," Thea blurted. "We'll be fine."

Below her, he turned, scowling. "You don't know the way."

Translation—she'd get lost.

"I do," Glen piped up. "You go on ahead."

Thea watched Logan's mouth work as if he was trying not to say anything.

"You can leave a trail of bread crumbs," Thea deadpanned, trying to keep the fact that the idea of being alone in the wilderness scared her spitless from showing on her face.

She must have done a poor job, because Logan shook his head and then started back down the mountain.

Thea thought she heard him mumble, "One rescue at a time."

LOGAN STAYED with Glen and Thea until he was within one hundred yards of the house. At that point, he couldn't hold back any longer. He sprinted ahead, stopping cold when he reached the front yard.

There was a beer can on one side of the driveway. The rear panel of Thea's Volkswagen was crumpled. Logan could picture Wes drinking his beer, tossing the can aside and then getting the girls somehow—that part wasn't clear to him. Then he must have pulled a U-turn in the tight space with his huge truck and clipped Thea's bright yellow car. The other Hot Shot trucks had been lined up along the driveway, out of the way in case they needed any emergency vehicles to come in. Logan's truck was in the garage.

Logan burst into the kitchen moments later, adrenaline fueled by worry for the girls making it impossible for him to keep still. He wanted to do something, run somewhere, hit something.

"I'm sorry, Logan…" Lexie paused, a spoonful of orange baby food halfway to Henry's open mouth. She looked as if she'd been crying. "We woke up and they were gone."

"The front door was wide open," Heidi added miserably. She didn't look much better.

Even Whizzer, sleeping in a patch of sunlight streaming through the open kitchen window, lifted his head and looked sad.

Logan mumbled something about it not being their fault. He didn't expect them to stop Wes if the dirtbag set his mind on taking back the twins, but Logan was determined to stop Wes this time. If he could just get his hands on him.

The baby gave a shout of impatience that got Lexie's attention. She delivered the orange stuff to Henry's mouth.

"Aren't Glen and Thea with you?" Lexie asked, craning her neck to look at the back door.

It suddenly struck Logan that Jackson's family— hell, any Hot Shot family—spent a lot of time waiting for someone to come home. The thought cooled his temper just a bit. If they could be patient and wait, if they could keep from going crazy with worry, Logan should be able to as well.

"They'll be here any minute. Glen's going to need an X ray of her wrist. I hate to ask—"

"Don't worry about it. You find Tess and Hannah." Lexie spooned another bit of food into Henry's mouth. "We'll take Glen to Doc Johnson's."

"Thanks." Logan rubbed the back of his neck before working up the courage to ask, "While you're there, can you ask him to refer her to a specialist for her little memory problem or maybe even a home for people like her?" Lexie had been the first one to suggest that Glen needed more help than he could give. And now, he could admit to himself that she was right.

"Of course."

He was extremely lucky to have friends like Lexie and Jackson. "Where's Jackson?"

"He and the others went into town to see if anyone had seen or heard from Wes."

"He used to hang out with Jerry Fischer." The father of the little boy that Hannah had fought with a few days ago. "He's the kind of worm that would help Wes."

Lexie smiled knowingly. "I think I heard Jackson mention his name."

Thea came in the door, steadying Glen's good arm. They both looked pale.

"What happened to my car?"

"We think Wes left his calling card. There's black paint on your fender," Lexie explained. "Sorry. The baby was fussy and we didn't get to bed until late. We slept like logs on the other side of the house."

"I didn't wake up, either," admitted an unhappy-looking Heidi. "When I got up, the front door was open and they were both gone."

Thea helped Glen sit down in a kitchen chair.

"Tess and Hannah have a lot of spunk. They'll keep that Wesley in line," Glen assured them. "It's the same kind of heart Deb and Logan had when they were kids, kept them going despite what Eldred did to them."

Something sickening churned through Logan's belly

at Glen's words, feeding his limbs with a nervous energy that demanded action. If Wes hurt them—

"I'm sorry." Thea sank into a chair next to Glen. "You may have told me this before, but who is Eldred?"

"Why, Deb and Logan's father," Glen announced as if this wasn't a devastating piece of news.

The phone rang, saving Logan from seeing the pity on Thea's face when she realized Glen had sacrificed a lot for her sister and her kids.

"Wes heard about Glen being lost through the police band at Fischer's house," Jackson said without wasting time on pleasantries. "He's headed for Boise. He plans to lay low until Deb's policy comes due on Wednesday. All we have to do is wait two days and meet him at the lawyer's office."

"Like hell." Logan wasn't letting Tess and Hannah spend more time than was necessary with Wes. "I'll call the police while you call Sparks."

Dale Sparks was a communications officer at NIFC in Boise. He could monitor local law-enforcement communications, alerting Logan and Jackson when the police found Wes. It shouldn't be that hard to locate a big semitruck with Washington plates and two kidnapped girls in the Boise area.

"Okay." Jackson sounded hesitant. "You want to tell me what you're planning?"

"I want to be there when they arrest his ass."

"As long as you promise not to do anything foolish," Jackson countered.

Logan made no such promise. He hung up. He was getting his nieces back today and getting rid of Wes for good.

"ONE LOUSY CHANNEL. That's all he's got," Tess grumbled as she sat on the little padded ledge behind the passenger seat.

Their father snored loudly on the bed behind a curtain. They were parked to the side of a freeway exit facing uphill. Their dad had snapped curtains over the outer windows, which cut out most of the morning light, and pulled the drapes closed that separated the living space from the driving space. He'd been sleeping for hours according to the clock on the dashboard.

"This steering wheel is huge," Hannah said as she pretended to drive the big rig. "How does Dad reach these pedals?"

"There should be some kind of button on the side or a handle in the front of the seat to move it forward."

Hannah pushed buttons, pulled levers and finally got the seat moved up. "Look, Tess, I can reach the pedals." Hannah pushed down on one of the three pedals.

"Great." Tess wasn't that enthused. Really, what was the point of having a TV with only one channel? She'd rather sit and watch cookies bake than watch the news.

"And in other news today, an elderly woman reported missing last night in the mountains above Silver Bend is safely home this morning."

"Aunt Glen?" Tess squinted at the snowy screen, unable to make out anything. They could have been showing Aunt Glen, and Tess wouldn't have known it. Were they going to say anything about Tess and Hannah being taken by their dad? Would Uncle Logan come looking for them?

Tess leaned farther forward just as the truck lurched backward. "Hey!"

"Ohmygod-ohmygod-ohmygod," Hannah screamed as they picked up speed.

"Brake, brake, brake," Tess shouted.

"I'm pushing in both brakes," Hannah cried.

Tess stumbled up, trying to see Hannah's feet. "No, there aren't two brakes. Let one go."

"Which one? Which one?"

"Both!"

Too late. They crashed into something and Tess was flung forward onto the gearshift levers.

"WHERE ARE WE GOING?" Thea looked at Logan so she wouldn't have to watch the scenery fly by. Somehow she'd convinced him to let her come along again. They'd left Aunt Glen with Heidi and Lexie. Then they'd barreled down the hill in Logan's big, silver truck way too fast.

Logan quit sucking on his cheek long enough to answer. "Boise."

"Why?"

"Wes has got to stay near the lawyer to collect Deb's money on Wednesday."

"We're going to check out hotels?"

He shook his head sharply. "A truck stop outside of town. I also know of a couple of ramps where truckers pull off to sleep. He was drunk last night and couldn't have taken them until after two, when Lexie went to bed. After the adrenaline wears off, he's going to want to sleep it off. Hopefully, he'll sleep long enough for us to find him."

"Are you still running on adrenaline, Logan?" Logan's face was set into tight, determined lines. Logan might be used to the brutal pace they'd been under the past day, but Thea wasn't. She longed to tilt her head back, close her eyes and drift off. But worry for Logan and the twins kept her going.

"I'll be all right." He went back to chewing on his cheek.

"I hadn't realized that Glen watched out for you even before you were born. It still weighs on her mind for her to talk about it like that, to tell all those stories." She held her breath for a moment before adding, "Stories about your dad." All this time, Thea had thought Glen had been talking about a former love, but it was Logan's father she spoke of—having to stay in Silver Bend because of him, Logan's father not pitching in or liking his children. Thea shuddered.

"I don't think you understand how strong the twin bond is," Logan admitted. "It's like knowing your left hand is there, even when you're not using it to take notes. Tie it behind my back and suddenly I can't concentrate, I can't function the same." He sucked on his cheek.

"So Glen stayed for her sister and you stayed for yours."

He drew his eyebrows tighter across his face, looking so determined to be strong that Thea longed to smooth her hand over his forehead.

"I'll be fine."

After surviving a rough childhood and a devastating loss this past year, Thea wondered how long Logan had been telling himself that.

"ARE YOU OKAY?" Hannah shook Tess.

Something warm trickled down Tess's forehead near her left eye.

Their father stumbled, threw aside the curtain and then loomed over them. "What the hell is going on here?

If you've damaged this truck, I swear you'll never see the light of day again."

Tess pulled her hand away from her forehead. It was covered with bright red blood, and lots of it.

"Holy crap, you're bleeding all over my cab! Get out!" Her dad grabbed a roll of paper towels and shoved it at Tess.

Hannah scrambled out. Tess tangled her legs painfully in the gearshifts before she could climb to the ground.

Clapping her hand back on her forehead, Tess swayed and Hannah steadied her.

"Look at this blood. How am I supposed to get it out of the carpet?" Dad yelled.

Hannah tugged Tess around to the passenger side of the truck. Tess squinted to see what they'd hit. Another big truck. This one hitched to a trailer.

Their dad was still cussing and stomping around in the truck when a huge man barreled out of the second truck.

"What the hell is going on out here? Look at this!"

Instead of looking at the damage, Tess leaned over, which was awkward considering her head started spinning. She turned her palm over, dumping a good bit of blood to the ground. To her horror, blood continued to drip in big fat drops onto the dirt.

"I think I'm gonna be sick," Tess said, wishing Uncle Logan or Thea were there.

"We should call somebody," Hannah said, pressing a paper towel against Tess's forehead. "Uncle Logan or 9-1-1 or something."

"We don't have a cell phone," Tess pointed out, staring at the dark spots she was making on the ground. Her hands were tingling and the rest of her body felt weird, almost light enough to float.

"Mister?" Hannah waved at the other trucker. "My sister is hurt. Can you call 9-1-1?"

"THAT WAS JACKSON." Logan snapped his cell phone shut as they approached the on-ramp to Highway 84 that passed through Boise. "There's a call out to 9-1-1 about an accident between two semitrucks. There's a reported injury. A little girl."

"Is she okay?" Just hearing that a little girl—any little girl—was hurt sent Thea's heart plunging to her toes.

"Don't know." His words were guarded, as if he didn't want to know, either.

"Did they say where?"

"On the west side of Boise, at an off-ramp."

"How far away is that?" They were almost upon the freeway on-ramp.

"Fifteen, maybe twenty minutes."

Thea didn't complain as Logan gunned his truck westward on Highway 84.

"SHOULDN'T WE GO to the hospital?" Hannah asked.

Tess and Hannah sat next to each other on the stretcher inside the ambulance. Tess was leaning on her sister and trying not to melt into a puddle on the floor.

"You're not taking them to the hospital." Dad scowled, ignoring the police officer trying to get answers about what happened. "It's just a little scrape."

"It looks like more than a scrape," Hannah said.

Scrape? Tess had never had a scrape like this. Her head throbbed where they'd applied a bandage and it was becoming a chore to keep her head up. It felt so heavy.

"Don't go making it more than it is," Dad snapped.

Tess's eyelids drooped. She should have been shaking fearfully with her dad yelling at her like that, but she wasn't. She was in another place. She just didn't know where that place was.

"What did you think you were doing?" Dad demanded, leaning into the ambulance.

"We were watching TV," Hannah admitted sheepishly.

"TV!" he stood and roared, then bent back into their faces, his breath just as unpleasant as Whizzer's sometimes was.

"Mr. Delaney, step away from the ambulance." That was the policeman. Tess couldn't really make him out anymore. He was just a dark blur outside the door.

"These are my girls and you can't treat them if I don't give my permission."

Most times Tess didn't like her father. He didn't act like a dad was supposed to.

"Mr. Delaney," the policeman began again.

Someone started to argue. Only to Tess, it sounded more like the cackling crows that she saw sometimes at school. And then Tess was sinking, not thinking about anything at all.

CHAPTER TWELVE

LOGAN AND THEA were nearing the highway exit where police cars and an ambulance were stopped, lights flashing. Logan had a decision to make. He wouldn't play this game with Wes year after year, wondering if that scumbag was going to take the girls in the middle of the night. But, Tess's note made it perfectly clear that the twins didn't want to be with him. She was right, he couldn't love them as much as they should be loved. He couldn't begin to imagine the type of life they deserved. What did he know about loving families, holiday traditions and little girls?

Thea turned her head to look over at Logan. The midday sunlight illuminated her face and turned her eyes to that deep milk chocolate that he'd come to love. She represented everything in life that Logan couldn't have because of who he was. Logan was the Tin Man, a heartless, selfish, irresponsible SOB who wasn't good enough to raise his sister's kids. When he and Thea made love, she'd known it. She hadn't been hoping he'd fall in love with her, she'd taken him on his terms. She'd seen right through him.

Thea was picket fences, apple pie and happily-ever-afters. Logan was hollow, shallow and selfish.

"I don't think I've ever thanked you for helping me

with the girls. It wasn't fair of me to put them in front of your studying," he said. "I hope that once you're out of here, you'll be able to catch up on your school work."

Thea tilted her head, as if trying to decipher what he was trying to say. He was trying to tell her he loved her without saying it in so many words. Guys like him didn't do the mushy stuff, particularly when they'd already been rejected.

"I wish you all the luck in the world on your test."

"Logan?"

"When I pull up, I want you to stay in the truck until it's okay."

"You don't have a gun, do you?" She looked worried.

"No." He'd never been much of a gun man. Just the thought of holding one turned his stomach. He'd always given out punishment with his fists. "If Wes hurt them…if Wes was the reason they called the ambulance…" Logan couldn't finish.

"Logan—" Thea's voice was soft as she took his hand "—I don't know who fed you those lies about your temper being dangerous, but I'd trust you with Tess and Hannah's lives, with my life." She gently shook his hand. "You're a good man."

The woman had no idea what she was talking about. He'd been avoiding responsibility and commitment since he was ten for fear that he'd screw up someone else's life.

"The important thing is to remember what's best for the girls. You will remember that, won't you?" She smiled at him, looking for reassurance.

Logan nodded in a quick, jerky motion. What's best for the girls was to make sure neither Wes nor Logan was ever in their lives again.

"YOU KILLED HER!" Hannah sounded more courageous than Tess had ever heard her.

Yet, Hannah's words chilled Tess's heart. *She was dead?* Tess tried to look around for her mother. Surely her mother would be here with her if she were dead. Only, everything was dark.

"Shut up." Her dad's voice.

"She's coming around." Tess didn't recognize the man's voice.

It hadn't been a nightmare. Tess groaned. Her father had taken them, again. Uncle Logan had been unable to protect them, again. And they'd wrecked Dad's truck.

"Tess, wake up," Hannah pleaded softly near Tess's ear. "Don't leave me with *him*."

Tess wanted to say she'd never leave her twin, no matter what. Instead, she squinted against the bright light as she struggled to open her eyes. She was in the ambulance. Everything was white and gleaming, and... But her eyelids were too heavy. Besides, if she opened her eyes, she'd have to face her dad.

"She looks like shit," Wes said. "Just give her a shake and she'll wake up."

"I'm going to have to ask you to back away from the ambulance, Mr. Delaney." The man spoke again. "Your daughter has a head injury that needs the EMTs' complete attention."

She heard Hannah's voice again, and it was kind of squeaky, but loud. "I'm not going to let Tess die. She's my sister and I love her." Tess felt her sister stand beside her.

If Tess had been scared before, she was terrified now. If she died, who would take care of Hannah?

"Oh, isn't that sweet." Only, the way her dad said it, Tess knew he didn't mean it.

Her head pounded and her mouth felt dry.

"It's that damn twin bond. It's enough to make you sick. My wife and her brother had it. I'm telling you, she'll be fine in a few minutes." But her dad's voice was getting fainter, as if he was moving away.

Hannah whispered, "He's gone. You can open your eyes now."

Cracking her eyes open, Tess reached for Hannah's hand. Leave it to her twin to know she'd been faking it, just a little.

"UNCLE LOGAN!" Hannah gave him little warning before the blond rocket slammed into him, wrapping her arms around him tightly. "I knew you'd come."

Logan resisted squeezing his eyes shut against an onslaught of jagged emotion and kept his gaze locked on the ambulance in front of him. He hadn't caught sight of Wes yet. Or Tess.

"I wasn't even scared." Hannah looked up at him, her face streaked with tears. Then she admitted, "Well, maybe just a little scared."

"Of course you weren't." He patted her back gingerly in case she was injured and just too young and excited to know better than to run around. The report had said a little girl was injured. Was it Hannah? Or Tess?

"Is that a cut over your eye? How did that happen?" she asked. "Are you going to get stitches, too?"

He ignored her questions, sinking onto his haunches and holding her hands. "Hannah, where's Tess? Is she okay?"

Hannah's grip on his fingers tightened. "She's in

there." She looked back at the ambulance, big fat tears welling in her eyes.

With quick strides, Logan was at the open ambulance door, leaning in. There was a little body on the gurney covered with a sheet. Logan could barely force her name past the lump in his throat. "Tess?"

She turned her sweet face his way. He took in the bloodstains on her face, the clean, white butterfly bandage on her forehead and the way her features crumpled when she looked at him.

Crap. What had he done? Logan's knees buckled. Slowly, he climbed into the ambulance and tilted her face to his. Her eyelid was red and swollen. She was going to have a doozy of a black eye. His sister's baby's beautiful face was marred.

"Hey, buddy, what are you doing in here? We're trying to get to the hospital," the EMT complained from behind him. "Mack, call that cop back over here."

"You found us," Tess managed to say with a look of wonder.

"Yeah." He couldn't get out much more than that at first. He was so relieved to see her. "Did he do this to you?"

Tess started to cry.

"I won't pay the bill if you take her to the hospital." Wes's voice grated over Logan's raw nerves.

His father's defective gene kicked into overdrive. Logan was going to kill Wes.

He'd experienced the rush of adrenaline when fighting a fire, battled the heat of anger boiling over in a bar brawl, but this was different. There seemed to be so much energy charging through his veins that Logan felt as if he could fly.

Wes stepped into view. All Logan could see was the

ugliness that was his father in a different form. Selfish. Uncaring about those he should most want to love and protect.

"It's not what you think, McCall," Wes, the lying, cheating, abusive asshole said, raising his hands and backing up.

Logan didn't give the man any more time for excuses. He catapulted himself out of the ambulance, bringing Wes down. They rolled a few times in the dirt before stopping. Logan landed on top and let a punch fly to Wes's nose. Blood splattered across Wes's face.

It wasn't good enough. The bastard had to die. He'd hurt Tess. He could have blinded her, or worse. He wouldn't touch the twins again.

Logan's fingers closed around the thick flesh of Wes's neck. Then he squeezed. And he shook Wes until the bigger man's face began to turn purple, until all Logan could see were his father's mocking features where Wes's face was supposed to be. Until Logan could hear his father's roar of rage when he hit Logan, Deb or their mother. Until…

Logan's fingers loosened. Not this way. He wouldn't kill Wes. He would not become his father. Yet, his rage wouldn't allow Logan to let Wes go completely.

Someone hauled Logan back. His hands fell away as he was pulled off. Logan watched Wes draw a shuddering gasp, filling his lungs with air.

He'd almost killed him.

"Logan." Thea's voice, her touch, so familiar now, on his face and shoulder.

"Back away, lady." The voice came from a beefy cop who still held Logan's arms. This must be the guy who pulled him off.

"It's all right. Please let him go. He's the twins' uncle," Thea tried to persuade the cop, and then looked at Logan, one hand still on his shoulder. "Logan, Wes is going to pay for whatever he did, but not this way."

Logan sucked in a ragged breath.

Not the way of Logan's father. Disgusted with himself, Logan's stomach lurched until he thought he might heave right there in front of everyone. He didn't fight the cop's hold. He deserved to be locked up. That way, the twins could finally get the family they deserved. He'd put Deb's money into a trust fund to keep Wes from getting it.

Wes staggered to his feet, one hand on his throat. "You saw him. He tried to kill me."

Thea whirled and stood in front of Logan, as if she was his shield. "Only after he saw what you did to Tess."

"That was an accident."

"You took the girls in the middle of the night. You don't even have custody." Her voice rang out with righteous indignation. She looked at the cop and pointed at Wes. "I want you to arrest that man."

"You can't be serious!" Wes threw up his bloody hands. "You want him to arrest *me* after *I've* been attacked."

The cop spoke into his shoulder radio about a domestic disturbance and needing backup.

"I don't know what's going on here, but I'm taking both of you in," the cop said in a deep baritone that warned not to mess with him. "And the EMTs are taking that little girl to the hospital. Now, is anybody going to give me any more trouble?"

Logan wanted nothing more than to take Thea into his arms and tell her he loved her, and that what he was doing was best for all of them. Tess and Hannah would get a real family. Thea would get her Ph.D. Glen would go to a home. Instead, Logan kept silent and nodded to let the cop know that he wouldn't offer resistance.

Thea's face paled as she looked into Logan's eyes. "Don't do this."

He pretended to be dumb and shrugged. "Do what?"

"Don't give up like Deb did. They need you." She blinked back tears, which did nothing to dilute the plea in her eyes.

Thea may have caught on to what he was doing, but she didn't understand. Logan wasn't cut out to be a family man. He'd resent Tess and Hannah if he had to be one.

"I left the keys in the truck."

"You knew you were going to come out here and fight him, didn't you? You knew…" Thea's voice cracked.

She was one smart cookie, his city girl.

"The girls are going to need you to be there." Logan looked at the pine trees on the side of the bank instead of at the handcuffs being snapped on his wrists. He risked looking at her one more time. "Please, just help them get through the next few hours."

"I DOUBT YOU'LL HAVE much of a scar." The doctor patted Tess's knee when he was done putting stitches in her temple. "But you will have quite a headache tomorrow. All we need now is to take some X rays, then you can go home."

Tess sat between Hannah and Thea, clutching their hands. All three of them kept sniffing. Every once in a while, Hannah would cry openly and Thea would wipe at her eyes.

"What's going to happen to Uncle Logan?" Hannah asked.

Tess had fallen on unsteady feet in the ambulance trying to get up and see Uncle Logan fight her dad. She hadn't wanted either one of them to get hurt. It was all her fault that Uncle Logan had lost his temper. She just should have told him it was an accident when he asked her if Dad had hit her. But she'd started bawling like a baby and he'd jumped her dad.

"He and your dad might spend the night in jail. I'm not sure." Thea's voice sounded funny. "What's important is that you two are together and safe." She didn't smile when she said it.

"You're here, too," Hannah said. "And Aunt Glen is waiting for us at home. Maybe tomorrow things can get back to normal."

Thea snatched a tissue from the small table next to the bed and blew her nose.

A woman peeked around the curtain. She had on large glasses and a brown skirt with a matching jacket. "Are you—" she looked down at her clipboard "—Tess and Hannah Delaney?"

Hannah nodded, a slight frown on her face. "Who're you?"

"I'm Edna Higgins, with Patient Services." She stared at Tess and Hannah for a while before looking at Thea. "And you must be the baby-sitter."

"We still have to go to X ray," Thea said quickly as she hopped down off the cart.

Tess noticed Thea stood up really straight, as if she were giving a report in school.

"Someone from Social Services will be here shortly. I'm just here to help the transition," the lady in brown said.

"The transition," Thea echoed. "I'm their nanny. I've been taking care of them for months."

"And I'm sure you've done a wonderful job," the lady said with a smile that made Tess's stomach upset. "Could you step outside with me for a moment?"

Thea hugged herself tight and followed the lady in the brown clothes out into the hallway. The bells on her feet barely made a sound as she left them.

"What's happening?" Hannah leaned closer to Tess. "Are they arresting Thea, too?"

"I don't think they're going to let us go home with her, or Uncle Logan," Tess said, feeling the tears streaming down her cheeks as her worst fear came true.

"They can't," Hannah wailed.

"They can." Tess sniffed. "Whatever you do, Han, don't let go of me, okay? We'll be all right if we stay together." Tess only wished it were true.

"GLEN? LEXIE?" Thea ran into Logan's house, still crying. Lexie's SUV was outside. Where could they be?

"Thea, shh." Lexie stood in the hallway, yawning. "Everybody's napping. Did you find the girls?"

"They took them. And he *knew* it was going to happen." Thea wiped at her nose with a balled-up tissue. "He knew."

Lexie led Thea to the couch. "Who knew?"

"Logan." Thea drew a shuddering breath. "He and Wes got into a fight when we caught up to them. Tess had this horrible cut over her eye and Logan thought Wes had done it to her. But it didn't matter because Logan wanted to get arrested. He wanted to prove to himself that he's no good for the girls..." She finally ran out of breath and gasped. "Or for me."

"Thea, where are the girls?"

"They wouldn't let me take them. I've watched them for months. And I've taken them across state lines, but that wasn't good enough for—"

Lexie gripped Thea's shoulders. "Where are Tess and Hannah?"

An overwhelming feeling of loss crept up in Thea's throat. "In a Boise foster home."

"HEY, MCCALL, you're being released." The jail guard opened the cell door with a clank of metal. Logan stood on stiff legs. After refusing his phone call and the right to seek bail, he'd sat on the cell bench all night between two drunks they'd hauled in after an extended happy hour. It was no more than he deserved. Even though he was exhausted, he'd been unable to sleep. How could he when he was letting go of everything that had meant anything to him?

Yet, what choice did he have? He couldn't go through life wondering if he was good enough for them, could he? Tess and Hannah would be better off this way.

He signed some papers, agreeing to appear in court for assault. It was nothing compared to the kidnapping charge he'd brought against Wes.

Thea was waiting for him when he walked down the jail steps. When she saw him, she threw herself into his arms and began sobbing. "They took them away. They took them away."

Logan went through the motions of putting his arms around her, but he couldn't offer her any comfort. His heart had been shattered yesterday when he'd made his decision to try to give his nieces a chance at a normal life.

She finally stepped back, blew her nose in a ragged-looking tissue and thrust a manila envelope his way. "Lexie helped me find the custody papers. You'll need these to get them back."

Logan slid his hands into the back pockets of his jeans. For a moment, he couldn't say anything. This was harder than he'd thought it would be.

"I'm not getting them back."

He hadn't realized she'd been staring at her feet until she turned tear-filled eyes his way.

"But the papers—"

"Mean nothing if I don't use them." He looked around the busy parking lot. Other people were being released and picked up. He wanted to get out of there before Wes came through. "Where'd you park the truck?"

"I thought...you mean..." She stuffed the envelope back into her big straw bag and started walking. "You had plenty of time to think it over in there."

"It's for the best. What kind of guardian would I be if I'm only there a few months out of the year? And when I'm home, I go ballistic on people who upset me."

"You think you're some horrible monster, like your father." It wasn't a question. She delivered the statement accusingly. "Don't judge yourself by the environment you grew up in. Look at your friends. They're not abusive dads or ax murderers."

She spun in a circle as if searching for an argument that would sway him. "For cripe's sake, you can *choose* who you want to be, Logan."

"Am I missing something? Didn't you see me try to snuff the life out of Wes yesterday? Can't you realize I'm not the man you think I am?" Who was he kidding? He wasn't the man his own twin had thought he was. He balled his hands into fists and put them behind his back.

"You thought he'd hurt Tess. I was ready to jump him myself. Any parent would have done the same."

"I don't think so." Logan shook his head, refusing to believe. His hands tingled at the memory of them clenched around Wes's neck, and he remembered how his brain had superimposed his father's face onto Wes's. Logan was one sick bastard and he knew it.

Thea turned on him, propping her hands on her hips. "I'll tell you what you are. You're a coward." She poked him in the chest.

"I am *not* a coward." It took guts to do what he was doing. It left him emptier inside than when Deb had died. "I don't know what Deb was thinking to give me custody of the girls. They'd be better off in foster care on their way to adoption. Hell, they'd be better off with you."

"You are so lost in your own sorrow that you can't see how beautiful you three are together."

He scoffed.

"Don't try that act with me."

"What act?"

"Don't try pretending you don't care. I've seen you skating in your socks with them. I've seen you hide Easter eggs for them. I've seen you comfort them at their mother's grave." She spun away. "Someday you are going to wake up and realize what a mistake you've made. It's too bad that day will be too late." Then she whirled, and walked away, in the direction of the parking lot.

Logan stretched his legs to keep up with her. They would have made better time in the mountains if she would have walked that fast.

Thea stopped at the driver's-side door to his truck, looking lost, looking as if she wanted to cry a couple more buckets of tears.

When she did speak, he could barely hear her from where he stood, five feet away.

"I promised myself I would not cry," she said half to herself, wiping none too gently at her eyes.

He had to hurt her, had to turn her pain into anger at him; otherwise, she'd cry all the way home. And he didn't think he could bear that. "Well, you've broken that vow already."

He could tell she was barely keeping it together by the way she had to swallow two times before speaking. When she finally spoke, he had to ponder a moment before her words sunk in.

"You didn't have to say goodbye to them." She dropped the keys into his hand, careful not to touch him. "I did."

It wasn't until she climbed out of the truck at his house after over an hour of silence that Logan realized Thea no longer wore her bells or her bracelets.

"WHAT ARE YOU DOING?" Logan asked, one hand gripping the door frame to Thea's room. Glen was napping and the house was almost painfully quiet.

"Leaving."

"Oh." He shifted his stance, cleared his throat. "You don't have to go. You can stay here and study until it's time to take your test." Maybe they could spend some time together. *Maybe...*

He bit back a curse. Was he so selfish that he could give up the girls and want to keep something going with Thea?

"Thanks. But no." She wasn't looking at him, or smiling, or making any noise.

"What about your car?" It hadn't been in the driveway when they got home.

"The garage in town—Al's?—they're pulling off the fender so I can drive it home. Jackson had it towed yesterday."

Logan considered cursing Jackson for his efficiency.

"I guess that's it. I owe you some money and then you can go." Logan didn't even attempt to hide his bitterness.

Thea took a deep breath but kept her eyes on that damn blue suitcase. The stab of pain in Logan's heart was from the knife he'd given Thea—he'd let down his guard and allowed her to get close and now she was leaving him. It was no more than he'd planned, but that didn't make it any easier to take now that the time had come to say goodbye.

"Don't you have something else to say?" he goaded, more than ready to fight, just to keep her there longer. This was their goodbye, right? This was where the good girl admitted she loved him and the hero told her that it could never work out. But life wasn't like the movies. He wasn't the hero and Thea had a promise to fulfill.

Thea raised her brown eyes to his and Logan couldn't help remembering how her body had felt wrapped around his in the shadowy night they'd spent on the bed not two feet away from him. Or how she'd gazed at him on the mountain with Glen between them. She loved him, he knew she did, but he wouldn't be the one to hold her back.

She didn't say a word, just stared at him with large, red-rimmed eyes.

She turned back to her suitcase.

Logan laughed, but he didn't feel any humor; in fact, he tried to feel nothing at all.

Thea's forehead creased. "You're making this difficult." She shook her head. "You made your decision. Face facts. There's no reason for you to stop being the Tin Man. Isn't that the point of the last twenty-four hours?"

"Yes." He hated how well she knew him.

A car pulled up the driveway.

"That would be Al with my car," Thea said calmly. "I've arranged to stay with a friend in Seattle, but if you could just write me that check…"

He couldn't believe she was leaving, even when an hour ago he'd convinced himself it was for the best.

"So that's it?" Logan felt empty when he handed the draft to her, drained of every emotion and all energy.

"It's what you want, isn't it? To be able to hide away in this house and be alone?"

He almost refuted her words, but that's the way it had to be.

She raised her eyebrows, clearly challenging him. Damn her for getting under his skin so quickly. Damn himself for being unable to just turn away and let her go. A sucker for pain, Logan crossed his arms over his chest. "I won't be around much once the season starts. I'm heading out tomorrow for New Mexico."

"Ah, yes. Your Hot Shot life. It's more important than the twins and Glen."

"It wasn't just that. You saw what I'm capable of."

"Poor Logan." Thea shook her head slowly, reaching up to cup his cheek. Her eyes were filled with sorrow. "Someday you'll come up with a more believable excuse for keeping your distance."

"Some people just aren't made for love." But in that moment, he wished that he was a fool capable of love

and forgiveness, capable of risking it all to have someone like Thea in his life. Because then he wouldn't have
disappointed two little girls.

FORTY HOURS OUT on the fire line and Logan was ready
to go home, if only someone besides Aunt Glen would
be there to greet him. And since he'd asked Lexie to
check into homes for the elderly, he wasn't even sure
she'd be waiting for him.

When it was time to sleep, Logan couldn't drift off.
He was tortured by the memory of the smiles Tess and
Hannah had given him on Easter. Had he made the right
decision? He wondered what Thea was doing, if her
studies were progressing according to that anal planner
of hers. Did any of them miss him? It was more likely
they cursed him to hell.

"Another round, Tin Man?" Chainsaw asked, rising
from their table at a Podunk New Mexico bar. The
place was typical of every other small-town bar Logan
had seen from Florida to Washington State—dark,
with a loud jukebox piping music through crackling,
horrible speakers, scuffed floors and duct-taped
booths.

Logan nodded. He was back to not saying much. His
throat felt rusty from misuse.

From three feet away, Logan could still smell the gas
fumes from Chainsaw's namesake as he passed. Not that
it mattered. They all smelled god-awful, of smoke and
sweat, of honest labor and making a difference.

*How important is your own child when weighed
against defeating such a deadly disease?*

Thea's words about her mother haunted him. Was he
really that noble that he'd given up his nieces so they

could have a better life? He didn't think so. He enjoyed his lifestyle—no ties, no strings, coming home to an empty house if he wanted or inviting people over early or late. That was the ideal bachelor life, wasn't it? And it had been enough before Deb died because Deb was his family. She'd grounded him. She'd been there when he needed her and had kept busy with her own life when he didn't.

"Who would have thought the New Mexico fire season would start so soon?" Jackson said from his spot next to Logan.

New Mexico had suffered from too many dry seasons and now an early spring, complete with lightning storms.

"Well, if we don't get released tomorrow, it's overtime," Spider said gleefully. The fire had been quick, quicker than anticipated and the ragtag response of certified crews from across the United States had been just as swift. Still, they'd finished their four ten-hour shifts and might be told to head for Silver Bend in the morning.

"I called home. Lexie said to tell you that she hasn't started looking for old folks' homes because Glen's new medicine is working," Jackson said. "Apparently, she remembered the dog's name."

With a shake of his head, Logan mumbled, "Whizzer." Logan had discovered him curled up with Aunt Glen after Thea left.

"You up for a little recreational action?" Dressed in a black T-shirt, with his hair slicked back, Spider eyed a woman across the bar speculatively. He'd somehow managed to shower and clean up before they came out to civilization.

Logan shook his head. He wasn't in the mood for company of any kind.

"Have you heard anything about the twins?" Jackson probed. "Heidi was asking about them."

Logan gave him a back-off stare, which his friend ignored.

"I miss the little angels, and Thea, too," Spider said, turning his attention back to the table when he got no response from the woman across the room.

"Everybody just lay off, okay?" Logan tossed his hands in frustration. "I made a decision that I thought was best for everyone. Need I remind you that Lexie left you last year because you were never around?"

"She took me back, though," Jackson noted with a superior grin.

"Just do whatever makes you happy," Spider added. "No regrets, no looking back."

Logan scowled. He wouldn't call what he was feeling even remotely happy. And he carried a ton of regrets.

Jackson hesitated, then looked into his beer. "Let me take a wild guess. There's a pain in your gut the size of a softball that won't go away. And you can't stop thinking about the choices you made, the corners you got backed into, wondering if they're thinking about you, playing conversations in your head when you aren't busy, apologies, defenses, confessions."

Spider made a noise suspiciously like an escaped laugh, and looked out over the crowd. "This sounds like a *moment*."

"That, my friend, is love gone wrong." Jackson slapped Logan on the back.

"Sounds like you two could use another beer. Where has Chainsaw wandered off to?" Spider turned in his seat and surveyed the room, but not before Logan caught the anxious look in his eyes. Spider was looking for more than Chainsaw.

The Queen came out of the rest room and Spider turned back around.

"Trust me. This is your heart's way of saying don't let them go." Jackson returned to his original conversation. "You need those girls and Thea as much as they need you."

"Can we change the subject? I think I have a tear in my eye," Spider deadpanned.

Jackson and Logan told him in no uncertain terms where to take his tears.

"You know why I can't be their guardian." Logan turned so that only Jackson could hear him. "You weren't there when I found them. I had my hands around his neck and I was squeezing."

Ignoring the hint that Logan wanted to keep their conversation between just the two of them, Jackson smiled at Spider as he spoke. "You're not your dad. I knew your dad. He was a psycho drunk. You, my friend, are anything but."

"You are so full of it," Logan said through gritted teeth.

"And you're blind." Spider grinned. "When we get back, can I get Thea's number? I want to ask her out."

"No!" Logan didn't even have her number.

Spider and Jackson both laughed.

Slumping in the booth, Logan listened to the music pouring through the crackly speakers in the cold, dilapidated joint and stared at nothing. He was bone tired. If only he could sleep. But it was worse when he drifted off, because he dreamed of Glen crocheting her endless chains, of Tess and Hannah hunting Easter eggs, of Thea's sunny smiles and limber back.

"I said no!" The woman's voice held a trace of panic underlying her command. "You're drunk."

"Baby, I'm not as drunk as I'm gonna be," promised a large hulk of a man.

"Arnie, I'm leaving." The woman's long features were pale, her slender body encased in a thick down jacket.

"No, you're not. We're having a drink. Come sit back down, Cindy." Arnie's big mitts pawed and pushed the woman in the direction of the booth they'd just vacated. "We'll have another drink, a nightcap."

Anger whispered through Logan's veins as he watched the couple.

Cindy resisted, trying to stand her ground. "Ow. You're hurting me."

Before he realized what he was doing, Logan shot out of his seat and grabbed the drunk by the arm. "You don't want to do that, buddy. Let her go."

For such a big man, Arnie was surprisingly quick, pushing Cindy down to the floor and spinning into Logan. In that brief instant, Logan relived the feel of his hands around Wes's neck, experienced the fear of what his temper could do. It took all of Logan's strength to receive the brunt of the man's energy and channel it against Arnie so that the drunk fell to the cracked linoleum floor. Alone.

Unfortunately, Arnie fell on his face. He rolled around, covering his nose with his big fists. "My node, my node. You broke my node."

"Nothing more than you deserve, chump." Spider tossed Arnie a handful of napkins.

"Never, *ever* force a woman. When she says no, she means no," Jackson added, climbing out of the booth.

Logan clenched his fists, half dreading Arnie would get back up.

Jackson helped Cindy to her feet. The woman sniffed and avoided looking at Arnie.

"But I love her," Arnie sobbed, still grabbing his nose. "And she's leaving me."

"You've never told me you love me," Cindy half whispered.

Logan wanted to roll his eyes. Instead, he kept them locked on Arnie, in case he got angry and tried something.

"I thought you were leaving me." Arnie wiped at the blood, which was really no more than a trickle now. He had a bloody nose, not a broken one.

Logan swore half to himself. Love made men into such idiots. "And if you want to keep her, you'll remember what I'm about to tell you." Logan leaned over Arnie. "You may fight, you may get drunk, but your woman is as fragile as china." Logan extended a hand to help him up. "Now, I'd offer to buy you a beer, but I think you've had enough. How about a coffee?"

Arnie continued to sit in a lump on the floor.

"I think I'll just take him home," Cindy said.

"Do you know what you're doing?" Logan doubted it. If he were a woman, he'd take the opportunity to make a classic exit.

"Yeah, he can't handle his booze, but he doesn't drink all that often. I was leaving him because I didn't think he cared."

"I don't think—" Logan began, not trusting Arnie. After all, the guy had shown he was capable of some ugly violence.

"Do you need any help getting him home?" Jackson exchanged an exasperated look with Logan that seemed to say he should have kept his butt out of things that were none of his business.

Cindy didn't even look up at Jackson from where she knelt next to Arnie, stroking his thinning hair. "Maybe just out to the truck, thanks."

"Well, Dear Abby—" Spider watched Logan slide back into the booth across from him "—that was quite touching."

"Not now, Spider."

"You'd be a lot happier if you'd take your own damn advice," he retorted. "Does Thea know you love her? Do the angels know you love them?"

Logan stared at his friend, seriously considering leaping across the booth to plant his fist in Spider's face.

Spider shook his dark head slowly. "Let me just say this one thing, in all seriousness." He sobered, which was a rare expression for Logan's teammate. "For a brief moment, you had it all. A home, kids and a babelicious woman."

"Spider—"

"Hang on. I've always looked up to the way you handle everything. You may lose your temper, but it's not as if you're gonna kill someone." Spider grinned. "We won't count that time you broke Kookaroo's wrist."

"You've had one too many beers." Logan's gaze sank down into his own empty glass. He'd wrapped his hands around Wes's throat. If that wasn't coming close to killing someone, Logan didn't know what was. But he loved Tess and Hannah so much, he was willing to protect them with violence, which was against the law just about everywhere.

"No, I haven't drunk too much. You could have beaten Arnie to a pulp and no one would have blamed you. Except maybe the local sheriff." Spider's grin faded. "Hey, we're all young men who believe in our own immortality. Bar fights don't count in the scheme of things. I heard about what happened in Boise with Wes. I would have fought off the cop to beat him to nothin'. The way I heard it, the cop pulled you off and you were cool as ice. That's not deranged in my book."

"Spider—"

"Take my advice or not, it's up to you, Tin Man. I had a taste of responsibility last year when you and Golden were out injured. I liked it. I've struggled to step back and, well, there's something that's been bothering me. And surprise, surprise, it affects my temper."

"A woman," Logan surmised, picturing Thea that first day he'd seen her, all color and sound and smiles, picturing her legs wrapped around him and knowing him so well that she knew exactly how to please him. If he lived a long life, he'd never get over his love for her.

Love. Logan snorted. Too little, too late.

"Yeah. Only it's not woman problems like you've got." Spider's expression remained stoic. His gaze drifted to a group of Hot Shots that included The Queen. "So you'd better reclaim those little angels when we get back, or I'm going to have to kick your butt. And I'll only give you one more chance with Thea."

"I missed all the action over at the bar. Had to talk fast to keep the bartender from calling the local law." Chainsaw set down four beer glasses he'd been balancing with two large hands.

"The damsel in distress is off in her four-wheel drive." Jackson slid in next to Logan and claimed a glass of brew. "Did we convince you to give fatherhood another try? Because Lexie said I can't come home until we do."

"This isn't such a good idea." But Logan liked it nonetheless. His friends were giving him their blessing to change. Not that he needed their permission, but it helped. He'd need their smarts, courage and heart to undo the damage he'd done to Tess, Hannah and Thea. He wasn't going back to being selfish and cool, but he realized he might be able to follow Jackson's lead and be a good parent while still being a Hot Shot. He'd need help being a dad, though. He'd need Thea.

He was going to propose again. Instead of the idea shaking him up, he was suddenly calm, filled with purpose.

"Well, you can step into the ring with me anytime you feel overwhelmed," Spider offered.

"And if you bring Thea back, she'll keep you in line," Chainsaw added.

Logan silently agreed. She knew him in ways Deb and his Hot Shot buddies never had. She'd seen the heart in him where Logan hadn't and he'd let her down.

"A toast." Jackson raised his glass. "To our love-struck, fatherly hero. The Tin Man finally found his heart."

"Pretty soon we'll have little twin Tin Men crawling around on the floor." Chainsaw laughed.

"Not likely," Logan mumbled. He had to win back three females—Tess, Hannah and Thea—not one.

"She loves you, man. Anyone can see it," Chainsaw insisted.

"You are sadly in need of a woman, Chainsaw." Spider looked at them all in turn, before he added, "And it's unfortunate that the woman you love married the wrong guy."

"Patience, my man, patience," Chainsaw answered, but he wouldn't look at any of them.

"Patience, my ass," Spider scowled. "If you want a woman, you've got to use the tools in the box to claim her."

Jackson rolled his eyes. "All you need to do is relax and go with the flow. You, most especially, Logan."

"Hey, Thea's quite a catch." Spider nodded. "It's not every woman that would climb a mountain in the middle of the night searching for an old woman she barely knows. Logan should fight to keep her."

Looking for Glen had been easier than winning his family back was going to be. "Yeah, her smile warms you in places, you know," Chainsaw said, then added at Logan's frown, "Not that way. I mean, she's sweet and all, but not my type. She's…she's…too loud, like you said."

They all laughed.

Jackson slapped Logan on the back. "We've got a couple of days off when we get back, so you can get your life back in order."

"Do you think Thea will come back?" Spider asked.

"Of course she will." Chainsaw elbowed Spider. "Soon we'll be calling you Tiger, not Tin Man."

"Won't work," Logan lamented into his mug, struggling for an answer to the problem before him. "Thea's afraid of tigers."

CHAPTER THIRTEEN

"HOW'S THE STUDY PLAN, Thea?" Amy asked as she set her groceries down on the kitchen counter and shook out her umbrella. She'd been in a couple of Thea's classes last fall and had offered to let Thea stay a few weeks to get ready for her exams.

"It's going." Slow. It was going slow because she couldn't concentrate at all. She'd been invited back to her study group, but hadn't worked up the courage to attend. She'd just drag them down with her temporary mental blocks, brain freezes and lapses.

"I heard that Dori's study group didn't pass the oral exam," Amy continued, unloading groceries. Amy was a real go-getter from Hong Kong. She'd announced Dori's failure as matter-of-factly as she might the morning weather. "They're dropping like flies."

Thea used to feel as if she could keep up with her friend academically, but not anymore. Now Thea's brain was on emotional hiatus.

"Did you hear what I said?" Amy asked.

"No. I'm sorry." Thea gave up the pretense of studying and put her pencil down.

"I said, are you still worrying about those little girls?"

"Could you tell?"

"Only by the fact that your textbook is open to the same page it was when I left."

Thea cradled her head in her hands. She missed the twins—their stubbornness, their sweetness, and the way they staunchly faced life. She missed Glen's stories and lovable oddities. She missed Whizzer's energy and Logan's soulful blue eyes. "What am I going to do? I only have a few weeks left until my written exams and I'm a mess." And she had no desire to pass. She couldn't make anything of herself when her heart lay in pieces back in Idaho.

"If this is so distracting, why not call Boise and find out what happened to them?"

"Oh, I don't think so." Her heart couldn't take knowing that Tess and Hannah were with strangers, couldn't take hearing their lost and lonely voices. She'd found the draft letter Tess had written in her notebook, had fingered the blotches she knew were caused by the little girl's tears, had cried a few herself. But she couldn't do anything for the twins. Only Logan could save them now. And he didn't want to be their hero.

"Maybe you could even talk to them on the phone," Amy said. "They'd probably love to hear from you. It's been a little more than a week, right? They can't have forgotten you."

But they might want to. Thea had been unable to keep her promise.

LOGAN SAT in the living room of the foster home where Tess and Hannah had been living for more than a week. His heart pounded and his palms were wet. He'd called in a lot of favors to even be allowed to see Tess and Hannah. This was the first step in them getting back together. The social worker had said that Tess would be the hardest one to convince, as if Logan didn't already know that.

"Here they are," the foster mother, Nancy, announced with false joy before leaving Logan alone with his nieces.

Tess and Hannah held hands as they stood in the living-room doorway. They wore matching school uniforms—blue plaid skirts and white button-down shirts. Their hair was braided neatly on either side of their ears. After an initial look at him, the girls stared at the television, which Nancy had turned off at his arrival.

If he'd been hoping they'd run into his arms upon seeing him, he was sorely disappointed. But their reaction was nothing more than Logan deserved.

"Hi," Logan said, deciding to be the first one to break the ice.

"Hi." Hannah barely voiced the word.

Tess said nothing. It was hard from this distance to tell if she was breathing.

"I…um…I came to apologize." It didn't matter that he'd practiced what to say. Nothing he'd practiced seemed appropriate now.

Hannah blinked in his direction. Tess just stared at the television.

"Have things been going well for you here?"

No reaction.

"You see—" he scratched the back of his neck, starting slowly "—I had a big hole in my heart after your mom died. She was my best friend in the whole world. We had a very ugly childhood and the only people I could trust for a long time were your mother and Aunt

Glen. And I couldn't get over your mom's death because I thought that left me with no one.

"I didn't have any experience raising two girls, and Glen was, well, you know how Glen was. I couldn't ask her for help. And there was this hole where all my emotions just leaked out." He pointed in the direction of his chest, and then looked down at his hands, feeling pretty damn stupid, hoping that Nancy wasn't loitering on the other side of the hall taking notes on his lame attempt to communicate his feelings. "I let Wes take you that first time because I thought that hole made me like a sinking ship or something. I thought you'd have a better chance with him than with me. A better chance at a normal childhood, which is more than I had."

Hannah caught him looking at her and turned her head to the window. Tess clenched Hannah's hand tighter but kept staring at the television.

"And then, somehow, even though I had this leaky heart, I kept on living. And I felt guilty about having let you go, but I had no idea where you were. It was like your dad had disappeared off the face of the earth."

He sighed. This wasn't getting any easier. All of this was painfully hard to admit.

"And then you showed up with Thea and I didn't know what to do with you or how to act around you because I'd been so lost before, I guess I lost the person I was. Lucky for me, Thea didn't let me get away with that." The confession came spilling out. "I think she may have tried to put a Band-Aid on my heart so that I could love you, but it was a Band-Aid and it didn't stick when I got mad at your dad for sneaking off with you that second time. I got so mad that I tried to hurt him— which was wrong—but then I thought that since I hit him that I could be like my dad, who used to, well, he used to hurt us with his fists." He hadn't meant to say that last bit.

Logan stood up and paced the small space between the couch and the low coffee table before he remembered that the social worker had advised him to sit down so that he wouldn't be so tall and intimidating. He sank back into the couch and washed a hand over his face. "And I read your letter, Tess, saying you didn't want me anymore."

Hannah's eyes opened wide, looking first to Logan and then to Tess.

"So, I didn't come and get you like I should have the day after the accident. I wanted to, and Thea wanted me to, but part of me was scared that I wouldn't be any better at taking care of you than Wes…er, your dad, or my dad. And then more days passed, and I couldn't stand coming home and not having you there. So I came home from fighting a fire and I called down here to Boise as soon as I got back to see if I could get a third chance with you, because I'd decided that I wanted to be a family man…I want us to be a family."

Hannah had tears trickling down her plump little cheeks. "You won't let us go this time?"

"Hannah!" Tess hissed.

"It's okay, Tess," he said. "You were right. I did care more for myself than for you."

Logan closed the distance between them and dropped to his knees. He wiped his palms on his pant legs before taking their hands gently in his. "But that was then. I'm not letting either one of you go. If Aunt Glen is stubborn, then I must be thickheaded, because it took me so long to figure out that this is how it's supposed to be—

the three of us together with Aunt Glen." He swallowed a couple of times before he could get the words out. "I love you too much to let you go."

"What about Thea?" Tess had her chin lifted.

"Thea left the day after the accident," Logan admitted reluctantly.

"I'm not coming back without her." Tess drew her proverbial line in the sand.

· "Much as I'd like to promise that she'll come back, I can't do that. She's got her mind set on passing those tests and then going to work." He might have lost Thea forever the day he'd been released from jail, but he wasn't losing Tess and Hannah.

"Not without Thea," Tess reaffirmed.

Hannah looked stricken. She stared at Tess and the tears came again. Logan recognized the twin pact. They were united.

"No," Tess repeated.

"I could find another nanny," he offered.

"She's the best nanny in the world," Tess said staunchly.

"Well, I have to respect your wishes. But I don't think I can convince Thea to come back alone. I was hoping we could work together." That was a spur-of-the-moment idea, but it seemed the right thing to say. He'd been going with his gut so far and it hadn't failed him yet.

Tess eyed him skeptically. "What do you mean?"

"Well, you see, it's kind of like fighting a fire. We have to plan our strategy, pick the best time to attack and then make sure we've contained her on all sides, so she has no choice but to come back."

After a minute, Tess nodded. "Okay, but you'd better make sure you know what you're doing."

Logan could no longer resist hugging them. For the first time since he'd come down the mountain with Glen, he felt the pressure inside his chest ease. "I think I know a little bit about women. Why don't you leave the planning to me?"

Tess and Hannah exchanged knowing glances and a nod.

DAYS LATER, Logan slouched on the couch next to Aunt Glen. The twins were doing homework in their room, but every once in a while he heard a shout of laughter. The sound reminded him that Thea had brought light and laughter to their house and then disappeared.

Glen got up, her balance steadier than he'd seen in months. The medication the doctor gave her had done what Logan assumed was impossible—given him his aunt back. Glen walked over to the living-room windows and closed the blinds, sending the room into shadow.

"Why did you do that, Glen?"

"Meg always liked her privacy. I think you need some time alone with your thoughts."

Logan suddenly remembered the darkness in his mother's house. He hadn't made the connection before between how he lived now and how he'd grown up. His mother had been unable to move on, unwilling to step out of the darkness and live the life she deserved. And although Deb kept her blinds open, she'd chosen to live in a house isolated from everyone else, as Logan had. They'd been in hiding.

Covering his eyes with his hands, Logan allowed himself a moment of self-pity. Thea had left him. Now the house was dark and silent once more. Just the way he'd kept it during the long months after Deb's death.

And Logan couldn't stand it.

Hannah's laughter echoed down the hallway.

The twins wouldn't want it, either.

Logan stood, fingering Thea's bracelets in his hand. He'd found them on the living-room coffee table the day she'd left. He carried them around the house like a love-sick teenager.

He caught a glance of himself in the hall mirror. Who was he? The son of an abusive man? A freewheeling Hot Shot firefighter? Or somebody else? Was he somebody Thea could love as much as he loved her?

You can choose who you want to be.

Thea's words echoed in his head. Was it that easy?

Whizzer trotted into the room, gave a soft woof and trotted over to the front door. It took Logan a minute to realize the little guy was asking to go out. In the time it took to walk from the couch to the door, Logan admitted to himself that he'd grown fond of the terrier. Thea must miss the dog, too.

Logan opened the front door for Whizzer, then opened the living-room blinds. The place was pretty darn dark. With just a bit more light, it wouldn't be so bad. There was a skylight in the upstairs bedroom. It was the sunniest room of the house. And Thea had probably never closed the drapes after Tess's meltdown. Logan glanced over at the stairs.

All Deb's pictures were up there.

He closed his eyes and took a deep breath.

It was time.

The stairs didn't protest as he climbed. It was only when he reached the landing at the top that he hesitated. *Maybe* Deb hadn't given up. *Maybe* she'd cranked up her morphine drip to leave on her terms. *Maybe* she'd wanted to make things easier for Logan and the twins by ending things early.

If he could choose who he wanted to be, he'd choose how he wanted to remember his sister.

Logan opened the bedroom door and welcomed the light on his face.

The sun was shining on his side of the mountain.

"How'd you do?" Thea embraced Amy lightly, careful not to wrinkle the suit she'd chosen to wear for her oral exams. Its soft blue reminded her of the melancholy blue of Logan's eyes. They'd both passed their written exams—Thea by some miracle of fate—and Amy had just finished her oral exams.

It was Thea's turn.

"It's brutal, but you can do it." Amy straightened Thea's suit collar. "I'll wait for you."

"Thanks," Thea mumbled with a premonition of failure, unable to remember why she wanted to get her Ph.D.

Blinking to hold the unexpected tears at bay, Thea turned away to give herself an extra moment to regain her composure. "On second thought, I don't know how long this will take. Maybe you should go back to the apartment. It's starting to rain."

A light shower pattered across the university grounds.

"How about I meet you at the coffee shop around the corner when you're through?" Amy waved and popped open her umbrella.

With a sigh, Thea turned toward the building where they were holding today's exams.

"We'd like to go for ice cream afterward," said a familiar voice.

Thea spun to face Logan, surprised to find him wearing a suit and tie, disappointed that her heart started beating double time at how good he looked. The rain came down harder and Thea took shelter under a tree, followed by Logan.

"What are you doing here?" And then something icy cold washed over her. "Of course, you're here for the custody papers." Thea's heart sank. She should have known he wouldn't come this far just to see her.

"What custody papers?" Logan frowned.

"The ones I took that day. I've still got them in my purse." Thea rummaged around in her straw bag, but just her luck, she couldn't find anything when she needed it. She was too conscious of Logan, the time, and getting inside the building the moment the rain let up.

The rain let up.

"I came to mark the day you'll start revolutionizing the textile industry." Logan smiled, setting off a familiar flutter in Thea's stomach.

"Hi, Thea. Uncle Logan, can we run up and down the stairs?" Hannah tugged at his jacket sleeve. She had on a pretty yellow dress, and carried a small umbrella.

"I don't know." Logan looked to Thea for her opinion.

"Of course you can. Just stay where we can see you." It was easier to paste a smile on her face when she wasn't looking directly into Logan's eyes.

Hannah whispered something to Logan that Thea didn't catch, and then the little girl was running up the steps. Tess, of course, was already there, wearing a red dress.

"Be careful," Thea warned. Reluctantly, she turned back to Logan. "How did you get them back? I have your custody papers."

"I have connections."

The proctor came outside and paused at the bottom of the steps, waiting for Thea.

"I need to go," Thea said, even though she was dying to know why Logan was here, and why he had changed his mind about the girls.

It started to rain again.

WHEN THEA CAME OUT, the sun was shining and Logan was waiting for her.

"Did you pass?" Logan asked.

"I don't know, but I found the custody papers." Thea waved the envelope in the air, feeling triumphant. "I kept thinking I'd send them, but I didn't have your address or telephone number."

Logan didn't even reach for the papers. "Actually, you took something else when you left, something that wasn't yours to take."

Thea couldn't imagine what that was. She'd left more in Silver Bend than she'd started with.

"We couldn't wait to get ice cream. The sun came out and it got hot." Hannah sat on a bench swinging her feet and licking a vanilla ice-cream cone.

"The girls are looking great." Thea couldn't help smiling at the twins, who looked happier than she'd ever seen them. Thea remembered how aloof and withdrawn they'd seemed when she'd first met them. "When did you get them back?"

"A couple of weeks ago," Logan admitted, not taking his eyes off her. "Can hardly stop them from talking, except when they're eating."

"And Glen?"

"She asks where the beautiful lady who used to hike with her is about ten times a day."

"Who's that? Deb?" It would be a huge blow for Glen to forget Deb.

Logan shook his head. "You."

"Me?"

Another nod of that gorgeous head. He looked so happy that Thea's heart nearly broke. Was she that easy to get over? Her heart was still in pieces over leaving him. "And Birdie says no one buys Strawberry Quik at the store now that you're gone."

"I'm not sure the twins really liked it."

"They miss you."

"They miss someone to make their cookies." Thea did smile then, trying to cover the pain she was experiencing. "Once you get a new nanny, they'll forget all about me."

"Nope, no one can replace you."

"I'm sorry, I need to go meet my friend, Amy," Thea mumbled, painfully aware that they were the focus of two pairs of very curious eyes. She wanted this meeting to go smoothly and end quickly, to end now.

Logan cleared his throat and extended his hand. "You left this at the house."

Her silver bangles clinked together as he held them out. She'd left them the day she'd lost faith in him.

She took the bracelets carefully, reluctant to have them make a sound. Everything was quieter now. She hadn't worn her favorite red sneakers or squeaky slippers since she'd left Idaho. They reminded her too much of the girls—and of Logan.

"How's Whizzer?" Saying goodbye to the little dog had only added to the heart-wrenching pain of leaving Silver Bend. But Thea knew that Logan needed the sweet terrier more than Thea did.

"He makes it through the night now without waking me up. He and I came to an agreement."

"That's great." She missed her little champion almost as much as she missed Logan and his family. Thea looked around for something to do, for someone to talk to, anything to take her from the intense pain of Logan's presence. It was torture being near him and being unable to touch him, devastating to realize he was so happy.

"Can I see those papers?" he asked.

"Sure." She handed them over.

He tucked them into his interior jacket pocket. "Can you spare a minute? I have something for you."

"Did I forget something else?"

He ignored her and headed to the bench where the twins were sitting, his long strides only stopping when he reached the gift sitting between them. He picked up a package wrapped in polka-dot paper and handed it to her.

"You're giving me a gift?"

He shrugged. "Open it."

Thea eased the paper off, careful not to rip it. If it was to be her only gift from Logan, she wanted to save everything, including the wrapping paper.

"Thea, just rip it off."

She ignored him and set the box down to fold the paper neatly.

"Open it." Logan picked up the box with one hand on the lid, ready to open it.

Thea put her hands on her hips. "Whose present is it?"

"Yours," he allowed sheepishly, handing her the box.

Thea tried glaring at him, but he looked so apologetic that she didn't have the heart to glare for long. With a heartfelt sigh, she flipped open the lid. "You got me shoes?" They were beautiful bright red sneakers with shiny sequins and silver shoelaces. Thea frowned. "I thought you hated my shoes."

"I didn't really hate them." He stared at her intently. "Do you like these?"

"They're fine. They're just..." So unexpected. He bought her a pair of shoes? Honestly, they looked too small for her feet. Thea tilted the box so that she might nonchalantly see what size was printed inside the shoes. Her finger pulled back the tongue of the shoe.

Logan made a choking sound.

"Are you okay?" Thea asked him. "Do you have allergies? I have some medicine in my bag." She set down the box and rummaged in her straw purse again.

The twins giggled. They'd stood up and flanked Thea.

Logan gently pulled her hands out of her purse and handed her the box.

"Maybe you should try the shoes on." Logan's smile was strained.

Thea was almost positive those shoes weren't fitting her feet. He'd obviously gone to a lot of trouble and she didn't want to hurt his feelings. "I don't think they go with this outfit." Blue suit? Sequined tennis shoes? Uh-uh. Not a match.

"Put the damn shoes on," Logan growled through gritted teeth.

"I—"

"Put them on!"

The twins' grins had faded.

"If it's so important to you, I'll slip them on. Sheesh."

Thea sat on the bench, plunking the box next to her. Logan stood a few feet away, arms crossed over his chest. Tess and Hannah, finished with their ice cream, mimicked his pose.

"I'd hate to see you on Christmas morning," Thea mumbled, knowing full well she'd love to see him on any holiday in any setting, but she'd never be able to.

"The shoes," he commanded.

With a sigh, Thea grabbed a shoe and began loosening the laces, because these shoes were obviously too small. But she didn't pay much attention to what she was doing. She was too busy drinking in Logan out of the corner of her eye. Even if they weren't her size, they were her kind of shoe. She would have kept them if they were mud boots as long as Logan was giving them to her.

One of the laces sparkled, catching her attention. Thea's hands froze in the act of pulling the sides of the shoe open. There was a diamond ring knotted in the shoelace. A diamond ring. A diamond. Ring.

"There's a ring on my shoe," Thea said stupidly, afraid to breathe.

"About time you noticed," Logan grumbled.

"Well, who could see it? The sequins are pretty dazzling," Thea snapped, still afraid to wonder what the ring meant. Did he want his nanny back?

He took two steps to stand in front of her. "I had envisioned this differently."

"Really?" She managed to lift her gaze to his.

Logan's expression softened. "Really." He dropped to one knee. "Dorothea Gayle…Thea…" His voice dropped to a mere whisper. "Will you marry me?"

"Oh, my." He was the Tin Man. He was the Tin Man. A man used to plowing through life selfishly, using people and breaking hearts. She had to remember that or he'd suck the remaining joy right out of her.

Dropping his gaze to the ground, Logan swore. After

a moment, he lifted his head again. "Sorry. I forgot." He wrapped one of his hands around each of her ankles, seeming to draw strength from the contact. "Girls, ske-daddle," he commanded.

Obediently, the twins ran over to the steps.

Logan gazed up at Thea.

"Have you ever wondered *why* you felt every rela-tionship wasn't right?"

"Nice to see you, too." Thea crossed her arms over her chest, ignoring the emphasis Logan placed on the word *why*, ignoring how his touch warmed her everywhere.

"It was because they weren't right for you. They couldn't appreciate you for who you were. They only wanted you for what you could do for them."

"And this is different than our relationship because…?"

"None of them ever traveled eight hundred miles to see you, did they? Don't you want to know why I'm here, Thea?"

With every fiber of her being.

"Ask me," he prompted. "Go on. Ask me *why* I'm here."

He was tossing her own logic back at her. She didn't want to ask, but oh, heck, she had to know. "*Why* are you here, Logan?"

He bestowed her with a satisfied smile. "I thought you'd never ask. I'm here because I went to New Mexico and almost got into a bar fight until I realized something."

Thea raised her eyebrows at him.

"I realized I couldn't live without you. You've given me the gift of balance. I've never seen my life the way you taught me to see it. I've never stopped to appreciate the sunshine, or a child's laugh, or the simple music made by a bell, not even when Deb was alive." He paused, lifting his face up to the rare Seattle sunshine. "I don't want to lose the man you saw in me. He's kind and patient and heroic and faithful. He's not the Tin Man."

"You've always been those things."

"No, I haven't. I've been a man without a heart. I don't want to go through life that way anymore."

His fingers slid up her calves to her knees. "Come back to Silver Bend with me, Thea. I was just starting to get the hang of me when you left. Please, come home."

Thea stared at him mutely. He'd said everything right. He'd said everything…but the words she needed to hear. He hadn't said he loved her. Thea wasn't going to be used by this man. "I made a promise. I need to make something of myself." The words sounded weak, and pitiful, coming through the tears she held at bay.

"I think you have made something of yourself. To us." He stared at her. "You made a huge difference in our lives. The house is too quiet since you've left. I look up from reading the girls a bedtime story and you're gone. Even when I fold the laundry, I think about you and how much you did for us. I know you want to revolutionize the textile world—"

"Was it that hard to find a replacement for me?" She cut him off. This was about child care. Reading books? Folding laundry? Oh, she was such a fool.

"Replacement?" Logan frowned.

"A new nanny." Who would take care of Glen and the girls when he went to the next fire? The man was hopeless.

"I'm not looking for a nanny. I want a *wife*."

Thea tapped his chest, knowing the custody papers were in his jacket pocket. "This is what you really came for, Logan. I'm so proud of you for getting the girls back."

He stood up, placing one hand on either side of her,

trapping her. He had that look in his eye, the spark that told of storms ahead. "I've been listening to my heart, Thea. The one you resuscitated when you crash-landed in my life several weeks ago. I've spent the past eight months wondering why I wasn't as strong as Deb was, why I couldn't give up like she did when everything seemed unbearable.

"But then, there you were and it didn't seem like giving up was a viable backup plan if I didn't find a nanny. I wanted to be better than that. I wanted to do better by them." He shook his head as if he was shaking off the dark choices he'd avoided for so long. "I love you, damn it. And if you know what's good for you, you'll admit you love me, too."

Thea couldn't find enough air to fill her lungs. When she did, she could barely squeak, "You love me?"

"Haven't you heard a word I've said? I'm willing to wait until you think you've fulfilled that promise to your mom and made something of yourself, but I think you've already done that. I'm so crazy for you that I can't live without you!"

"Oh, my," Thea whispered.

"You can say that again." Logan glared at her, but there was a different look in his eye now. The same glint that had captured her heart that precious night before Easter. "Kiss me, Thea. Kiss me as if you need me more than air."

And she did.

EPILOGUE

"HURRY UP, girls," Thea called out of her SUV window a year later. She'd traded in her dented Volkswagen for a more practical Idaho vehicle.

Tess and Hannah walked slowly down the school sidewalk, hand in hand. Exchanging glances, they giggled when two boys ran by, and then ran the last ten feet across the bright green grass to the SUV.

Whizzer sat in the front seat, tongue hanging out and tail wagging. Hannah climbed in the front seat with Whizzer, while Tess hopped in the back.

"Is it today?" Tess asked.

Thea nodded. "They'll be at the Painted Pony any minute now."

Thea waved at Lexie and Heidi as they pulled past them. The Silver Bend Hot Shots were returning from the first fire of the season and all the fire families in town were excited.

"Did you finish your dissertation?" Hannah asked, just as she did every day after school.

"Nope, but I'm a little bit closer." Thea was composing a paper on the opportunities to improve the durability of fire clothing. Of particular interest lately was a new pulp product she'd read about on the Internet. It had the potential to increase the life of a firefighter's fire-resistant clothing. Two prominent labs had already contacted her, interested in her theories, and she wasn't even close to exploring the various discoveries by other scientists that she thought might apply to her paper.

But Thea wasn't pushing herself. She had the family of her dreams, a mantel filled with family photos and all the time in the world to submit her dissertation.

"SPIDER, I'D LIKE TO make it home in one piece," Logan cautioned from the back seat of Spider's pickup. They'd made it from the Boise airport in record time, but Logan didn't want to end up in a ditch just a few miles from home.

"Like you don't want to see Thea and the kids." Spider barely slowed down to take a corner, sending everything in the truck, including the men, listing to one side.

"Spider!" Chainsaw, Jackson and Logan yelled at the same time.

"Sheesh, all right. We're at the city limits anyway."

Logan leaned forward, trying to catch a glimpse of Thea's bright yellow SUV.

"The kids should be out of school," Jackson said.

Sure enough, two SUVs crossed the road ahead of them and pulled into the Pony's parking lot. Jackson's and Logan's families had arrived just in time to welcome their men home.

It wasn't as if Logan hadn't been apart from his family last fire season, but he'd been home so long that this first separation of the year was tough.

Spider had barely put his truck in park before Logan was tumbling out and heading toward Thea's SUV.

"Uncle Logan!" Tess saw him first. She ran into his arms.

Logan swung her around and then hugged her tight.

She may have put on a few pounds and grown a few inches since last year, but she was still slender.

"I made the math club." Tess squirmed out of his embrace, but grabbed his hand and tugged him toward Thea's car.

"Uncle Logan!" Coming from the direction of the kennel, Hannah wrapped her arms around him.

He lifted her just as easily as he had Tess and spun her around.

"We missed you. I wasn't sure you'd get home in time for the 4-H show on Saturday." Hannah had joined the 4-H Club to learn more about raising animals. She currently had a pygmy goat, a dozen bunnies and a large goose. Being happy, keeping busy and another year's growth had slimmed Hannah a bit.

"You know I try hard to get home for the important stuff," Logan said, letting each twin take a hand. He purposefully slowed his steps so they had to tug him along even though he wanted to run to the SUV.

"Uncle Logan!" they both complained in unison. "Hurry up."

"Yes, Uncle Logan," Thea called from her SUV. "Hurry up or the girls will miss ice cream."

"I hope they save some strawberry ice cream for me," Hannah said.

Logan approached from the passenger side of the car. Thea stood on the driver's side. Her smile had that same hint of sunshine that had captured Logan's attention a year ago.

She opened the back door on her side. Tess opened the back door on their side.

Thea and Logan smiled at each other across the toy-cluttered back seat.

"Hello, honey." Logan almost couldn't stop himself from climbing right across the seat to take her into his arms. Thea was his oasis from the outside world. Her love and the love of Tess and Hannah had taught him patience, which made his temper flaring a much rarer occurrence.

And then there were the twins.

The new twins.

Mikey and Matt.

Mikey shifted in his car seat and yawned, blinked, and then let out a hungry yowl, brief but effective. It woke Matt up.

"Let me take him." Tess pushed past Logan and started undoing Mikey's car-seat straps.

"Tess, would you like to carry Matt for me?" Thea asked, giving Logan the opportunity to hold one of his little guys.

At two months old, the twins were still just wisps, barely ten pounds. But they were healthy and thriving.

With extreme care, Logan lifted Mikey out of his car seat and cradled him in his arms.

"Were you good for your mom, kidlet?"

"Him?" Hannah snorted. "No way. He lets us know when he's hungry, when he's wet, and when he's gassy. The kid is louder than Mrs. Whipple." Her goose. Hannah reached up and chucked Mikey's delicate chin. "But you're still cute, aren't you?"

Logan's family of six started slowly toward the Pony. Aunt Glen stepped out on the porch to meet them. Other families were drifting inside.

"Hurry up, Logan, or you won't get any of the apple pie Thea and I made," Aunt Glen said.

"I saved you a slice at home," Thea whispered.

"Do we have to stay long?" Hannah asked. "I really want to go home, just us."

Logan drew his niece closer, enjoying the feel of the spring sun on his face, the baby in his arms and the spunky girl at his side. Sometimes he wished he had enough arms and lap to encompass them all at once—Tess, Hannah, Mikey and Matt.

He shared an intimate glance with Thea.

And other times…

Thea cupped his cheek with the palm of her hand, simultaneously welcoming him home and promising him a more intimate homecoming later.

"You know, kidlet," Logan said, "when we're together, anyplace is home."

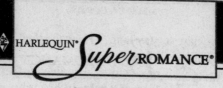

HARLEQUIN *Super*ROMANCE®

YOU, ME & THE KIDS

Along Came Zoe

by Janice Macdonald

Superromance #1244

On sale December 2004

Zoe McCann doesn't like doctors. They let people die while they're off playing golf. Actually, she knows that's not true, but her anger helps relieve some of the pain she feels at the death of her best friend's daughter. Then she confronts Dr. Phillip Barry—the neurosurgeon who wasn't available when Jenny was brought to the E.R.—and learns that doctors don't have all the answers. Even where their own children are concerned.

Available wherever Harlequin books are sold.

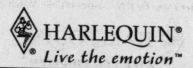

HARLEQUIN®
® *Live the emotion*™

HARLEQUIN *Super*ROMANCE®

A six-book series from Harlequin Superromance.

Six female cops battling crime and corruption on the streets of Houston. Together they can fight the blue wall of silence. But divided, will they fall?

Coming in December 2004,

The Witness by Linda Style
(Harlequin Superromance #1243)

She had vowed never to return to Houston's crime-riddled east end. But Detective Crista Santiago's promotion to the Chicano Squad put her right back in the violence of the barrio. Overcoming demons from her past, and with somebody in the department who wants her gone, she must race the clock to find out who shot Alex Del Rio's daughter.

Coming in January 2005,

Her Little Secret by Anna Adams
(Harlequin Superromance #1248)

Abby Carlton was willing to give up her career for Thomas Riley, but then she realized she'd always come second to his duty to his country. She went home and rejoined the police force, aware that her pursuit of love had left a black mark on her file. Now Thomas is back, needing help only she can give.

Also in the series:
The Partner by Kay David (#1230, October 2004)
The Children's Cop by Sherry Lewis (#1237, November 2004)

And watch for:
She Walks the Line by Roz Denny Fox (#1254, February 2005)
A Mother's Vow by K.N. Casper (#1260, March 2005)

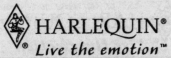

HARLEQUIN®
Live the emotion™

www.eHarlequin.com   HSRWOMIB1204

HARLEQUIN *Super*ROMANCE®

Visit Dundee, Idaho, with bestselling author

brenda novak

A Home of Her Own

Her mother always said if you couldn't be rich, you'd better be Lucky!

When Lucky was ten, her mother, Red—the town hooker—married Morris Caldwell, a wealthy and much older man.

Mike Hill, his grandson, feels that Red and her kids alienated Morris from his family. Even the old man's Victorian mansion, on the property next to Mike's ranch, went to Lucky rather than his grandchildren.

Now Lucky's back, which means Mike has a new neighbor. One he doesn't want to like…

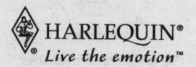

HARLEQUIN®
Live the emotion™

www.eHarlequin.com

HSRH001204